GLYN HUGHES

Glyn Hughes is the author of five novels. His first, WHERE I USED TO PLAY ON THE GREEN, won the Guardian Fiction Prize and the David Higham Prize for Fiction and was followed by the highly acclaimed THE HAWTHORN GODDESS, THE RAPE OF THE ROSE and THE ANTIQUE COLLECTOR, which was shortlisted for the Whitbread Novel of the Year award, the James Tait Black Memorial Prize and the Portico Prize. He is also the author of several works of non-fiction and three volumes of poetry.

Glyn Hughes

ROTH

British Library C.I.P.
A CIP catalogue record for this title is available from the British Library

ISBN 0-340-58601-X

To Bernard Jacobson – who represents
in every particular
the antithesis of Pericles Rosblum.

And to Jane,
who has contributed so much
to the writing of this novel.

I do not have a choice. If I am to live at all, I must act according to my instincts for the pictures I might paint.

Jackson Pollock

1

The dawn of Roth's last day was not a private view. At five o'clock in the morning, the whole of a Hertfordshire village dragged themselves from their beds to watch the painter being led to the ambulance. United in their fascination with catastrophe and wealth, they stared at the vehicles surrounding the church: two police cars; the ambulance at the gate; Dr Kaplan's Rover; and at a discreet distance, close to Roth's studio beyond the church, the Rolls-Royce in Van Gogh yellow belonging to the art dealer Pericles Rosblum.

'At his age!' one of the crowd remarked upon Roth's predicament. 'But we all saw it coming.'

Standing in the lanes or under a rim of gargoyles, they contemplated the wreckage that Roth had made of their churchyard: the muddy curves and circles drawn in the turf by his Laverda motorcycle. It was for this sacrilege that the police had been fetched to assist Mr Roth.

The tall figure of Leonard Roth, unhelmeted but clad in travel-battered, dirty black leather, bits of twigs and leaves clinging to him as to a mythical green man, was led away, muttering about 'Arts Police'. His face was of a metallic intensity, white from a year in the studio, greasy from bike travel: Yorkshire and back without wash or rest in almost twenty-four hours. His hands and nails were black with earth from skidding through the graveyard. As usual, a fine sweat prickled his brow. His mouth was dry and his heart was pounding.

Roth's impulse for freedom and for another perspective had once driven him to take to the air and paint from a glider. At last, at the age of seventy-one, he'd stopped struggling, ceased flying. He was resigned, tired and earthbound as Dr Kaplan, his psychiatrist, cajoled him into the ambulance. From the step, Roth did take one look back – aloof, distant, perhaps frightened – over the wrecked graveyard, the flashing blue lights, the puzzled villagers and, finally, down on to the dome of Kaplan's bald head some distance below his chin. He had the look of someone without a parachute about to throw himself from an aeroplane. To that far prospect of the world he was leaving, Roth growled his summing-up of his lifetime's relationship with picture dealers, buyers, accountants, doctors, et al.:

'Those who haven't been in the battle don't understand the war. Okay?'

Dr Kaplan answered not a word.

'Okay, okay . . .' Roth trailed off, retreating back into his head.

In there was the face of Dorothy, his wife from whom he'd been separated for a year.

People whose limbs have been amputated may continue to feel pain in them, and he could still feel her body and her touch. Especially her light touch yesterday as they had sat together on the carpet, in Leeds, in a pool of calm; her party left to take care of itself around them. Keep hold of that, keep hold of that. Okay? Okay.

There was something crucial left over from yesterday. Something unexplained from that meeting. At first, as they sat by the fire after he had arrived on her doorstep so surprisingly, she asked him to stay for the night. He hadn't answered straight away, because he had been overcome. He had found it the more moving because, despite all the destructiveness of their thirty years together, she must have wanted him simply for the old joy of holding, touching, murmuring.

Or had it been pity?

No, Dorothy would never reduce his dignity with her pity.

While he had been pausing over her offer, he had seen her face tighten. Did she think he was being arrogant, calculating her desire?

As so often in his life, he had not faced it, but had fled.

That was last night. Now – *the bag . . . where is the bag?*

'My bag,' he growled at Kaplan. 'A black case in the bedroom.' Roth fumbled for his key and gave it to Kaplan, who accepted. 'Someone must fetch it for me. It has my spare clothes and . . . things.'

Dr Kaplan gave the key to an assistant, who hurried towards Roth's cottage.

In the yellow Rolls-Royce, parked at the far side of the church while Roth was led away, Pericles Rosblum, owner of the Station Gallery, sat next to his chauffeur, with two large men squeezed into the back. These two pacified themselves by sucking cigars. Rosblum, ascetically, never smoked, nor did he drink alcohol. The interior of the Rolls offered him sufficient comforts. It was decorated like a Greek taxi. There dangled a St Christopher medal and a row of portraits of the Rosblum family: wife, daughter, son. (Pictures of father, mother and other relatives had been looted en route for Auschwitz.) Seen through its windows, the real life of mud and wind and a chill June dawn were turned into a remote fantasy of struggle and labour – even to these four toughs, who had clearly been bruised by plenty of reality.

Yes, four, for Rosblum himself, in posture and build, looked like a smaller version of his henchmen. He was muscle-bound, though turning to fat, and often either aggressive or unneces-sarily defensive, like a man used in his past to holding his own on construction sites, or to putting his foot in doorways.

Arriving at half past three that morning, they had cleared out Roth's studio by half past four. They were in too much haste for proper crating. 'C'mon! C'mon! Le's ge' this show on the road, will yer, fellars?'

(Rosblum, a Jewish-Greek ex-waiter, survivor of the German transports from Salonika, had learned his English from the cafés and the movies.)

Rosblum and the boy, Adam, had pulled the big self-portraits out of their racks, taken them from where they rested against the walls, or lifted them off the easels. While the big fellars, more nimble than they looked, quickly taped the pictures in bubble wrap, Rosblum had compiled an inventory. Two teams, two men in each, had carried the vulnerable canvases on their stretchers, five feet by four feet, six feet by five feet, into the gallery's largest van, and chocked them into secure positions, quietly, without much disturbing the villagers – who had assumed that almost nothing was unusual at 'the artist's place'. Adam had been trusted to carry out piles of watercolours and drawings, which flopped in his arms like so much washing. Then the boy, a cheque in his pocket, had walked to his home in a nearby village. The loaded van, with a crew of two, had sneaked its way through lanes and dark villages towards the M1 and, finally, to Rosblum's nondescript but well-guarded warehouse on an industrial estate in Slough (handy for Heathrow airport).

Meanwhile, the chauffeur, on lookout, had dozed in the car.

The two men remaining in the studio had talked about 'coffee', while in truth they were rifling the makeshift kitchen for booze.

Rosblum had let them do it, while he searched for final pickings for half an hour. At the back of a drawer, otherwise filled with paint tubes, he had pounced on Roth's tatty and half-heartedly kept account book. In another drawer, what looked like a rat's nest had turned out to be some much-stained correspondence between Roth and his wife. Stained – what with? Linseed oil, turpentine, certainly. Rosblum hoped that analysis would prove there were tears. Private revelations sell names, sell pictures, and the letters would end up in Sotheby, Parke Bernet's manuscript department. Rosblum also stowed into his briefcase (kid, by Gucci) several small notebooks.

By the time Roth turned up at half past four, there had been little else left for Rosblum to do. The tables, shelves and cupboards were so crammed with oil paint, acrylic, jars of pigment waiting to be ground, brushes, rolls of canvas and unassembled stretchers that it had been clear that the secretive bloody liar had been planning to continue an intense period of work, yet Rosblum had left behind the materials for paintings that would never be executed. The books, too, had drawings or paint daubs on the pages, and even a folder of bank statements was transformed into a sketchbook of gouache studies, for Roth had been able to leave nothing alone.

Rosblum had paused for some time, between the stereo speakers on either side of the studio and by the three huge mirrors in which the lonely man had faced himself, day after day, and the nights too, sometimes. He had looked over the enigmatic mandates that Roth had scrawled upon the walls:

COLOUR   – FLOAT
STAIN AND DRIFT
FIRM-EDGED

Now that business was over, the hard-headed dealer had been moved by this stripped and desecrated room. A wounded bird had fluttered in his stomach. He could have cried.

'Worra price he paid to do this,' he said, reverently and, for him, very quietly. 'And Dorothy, too.'

The guys had found an unopened bottle of cheap Yugoslavian wine, and a part-consumed bottle of high-quality malt whisky, and they had not replied.

But when from inside the studio they heard the powerful bike, they had been instantly at the door. 'Mr Rosblum, it's Mr Roth! He's tearing round the churchyard like a loon!'

Using the tone of those uncertain how to treat one who has flipped his lid – not sure whether the situation is grave or comic – Rosblum had ushered the men out. He had switched off the lights, treble-locked the doors, and while the men watched the black, bucking figure of Roth from a distance, Pericles Rosblum had used his car phone to call the police, at the same time informing them for the second time of Roth's attack yesterday on his assistant, Adam.

Next, Rosblum had woken up Kaplan (whom he unblushingly referred to as his 'tame psychiatrist'). Kaplan had been at his clinic in Kings Langley.

'Get here fast and have this guy certified once and for all, Kaplan! You'll be here in half an hour at this time o' night. Tell the police you're on your way and arrange an ambulance. When it's done, there's a couple o' prime Roths waiting for you.'

Then they had bundled into the Rolls to watch. At four

forty-five, the ambulance and the police arrived. Kaplan had turned up ten minutes later.

'I tell yer sumpon!' Rosblum lectured his boys in the back as they watched Kaplan and the police dealing with Roth's departure. 'Sixteen years after Pollock was killed, his paintings sold for one million, yet the guy never had much dough. Fifty years after Van Gogh shot himself, a morning's work of his sells for twenty-five million. A picture he daubed of his shrink in two hours goes for eighty-five million. What happens in between? We dealers do *our* creative work. We have to be in no hurry to sell, only to collect. Tha's the moral!

'If there *is* any morality in this game,' he added, as if he needed to think about it. 'Let's get moving, boys!'

2

What the *fuck* is *that*?

Shaken by the noise of a helicopter drumming over the village,
on the previous morning Leonard Roth had arisen soaked in
nightmares. Helicopter and nightmare ran together.

It had been his lifetime's habit to dream of paintings, waking
with them clear in colour, form and tone. He might be teased
by these images for days, before being compelled to put brush
to canvas. Now it seemed that through dreams he was settling
his score with life. Or life was settling its score with him.

There are nights of dreams which leave one restored,
refreshed, healed, confident that a new life has begun. There
are other sleeps from which one awakes exhausted, tormented,
nervous, unresolved and hardly brave enough to face an
ordinary day. That was the state in which the night had cast
him up.

Once again, he'd dreamed of Dorothy. More and more frequently he'd suffered nightmares about her and most commonly
they were ones in which he could not find her.

This basic type had occurred repeatedly over the thirty years
of their marriage; prophetically, he now realized. Sometimes he
lost her in jungles of airports or supermarkets. Mostly it was
among the rambling streets, waterways and hills of his childhood home in the Jewish area of Leeds; a place maddeningly
familiar, yet every path was blocked by a strange obstacle. He
would take long, circular routes in searching for her, but find
himself back at the same spot, without success.

He understood what was reflected by this nightmare. It was
those moments when their quarrels would erupt. From the love

with which they normally cosseted one another, so familiar, so warm, so like an animal's burrow or a bird's nest, their arguments would throw them into an emptiness in which they could not find one another; could not touch, make eye contact or give words of comfort.

Last night, Dorothy had appeared to him a hundred years old. Her skin was creased, yellow and leathery, her hair had turned grey and scraggy. Her once delicate ways had been transformed into mad, erratic gestures. Her features were glaring, angry, slobbering bits of blood from the gums, while saliva dripped through rotten teeth.

It was a shocking image of the reversal of his love. Did he love her? Love the gender: woman? He believed that he did, but women made him unsure of it. At any rate, he was passionate about them, otherwise they could not have hurt him. Otherwise why was he thinking about her all the time, just as if she were a place, a landscape that was on his mind?

It was a dream out of his other self.

It was also like one of Dorothy's own paintings, which were anecdotal and often based upon subject matter that was women's property before, as it was put, 'the millennia of male-dominated art': fairy tales, especially those representing the male as sinister and voracious, in the guise of a wolf or bear, and the female as either victim or powerful witch. They were hyper-real and surreal canvases, as nightmares and fairy tales are. Quite different from his own near-abstract landscapes.

Their joint work had represented two sides of a dialogue. Now it was as if, having ceased to pursue her own career because of him (as she claimed), her alternative was to paint inside his mind, creating dreams.

Dorothy transformed herself into Victoria Voyce, Rosblum's gallery director; melted into the form of Hannah, his sister; then she became Dorothy once again.

He thought it was when this female monster was assuming Dorothy's form once more that, grasping a carving knife and swearing to kill him, she stumbled and grabbed him around the knees. She tried to hide her face from him. She was weeping.

In another dream, Dorothy and he had been in one of the

places that used to frighten him as a child, behind the huge engines, black and shaking, smelling of oil, in the dark outer ring of a fair; a place for crimes. Her eyes then, too, had gleamed viciously and her fingers had turned into threatening iron spikes. Dorothy and he had been locked in a terrifying dance. Without touching one another but with hands outstretched they circled each other, at the same time as they also circled the perimeter of the fair, where the merry-go-rounds were.

This one was a dream of cycles within cycles. He realized that it was a dance of death. It was a parody of the circular patterns of life and of seasons turning which Dorothy and he must keep up until one or other of them dropped dead.

He remembered what might be the origin of his dream. Dorothy was not the screaming type. At least when he had first known her, she had been the calmly affectionate sort of woman who knows her husband's measurements so that she can buy clothes for him while out shopping. Yet she had reached an expressionistic limit that had horrified Roth on that last trip to Greece.

Is our life to be a fight to the death? she had burst out at him. *Are you going to watch and watch me, stare at me with your terrible eye until I've melted like wax and there is nothing left of me?*

The helicopter landed beyond the sheds. Creative programme organizers? Visual-arts officers? Media directors come to interrogate him? The Arts Police arrived to deflower his talent?

It was only Mr Sandbach, the farmer.

Roth flung back bedcovers, turned and looked. Not out of the window – he couldn't bear the sudden light. At himself. Roth slept naked. Having always claimed that he painted with his penis, he could perceive (if he thought about it; he often did think about it) the history of his life and art encompassed in his genitals, from his surprise at the age of thirteen on seeing the hairs growing, to the present day shrivelling. As a boy, he had thought of his penis as an animal attached to his body. It had been an unruly fountain that spouted under the stimulation of the Leeds City tram. He had been unable to paint a tree without depicting a rampant penis. Today, he believed that art should use sexual energy, but not be about sex, necessarily. Was that merely reconciliation? The gap between the two was his life.

By his bed, there was a glass of water, the paperback that he had been reading, and many packets of pills.

Also nearby was a small black leather case, locked with a combination lock and containing a hoard of pills buried among pyjamas and underclothes. This was his emergency kit for an overdose if they carted him off and he couldn't control the situation. There was a mirror, and a sketchbook in which to portray his end. He would watch his face until his eyes closed or the pencil slipped from his grasp. No artist had ever done that.

The book contained an essay by Carl Jung about growing old gracefully. Roth thought it a good idea to read about what for him was so unlikely. The professor's advice was to treat age as a blessing. Live this stage, as one should live all the others, fully according to its potentials. Roth had tried living with impotence (impotence was Roth's definition of age) and it had turned into a hell.

With age, couples grow more like one another, the Swiss professor pointed out. With weakened libido, men become like women, women take on the characteristics of men. How often one observes it! How true! Did the feminine emerge more strongly than ever in Roth's art today?

Sitting on the edge of his bed, sweating already, heart pounding, eyes hurting, Roth carefully arranged three capsules of Valium, his tranquillizer, and three of the red-brown, triangular tablets of Tofranil, his antidepressant, in first one and then another symmetrical pattern on the bedside table. This ceremony took some time. He swallowed them, with the water. His eye caught:

Two of his paintings of her on the wall. Three photographs of her by the bed. Muse; short and fair; preserving a rosy rather than a brown skin, despite their long stays in sunny places abroad. Nothing of the middle-class leather brown about *her*! In one, her hair was shoulder-length, in another it was short, and in the earliest photograph (standing by her bicycle) she wore a Fifties fringe and ponytail.

Roth despised photographs. Compared with paintings and drawings they were flat and illusory, because no analysis of structure went into making them; they were seizures of appearances, merely. He had selected these – one from Greece last year; the earliest from Hampstead Heath, taken when they had first met in 1951; one from Spain in the middle period – because in all three she was giving him that look which he had never been able to grasp in paint, yet for which he would gladly die. All men know it, when they have been loved.

It's all eyes and visual glitter with you, isn't it? she said. *If ever you want to tell me I look good in a photograph, you say that I 'look like a model', but I only . . . I only want you to say that I look good as* MYSELF, she said.

Roth stood and stretched. Without ceremony he threw himself into stained Y-fronts and paint-stained clothes – old corduroys and a woollen check shirt with a frayed collar – as one might stuff straw into a sack. He had not attempted to be sartorial since his army days in the Forties. Big men didn't much need to dress up.

Bare and dusty boards creaked as he followed the passage to the bathroom, ducking under low ceilings.

For the last year, since they went to Greece together and came back separately, he had been living in this rented cottage. Aloneness had been a relief at first. No more carpet-bombing with emotions. The final result was shivering neurosis, with heavier and yet heavier doses of drugs. He who since he was a kid had been given to escapades on a motorcycle, later to the ecstasies of flying, now huddled in one of the cosy counties, in the village of Ashby Green (also known quite simply as Ashby), half-afraid to mount his bike and terrified of spaces.

Dr Kaplan had recommended that he 'find somewhere peaceful, stop drinking and cease having anxieties'. As Roth was clearly beyond looking for a home for himself, was more or less beyond doing anything except painting, Kaplan had found the place for him. In this cottage in the midst of nowhere, as it seemed to Roth, he had been peaceful enough for many people to think that he was already dead. It was not only readers of art magazines, visitors to galleries and lovers of landscape paintings who thought this, but also friends and those who had been to his parties. (They had been famous parties, he remembered with relish.) Now there was pleasure in choosing to be forgotten, which was the reverse of the delight in being 'famous'. It was like a sour taste after a sweet one.

Unfortunately, being without a wife and a community of acquaintances, he was unable to disperse unrealistic, unspecified fears and paranoia. That encouraged him to drink.

Neither had Roth escaped anxieties, and why should he? His whole life and work was made out of them. Anxiety was his creative element.

They had been apart half a dozen times over their thirty years, never managing to keep it up for more than a few months before they locked together again, soul twins.

For instance, in 1963 at the foolish age of fifty-three, he had shacked up in an attic in Bath with a twenty-year-old kleptomaniac, Rebecca Marks. It lasted for only six months of hectic lunacy.

Two years later Roth had fooled himself with exotic illusions about Mrs Kilburn, who set her breast-feeding infant aside in a cot by the bed among the bead curtains where they made love every afternoon, before her husband who worked for the Water Board returned for his tea. Twenty years younger than Roth, she seduced him and taunted him at the same time, with a central-heating system that compelled undressing, but that also would dry his balls to raisins. A 'pagan' with a bandanna of Indian silk around her black locks, long earrings and sandals, Mrs Kilburn had gained quite a grip on him. He started wearing sandals himself, and talked of keeping goats. Planned to follow the hippy trail to Wales, or to travel around in a converted van with her. She owned a Palaeolithic Bedford with pot plants around the windscreen.

At other periods, Roth had fled the strains of relationships altogether. Wasn't it true that all the married people were envying the unmarried ones, and vice versa? Therefore he would decide to make the most of a separation, go on a bender and relive the joys of bachelordom.

Didn't work.

Half of Roth's trouble had been that his fear of going to pieces when not anchored to Dorothy's love appeared to be self-fulfilling.

Escape from himself had proved useless. His underlying ache created its neurasthenia beneath the frivolity. Secretly he waited for his wife and wondered about her. He developed an instinct for knowing what she was doing and where she was. This had been confirmed many times.

There had also been days when he had been possessed by an insecurity that was without reason, and he had discovered later that this was when Dorothy, far away, had done something erratic and unexpected. He had been reacting to having lost his bearings. Always he was anchored to her. There was no experience, no taste, quite like that of their coming together again.

He was old-fashioned; at his age, he could be excused. Though feminists disliked him for holding such ideas, she was his anima and his muse, as well as his flesh-and-blood woman. As he had been part-animus for her. Some would say it was that fantasy which was the cause of trouble between them.

Today, all his demons poured in through the gap that Dorothy had left.

When the phone rang, his heart leaped.

He had two choices: either pull the receiver up by the root like someone wrenching out a bad tooth and determined to get the pain over, or prowl around it with his heart beating and the chance of the caller ringing off. This would be partly a relief, but leave him wondering who it was and what it was about.

Roth had become a hermit, yet depended on injections of contact through telephone calls, as if they were another drug. He managed to keep the phone ringing. He tormented himself by willing people, and making it necessary for them, to phone. They were anxious about him. (They might well be.) Perhaps there was money in the offing? Pictures? There were business deals left hanging.

Roth let it ring. As it did not stop, he abandoned his ablutions to hasten and wriggle down the low-ceilinged, narrow stairs.

3

'Len?'

It was not Dorothy. Roth recognized the voice of Sam Fall, his accountant; his voice not at all unsteady from the whisky he habitually consumed for breakfast.

Roth pictured Sam, dear complicated Sam, the stupid old bastard, blinking through thick pebble-glasses out of a near-circle of lank, grey hair, like an intellectual half-blinded with books. But he would probably be clad in a leather jacket, leather trousers or tight designer jeans, although he was sixty years old. His ample London office would be in bachelor disarray, not with junk but with a large collection of contemporary art works; a million quid's worth, it had been estimated. He wasn't such a fool as he looked.

That is, as Roth pictured him: rocking back and forth on the rear two legs of his desk chair, the white phone on his knee like a pet cat.

Fall was one of the few people who still called Roth 'Len' as if he were a child. It was Roth's own fault. He'd always had a weakness for allowing others to straighten out his life. His mother; his sisters; Dorothy; dealers. If Roth should be put away, he planned to depend upon Fall to smuggle in a bottle of whisky to wash down the final overdose (though Fall did not yet know this).

The accountant telephoned often. The men were linked by friendship, and by Roth's investments, which Fall handled.

'Sam Fall here. How are you?'

'Okay, Sam. Fine. I'm okay. Mustn't gringe.'

'Sleeping any better?'

'Not much. The pills and the drink wear off in the middle of the fucking night and I can't wait until morning for another dose. I think they make me dream. I have terrible dreams, Sam. They never stop. They persecute me.'

'You're still on the Tofranil prescribed by Dr Kaplan?'

Sam sounded anxious, but also impatient to be assured that Roth was on the track he recommended.

'I think it's having side effects and brings on these nightmares. When I was a kid in Leeds, I called my first studio that my mother gave me in the attic, my "Dream Room", because up there I used to . . . fuck it, I used to like dreaming.' Roth's deep voice quavered and fell limp. He was glad that Fall could not see the increasing wreckage: his sweating, nervousness and palpitations. His swearing, and the quaver of his voice, delivered their clues over the phone clearly enough. He couldn't help it, though it gave the advantage to his combatants, fuck it.

'Kaplan is the best psychiatrist in London for your condition, Len. It's only because I hold his account that I could get even you on to his books.'

'Do *you* think you can cure my destructiveness with drugs, Sam? I don't want anyone telling me any more that yesterday I beat them up, when I can't remember anything about it. Nor that I was grovelling in my own sick, in some place I can't even fucking remember. When we were in Greece last year, I woke up with my hands around Dorothy's neck. She was terrified that she wouldn't be able to wake me in time.'

'Lots of people get locked in a situation, alternately loving and hating, gnawing destructively at each other. You know as well as anyone that it can go on through a lifetime, yet couples stay together. But keep on the Tofranil, Len.'

'My damned heart never stops hammering.'

'*Are you still taking it?*'

There poured through the telephone all the impatience and articulate simplicity that Roth recognized as belonging to those still pursuing careers; how far away that seemed.

'Yes.'

'That's a good boy, Len! The Valium helping?'

'No, I don't feel so fucking tranquil. I heard the other

day that it has side effects, too. Blurs vision, deranges the senses.'

'Who's giving you all this weird information?'

'Dorothy.'

'So you *are* communicating?'

'Not much. It's difficult over the phone. Conversations always break down and we start arguing. Or crying. We've more or less stopped talking any more.'

'You're a naughty boy, Len! Be careful. You can't believe anything a woman says who's your opponent in divorce. These women are wily. She might be wanting to kill you. Encouraging you to drive yourself mad. Side effects only touch a small percentage of cases. If you weren't taking the drug, you'd be worse.'

'You're talking nonsense, Sam. Dorothy's not at all like that. You know the kind of woman she is. She's been asking around on my behalf. She was telling me about someone she's met who's on similar drugs. I forget what else she said. It's half past eight in the fucking morning and I haven't even washed yet, Sam. I've got these damned flies in my eyes.'

'Flies in your eyes?'

'A plague of them out of the rape and the corn.'

'You're joking.'

No, he was not joking. The flies were bloodless, sharp as splinters of ebony, and they were everywhere, sticking to fresh oil paintings, getting into the frames of watercolours, invading his bed at night. After he'd been for a walk he washed them off his skin, and with the soap they turned into black cream.

'What's the point of painting landscapes when the land's fucked up? The goddess has flown, Sam! The goddess has flown!'

Sam was used to this flowery language and took little notice.

'Can you hear those guns popping?' Roth asked.

'Yes. What are they?'

Outside, scattered on the flat fields, were guns designed to frighten rooks and pigeons from the crops. Fired by regular explosions of bottled gas, they went off every few minutes, pop! pop! As they had done all night, entering his dreams.

'Bird-scarers. I'd sleep better without that.'

'You'll soon recover your nerves, Len, so long as you keep up the treatment.'

'But you haven't phoned me before office hours to give me medical advice, Sam.'

'How is it with Dorothy?'

'I think she's doing okay. Full of anger, but she doesn't say she's short.'

'Len, we have to talk about your estate. I think you're going to have to take Dorothy out of the trusteeship. Forgive my being blunt, and I know we've talked this through before, but you've got to *do* something, Leonard Roth. Yes, *do* something. There's no knowing what association she'll form now, or what influence a new man might have on her. Even at her age anything can happen, especially with an estate in the offing. Just leave it to Rosblum and myself and maybe one other person – we could talk about that – to carry out your wishes and to fulfil your provision for Dorothy. All you've got to do is make up your mind what you want to do.

'And there's another detail that I must point out, Len. It's important that you don't stipulate too much about the destiny of the pictures – how they are to be hung and where. I appreciate your anxiety but it hinders the probate, and conditions attached bring the prices down.'

Roth wasn't listening, his mind deep in something else. He hesitated, then he plunged. He knew these hesitations, followed by dives straight into a mania. It was like the act of painting.

'Sam! She's holding a party tonight, up in Leeds, at Prospect Terrace.'

'I know. You told me about it yesterday. And a couple of days before that. *And* last week, after you left the clinic. You've forgotten.'

'I keep thinking that on the bike I could be up there in three hours. Home! Home, Sam! It'd be our first meeting in months. A chance to talk it out apart from over the telephone. I could celebrate with her. Enjoy the old fun times again. It would be a nice surprise.'

'Don't do it, Leonard! You know that in your condition you

shouldn't be going on that bloody bike. Who the hell else careers around on a powerful bike at the age of seventy-one? And you're already getting too excited to be able to talk to Dorothy. I can feel it at this distance. Leave it to the lawyers to sort her out. Leave it to us and to the gallery. We'll gladly take the burden from you.'

'You don't understand! I *want* to talk to her. We need each other.'

'Don't even try! I'm sending her the allowance you agreed. It's more than generous. She's sent me on her quarterly bills.'

'You just pay them. If they get over the top, let me know.'

'They're over the top already, in my opinion, and you're setting a precedent. How's Krupnik handling the divorce proceedings for you?'

'He writes a lot of fucking letters, which are a lot of fucking rubbish because there aren't any *proceedings*, yet. I've told you enough times, you mad old bastard, that I don't want to start them, and Dorothy isn't interested either, and I don't want to hear you fuckers talking about it any more. I'm not interested! Why can't you listen to me? A lawyer coming into it, sending out what he calls "warning salvoes", is making things worse between us. Why have you been pushing him on me? I wish you'd all stop fucking *pushing*!'

Leonard felt hot. His piles of tormented and tormenting letters – between Dorothy and himself, between himself and the gallery over his contract with them, over his will and his trust fund – had grown to the thickness of *The Brothers Karamazov*. Instead of knives, the knives of his dreams, there were letters aimed at his gut. He didn't want any fucking letters. He didn't answer them. Some he didn't open. Words weren't Roth's medium.

'You're an impossible person to take care of, Leonard Roth! Remember you've a sizeable estate that will need looking after and you can't afford to leave all your business to chance. An artist doesn't have to have a filing cabinet and a secretary if he doesn't want them, but – '

'Thanks.'

' – But it's a good job you have friends!'

'Sometimes.'

Sometimes Roth detested the way that Fall had swallowed responsibility for his family, health and psychological problems, as well as his accounts and investments. He hated him for it, yet suffered what Kaplan's cliché termed 'classic dependency syndrome'.

Roth often wondered how he had got himself into this position, and he didn't see how to extricate himself.

Anyway, Fall had his good side. He was interesting, and Roth's imagination was fed by his lifelong sympathy with mad, interesting old fuckers. Fall had a curious face that was worth painting. It was as if there were half a dozen other faces squeezed in behind it, struggling to get out, fighting at the doors of eyes and mouth.

Anyway, it was too late to go hunting for another accountant. Imagine the paperwork, the time, the complications. Sam Fall had embedded himself too deeply. Imperceptibly, while Roth had been off his guard, every strand of his life had become tangled with Fall's office. His relationship with his accountant was itself like a marriage, built upon consideration and affection, after which cruel liberties were practised. It was a love-hate relationship in which Roth still depended upon Fall to become the agent of nemesis.

Whenever Roth became irritable with the trap, Fall remained amiable and considerate. He would chide the painter as if he were an infant. *Temper, Len, temper! We've known each other a long time!*

'Your gallery was on the phone to me yesterday, Len. Where are the new landscapes? Did you bring so little back from Greece? Done nothing since?'

'I'll tell you some day about what happened.'

Roth managed to speak with the old growl that he'd always used to shake off unwanted enquiries; it was Roth's technique for remaining a private man.

'The Station think you are not releasing work and that they have a right to see some,' Fall persisted smoothly.

'They never exhibit or sell for me these days. I don't know how much they're storing. Whenever I ask, there's always some reason why I can't get to see it.'

Roth continued to growl. If he had been physically present to
Fall, he would have been threatening, still with something left
of the bulk of a rhinoceros.

'I'll look into it for you.'

'You've promised that before, Sam, you scatterbrained bastard!'

'Hold on a minute. I'll make a note this time.'

Roth heard the two front legs of Sam's chair hit the floor.

'Besides, my contract lapsed three months ago.'

'No, it didn't.'

'Yes, it did!' They had discussed this before. 'I'm sick of
them! My decades of slavery were up three fucking months
ago. Okay?'

'Len, the contract you signed was automatically renewable for
a further two years, unless you gave at least six months' notice
of your intention to conclude it. In writing – not just grumbling
about it for a couple of years. You didn't do that.'

'You didn't warn me.'

'You didn't ask me. Not specifically, to actually *do* something.'

'How was I to know the rules? *You* keep the contract. You
sound like the fucking Arts Police yourself.'

'Len, you're just not in touch with reality. *Reality*, Len! You
spend too much of your time worshipping nature, or whatever
it is you get up to. The position, which may be a sorry one
from your point of view, is that you owe them some work, and
you can't sell from the studio, as they suspect you of doing,
without their at least knowing about it and getting commission.
That's the position for another two years. As your accountant,
I wouldn't have a leg to stand on in presenting any other case.
Anyway, the Station have done very well for you for the past
quarter of a century. They've made your reputation. And if you
do sell without their taking an overview, you might well devalue
your own work by creating a glut.'

Teaching his granny to suck eggs, Roth thought.

'How's the painting going, now you're not fighting with
Dorothy every day, or whatever it was you've had on your back
recently?' Sam asked benignly, feeling he'd got his point over.

'I *am* fighting her every day. In my head. And I'm fighting myself, too. I'm not doing much else. A few small sketches, bits and pieces. Some drawings. The studio's empty, I'm afraid. So you might as well keep all your fucking noses out of it,' Roth added, genially. 'It would only depress you.'

'Well, we'd both better get on. Some artists do their best work when they reach your age. They turn out the stuff that clinches their careers. "Painting's an old man's passion," as someone famous said. Was it Monet? Keep hold of it. Have a good day.'

'Have a good day.'

Sam Fall put his phone back on his desktop and continued to steep himself in post-breakfast Glenfiddich, meanwhile staring at a framed Hockney crayon drawing of seductive boys by a swimming pool. Recently acquired, it leaned against a bookcase for constant contemplation.

——Roth is more similar to an American frontiersman than to any British painter. That's the truth of why he gets into such a pickle here. He's never been comfortable in Britain. It's not big enough. It's like having to make love in too small a bed: from time to time his limbs are out in the cold. One reason why he's travelled so much.

His great mistake was not to have settled in New York, with its room and encouragement for size and gesture. Unless instinct told him that New York would kill him. There'd be no restraint, he'd feel so much at home.

I wonder if Roth's kinship with Pollock, Gorky et cet-er-a (hiccup), pardon, has to do with his parents?

I never met either of them, but I know that his father hated art. His mother loved it. Loved what he did even as a tiny kid. Loved everything, the way mothers can.

They can give you a complex, too. A man never straightens out his relationships with women after a possessive mother. The archetypal mother is all that he understands.

That's the American frontier brew for producing an artist. Pollock's biography. Art, feeling and literature were the woman's domain in the parlour, so a man who went in for it soon felt he had to make sure he outshone the men at their game, too.

In the Jewish community in Leeds, and poking his head out into the gentile one, Roth had to keep proving he was a man, as much as if he had been the son of a storekeeper in Nebraska. Not, heaven forbid (blurp – pardon), a poofter.

Made him very attractive. But I could never get him interested. He was exclusively into women, if I may put it that way.——

4

Roth was, indeed, aware of how the Station Gallery had 'done very well' for him.

They had started showing Roths in mixed exhibitions as soon as Rosblum opened solo in England in the late Forties, after first establishing himself in partnership in Paris. His London advisers told him to specialize in the romantic postwar boom in landscape art.

Rosblum wasn't much into landscapes himself. It was too English a taste for him. Rosblum's Neanderthal hunch, Roth discovered, was to go for 'big, excitin' pictures, to fill big places'.

Roth's work was suitable in both ways. Also his expressionist trends fitted in with the speciality of Rosblum et Jordain of the Rue des Beaux Arts, first set up to sell a postwar cache of Soutines. Roth, a hardly exhibited artist, came to the Station like a virgin to a marriage, satisfying on all counts.

Between 1949 and 1951 Roth went through one of his transformations, from precisely observed landscapes to abstract expressionism with affinities to some of the St Ives painters, especially Peter Lanyon and Roger Hilton. A wilder element was close to the maverick David Bomberg. At the time, all these artists were still on the fringes of popular taste. The St Ives painters had seemed to Roth then, as they appeared to him now, the most pregnant and forceful British painters of the century, when considered as a school. Looking over their shoulders, Roth caught his first glimpse of New York abstract expressionism.

Roth was given his first one-man show during the auspicious Festival of Britain year, 1951; that was when he met Dorothy, who then was exhibiting with the same gallery. The Station was happy to put him on contract. Hard to believe that it was thirty fucking years ago.

Artists then were naive about the long-term contract, which was a new method of 'handling' painters. Paying him a retainer fee and taking in consignments of Roth's output, the Station held back many pictures from exhibition while they worked on influential people who would raise the value.

Paradoxically, they also encouraged him to be prolific. Sparsity gave them cold feet about his career, too – and it had been to stimulate his energies that he had first been encouraged to experiment with drugs. The gallery got academics to buy cheaply or to accept gifts of minor canvases, which were really bribes for them to write monographs; to create a myth about the artist and raise his worth.

Rosblum, arriving in Paris after the liberation, had learned from Left Bank intellectuals the value of friends conversing and writing about one another. Society figures were encouraged to become collectors and then to name-drop 'Leonard Roth' into the ears of gossip writers. With meals, flattery and small gifts of paintings, young, aspiring journalists were easily corrupted. In the Sixties, the first television arts journalists and the first officers of arts organizations began their careers, keeping their ears to the ground and picking up retailable names, buzz words and catch phrases.

The demands had torn some artists to shreds: those, such as Roth, who looked tough, but were more vulnerable than they appeared.

The publicity divided Roth from himself so that he did not know who he was. The Station knew what they wanted him to be. Photographers were briefed before visiting his studio. Afterwards, intelligent, busy people in the gallery's back room devoted hours to cropping prints in order to 'project the right image'.

The marketing strategy for Roth contrasted him with the escapist landscape artists who were satisfying a reaction against the war. Rosblum's business instinct overriding that of his gentle-manly advisers, the Station dropped most of the romantic painters, one by one, slowly, without informing them. It ruthlessly, although not openly, denigrated its erstwhile stable in order to promote Roth.

It could take several years to wreck a reputation, as it could to create one. The Station's behind-the-scenes work, using arts magazines, adverse marketing and innumerable small forms of neglect to stab artists in the back, cost Leonard many friends who blamed him, not the gallery, for his promotion and their own neglect.

Roth disdained to keep a cuttings book, but on looking through the Station's he saw that his newspaper images had belonged to two categories.

One was the toughie: the individualist who held affinities with the artists of St Ives but did not go there, eschewing the comforts of group companionship. He was portrayed as a fighter and an adventurer. He was photographed with his then black hair tousled over his heavy-jowled, heavy-eyed, brooding face. In the earlier years, before he gave up smoking, they would show a fag drooping from his mouth. Wearing 'the slouched but alert expression of a jungle cat', he was set up in a Soho street. It was around this time that he began to wear black leather motorbike gear, even for gallery openings. Eleven years ago, at the age of sixty, he was posed wearing flying kit before the plane that had taken him up to his first aerial landscapes. 'The artist who said, "Turner would have loved an aeroplane,"' the caption read. He was posed in paint-encrusted jeans, hands on hips, standing aggressively before his pictures. Photographers wanted to show in the background only his biggest paintings; only size was dramatic and ambitious to them.

In the late 1950s and early Sixties, Roth, forty to fifty years of age, had been made to look like a Jewish James Dean. Reporters expected him to be rude to them, to be late for appointments and drunk. Otherwise they never came up with the copy that sold pictures. The best article of all was written after he had beaten up the reporter.

The other popular image was of the racked, introspective artist. In one famous shot (first published in a limited-edition volume covering six artists, at £100 per copy and now worth £1,000 if signed by some of the painters), this message was fortified by photographing Roth from the back, apparently brooding over huge canvases, curls of cigarette smoke rising meditatively. He was often shown with a collection of whisky bottles and glasses among the brushes and paints.

Because of this myth-making, lovers of his work were baffled when Roth, crudely defined as a 'violent' painter, also painted small, delicate watercolours.

Roth had been forced to dress in certain ways and express particular opinions. He had seen that 'Leonard Roth' on television. Today, he could watch him on videos. Late at night, the old man might keep company with a stranger who was yet himself, darting at a canvas with what now looked such a quaint and dated eagle expression. In his midfifties, he had seemed bulky and confident on a chat show, comfortably filling his chair. There he sat, with whom? Poets, novelists, politicians, *names*, who like himself were pushing for opportunities to speak. In one video he explained why, although there was a link between St Ives, Cornwall, and the gloom and soot of West Yorkshire – some St Ives artists were born in Yorkshire or had lived and worked there – he himself had not made the move. He glamorized it as independence. He knew it had more to do with insecurity, working-class background and lack of social graces.

The St Ives painters were, relatively, gentlemen. Also, Roth never overcame his feelings of being an outsider because he was Jewish. It was aggravated because he had not lost the accent of the Leeds Jews, which was a mixture of Yiddish and Yorkshire. He bluffed his way before microphone and camera, feeling the worse for sensing the gallery at his back. With the duty to entertain or shock on his mind, he would say more than he meant, and be trapped into aggressive hyperbole. Very working-class, that. No one seemed to spot his unease.

He even swore on early television. Alas for publicity, he was not the first to make his mark this way. Brendan Behan had been the first to swear on screen.

Alas, too, for Roth's career within the framework of 'working-class art', he did not produce the correct kitchen-sink, social-realist iconography expected from painters of his background, either. He remained a loner. That was his strength.

The difficulty was that Roth, like any artist, grew not because of his certainties, but through his doubts. Doubt was the last thing that a dealer, or what Victoria Voyce of the Station Gallery termed a 'committed collector', wanted to hear about. And a big man, especially, was not supposed to question himself.

The gallery was in the same trap that it devised for its artists. Operating in an unstable market, they were compelled to be assertive in selling a product which they knew thrived on self-questioning and on changes of direction. Their own insecurity made them nervous when their artists changed tack.

'Decide who you are, Leonard Roth, otherwise we can't sell you!'

To avoid being stereotyped, periodically he had gone into hiding, keeping new work secret until its content had grown stale.

Thus Roth had to cope with being split into two people: one of them the public myth and the other his private, creative self.

Perhaps there were many divisions in his character. He recognized a split between the masculine and the feminine. He saw that, in inspiration, his painting was feminine – the colour, the poetry, his loose and easy draughtsmanship, the loops and arabesques of his forms, the dependence upon nature – though expressed through a male drive at the end of his paintbrush. He kept the feminine for his art; the masculine as his shell to face the world.

Now, after thirty years of acknowledgement, he was paying the price. If he was indeed ill, division in his personality was at the root. Could that be healed with Tofranil and Valium? Even Roth often doubted.

'Who are we today?' Dorothy had joked, acidly, at the end of her tether.

This was when the shadow was beginning to cloud her eyes and it was becoming clear that the Station, supposed to be exhibiting and promoting her, too, was interested only in her

husband. She said it years later also, when angrily she had cut
her hair short and refused to dye it, perversely glad that this
savage hacking did not 'suit' her.

She echoed the very words of his gallery when they were
confused in their struggle to stereotype him.

At last he realized that a split, in need of healing, was being
encouraged by the Station. One character, true to himself, had
to be kept private; the other was a public being, but a fake.

5

' "Do not go gentle into that good night." '

Roth was in a rage against God, age, fate, and death. If only I could get my hands around His whiskery old neck, I'd strangle the fucker. Old Jehovah. Old Nobodaddy.

He had once believed that we are granted the time we need to complete our work and that it is when our life's task is over that we begin to die. Try to imagine Van Gogh, Dylan Thomas or Keats as old men. Now Roth found that he was still full of intentions.

On his turmoiled route alone from Greece on the Laverda almost a year before, Roth had called at La Ruche in the Passage Danzig, Montparnasse, in order to see if his old friend, the painter Marcus Reinhardt, was still alive.

During the Thirties they had been impoverished neighbours in the famous nest of rickety studios previously occupied by Soutine, Chagall and Modigliani. The district was still seedy, though now it was in a 1960s–70s way rather than a between-the-wars one. The greatest difference was that a dull park replaced the massive abattoir where once everything from chickens to horses had been slaughtered and where Roth had strolled with Chaim Soutine. Roth had used his bulk to defend his quarrelsome friend in his shouting matches with the slaughtermen from whom he wanted the rancid chickens and lumps of bloodied meat that he painted.

La Ruche – 'the beehive' – was a rickety tower of some sixty studios, built by filling in the iron girders of a small companion piece to the Eiffel Tower that was transported to Montparnasse after the 1889 exhibition. It struck Roth as being like a birdcage.

From its neglected garden Roth could see the artists, busy as pecking birds behind the huge studio windows on each flattened segment. The studios, tapering towards the doors which opened on to the central staircase, were shaped like wedges of cake.

Nowadays, though the garden was overgrown and the little theatre that had been there had vanished, the building was tidied into smart apartments. Where had all the stovepipes gone? There used to be one sticking out of every window. What had happened to the fire-hazardous loops and meanderings of the electric wiring, which everyone connected for himself to the main supply?

More than anything else, that had imparted a lively feeling of life's chief lesson: that it is transient. The rickety electrics worked at some varying point of balance between not functioning and going up in a blue flash. The day-to-day risk of fire turned the studios into a treasure ship voyaging upon incalculable waters.

Until the 1980s, art had a way of shifting its centre. Florence, Venice, Paris, New York and London took their turns. It was not Paris's turn any longer While much of Parisian painting descended into stylish pastiches of cubism or into other, derivative, pretty versions of the greater decades that had passed, Marcus had kept his integrity, and had stayed on at La Ruche with dignity.

Roth might be troubled by age, but Marcus was eighty: ten years older than Roth. They had known each other before the war. Marcus, unlike Soutine, had survived the German occupation. In 1980, Roth was still strong but Marcus was frail, thin as a small sick bird and almost blind. He had never enjoyed as much acclaim as Roth, yet his atelier was crowded with paintings and with his lifetime's other accretions, mostly books and framed honours for his courage.

Marcus could hardly see them any more. He was aware only of vague shapes and suggestions of colours. The only true remaining possessions, the ones of which he had a grasp, were the blankets on his bed, his walking stick, his clothes, his bag, invariably with a bottle or two of wine sticking out of it, and the multiple locks that he could still manage to fumble for on his door.

Roth found in the studio brilliant landscapes and sensual nudes from years before when Reinhardt had possessed his full sight. They were harmonies of chrome yellow, gold and crimson. He had also painted flowers, which he called 'angels'; their colours so light, numinous and fluttering that they appeared winged visitants.

Today, Marcus had to run his fingers over them merely to recognize the textures of glass or board. The man who had painted with colour and sensuality had nothing more to do with his pictures any longer, other than to fumble for surfaces and edges. He valued them only as tokens of what he remembered.

Was this all that artistic striving was worth?

Roth had felt one of those inexplicable shivers that in the north of England makes one say, 'A ghost walked over my grave.'

It amazed Roth how old people clung to their baggage more pathetically than did the young, who had some future use for objects. He himself wasn't any different. Today he was fuelling his illness by worrying about the destiny of his pictures. Old couples, who once loved one another, squabbled over sixpences while death stared them in the face, and apparently death made them like that. One would think they'd appreciate ephemeral joy and beauty the more; would realize that happiness consists of living in the beauty and eternity of the present. Instead, fear that life was nearly over made them cling to meannesses.

Roth was haunted by photographs of Jews clutching their suitcases while being hustled to the death camps. Some had been his relatives; old couples and children of the Pale who had been dragged out to be hanged outside their huts.

Other events were so awful that they could hardly be forced to rise into consciousness. There was the fate of his sister Rachel, a communist, trapped in Poland at the outbreak of war, who was condemned to dance on broken glass before she was executed 'by Germans who smiled', so Roth had been told.

He imagined these people before they left their homes, scrambling and worrying over precious things, a grandfather's watch, a piece of embroidery, their fear of forgetting an heirloom stealing away their last hours of life. They might as well have laughed for one last time. Did anyone ever laugh on the way to Belsen or Auschwitz?

Such people, who could truly live in the present moment, did exist, Roth was sure, although he had never met one.

Roth had once rejected the possibility of a geriatric old age. Not for him his own armchair in a crumblies' rest-home among the Surrey pines, humoured by nannies while he faded out, stifling his pain. He would consider himself dead before he was wheeled in through the gates.

Instead he had in his fifties formed a strategy, which he had announced to friends as they sprawled their elbows in the pools of ale spilled on a garden table, or relaxed on the Rectory lawn in Wiltshire with their wine glasses shining in the sun.

'We should buy a house between us,' Roth suggested to a circle of notoriously drunken painters, plus a haphazard band of lunatics such as artists tend to gather, their trades and professions incongruously ranging between builder's labourers, actresses, accountants and poets. 'We should drink as much as we can, smoke, enjoy as much sex as we are still able for, paint, write and follow only two rules, *no gringeing and no cosseting*, until each of us goes out in noise and glory and fucking.'

Now that age was with him, the course was harder to follow. Roth's capacities for sex and ale had faded remorselessly, and friends had disappeared. Several were dead. Others had gone to distant places, had entered the reserves of marriages that were inhospitable to survivors of the old, wild circle, or they had been swallowed into careers that made them strangers to him.

Over the last decades there had been two phases in their decline. In the 1960s and early Seventies, one had died of what was now known to be AIDS, one had become a disciple of Bhagwan and lost his possessions in California, one was incarcerated with DTs and another with heroin addiction. That period had ended with many liberal-minded talents dragged down in a vortex of sickness and/or failure. In more caring or, perhaps, simply more prosperous times, they had formed false hopes that couldn't be fulfilled as the empire declined.

Britain had wasted its taxes on pretentious, absurd adventures
– the Brabazon aeroplane, Suez, Concorde and building up
an overarmed island. During the same period the quality of
education, hospitals, housing and finance for the arts leaked
away, and the good things in life shifted to countries that didn't
take part in the arms race. That was when the Station first cannily
exhibited Roth's work in Japan and Australia.

In the second phase, starting in the late Seventies, friends less
frequently faded into drug addiction or loony religions. In the
present years of praising 'enterprise', oddly it was risk-taking
and all forms of liberal or adventurous thought that were leaking
away. It was a mark of the era's philistinism and mercenariness
that artists had become financially 'hard-nosed'; that very term
had arisen recently. The scope of all the arts was narrowing in
the interests of balancing the books and crowd-catching. One
painter turned into a fund raiser – that, too, was a profession
risen to prominence. Another became an administrator, his
talk rigid with artspeak. What was priced but not valued – a
picture locked away in a vault – was measured in percentage
returns. Desperately, artists talked more of making money, less
of making art.

Yet Leonard Roth, who hadn't a clue how to make or save
money, acquired it in quantity from the Sixties onwards. It
fell into his gallery's office from exhibitions, some of which he
didn't even bother to visit, in Munich, Sydney and New York,
where famous collectors 'acquired him'. Now the Saatchis had
appeared, looking for Roths, persuading the Station to release
some good ones – if they had them, that matter being ever
surrounded with mystery. Roth had kicked off in the Fifties
and Sixties as an 'English phenomenon', and he felt that he
had crashed through the ensuing decades as if mounted on
his bike.

Looking back over his life, that was his prime image of himself:
he never seemed to be off that crimson, thrusting, powerful
bike, even when mounted on a paintbrush or curled up with
Dorothy.

Meanwhile, the period from the late Forties through to
the Seventies was punctuated by the deaths of burned-out

artists. They were fabled deaths that managed to be both
sordid and magnificent. Arshile Gorky hung himself in 1948,
Jackson Pollock crashed into a slender tree in 1956, Sylvia Plath
gassed herself in 1963, Mark Rothko died with slashed arms
in 1970, John Berryman leaped, waving, off Brooklyn Bridge in
1972. These were among the ghosts who haunted Roth in the
Hertfordshire countryside.

Less glamorous friends merely faded away. Old ones, artists
neglected by the Station perhaps, ceased to suggest walks,
expeditions and drunken get-togethers. The rougher ones
stopped coming to his parties, and left them to the suave picture
buyers. He needed those rough, unmanageable friends.

It was when his acquaintances withdrew that Roth began his
dependence on the telephone. Increasingly he made a virtue of
necessity and became a hermit.

Before that time he used to believe that 'spectral images of
death' was a romantic figure of speech. Death was real enough
now, having presided over the diminishing of his faculties
during the past years – his fading memory, his breathlessness,
the aches that lived permanently like alien ghosts in his muscles. Roth, like a medieval artist, saw Death as tall and even
thinner than he himself had grown; skeletal, with a grey wool
shroud. Probably he had a complexion like Roth's: grey skin and
bloodshot eyes that frightened people whom he met in the street
and pub. Death followed him on the stair and looked over his
shoulder at his easel as he worked in the night. Death peered
down at his shrivelled balls in the bathroom.

Now, instead of sharing his deepest feelings with friends,
Leonard Roth, like most old people, tried to keep his craven
fear of death to himself.

6

——Think of the early days. After making love, Dorothy would curl under the covers, turned away and perhaps humming. The sight revived my blind absorption in her. I never knew what I was feeling. I was feeling everything in the world, in one huge torrent, drowning. Sore maybe, when I thought that nothing more could revive me, I would lie upon her yet again, though limbs were warm and fulfilled. I did not care how I lay. I fitted into her as snow into flowers.

It was the ultimate contentment, like that of someone who has been drowning, fighting the sea and exhausted, but who has at last been cast upon warm sand, in peace, under the sun, hearing far away the ocean that cannot reach him any more.

For days, weeks, months on end, I felt that I had a sunflower, a dandelion, a Greek-spring glow of a flower in my heart. A gold coin to buy me the whole world. The things I would otherwise have hated, such as shopping in a crowded supermarket, brought me joy if I was with Dorothy. Every moment of the day was invested with love. Everything brought us joy. Pleasure is too slight a word for it. The sight of pots in the kitchen, flowers in the garden, the voices of friends.

On the days when we had painted side by side together, there was an aura of happiness around us that excluded the remainder of the world.

Oh, what have I done to her? What have I done?——

Roth made it to the bathroom at last.

He had to wash off not only the summer's plague of flies, but also those dreams clinging to him like sticky sweat.

He brushed his teeth and the sound in his head filled the lonely cottage. He buzzed an electric razor over his face.

With his free hand, he twisted his features before the mirror. He was attempting to take himself by surprise; to pounce upon a new shape, a new image, as one has an insight about a stranger at the moment of meeting, losing its sharpness later. After he switched off the razor he continued to pull his cheeks, his mouth and the skin of his forehead, so as to exaggerate his expression. Fifty years of landscape painting had come to an end and he was looking at something else. Because he needed to know himself, Roth was painting self-portraits.

Each one showed a different face. For most of his life he had been intrigued that everyone had seen him as a different person. This was especially true of women, because they came closest and scrutinized the most. Possibly, too, they had the greatest stake in reinventing him. Mrs Kilburn had seen him as 'unearthly' and a 'planetary visitor' – which meant nothing, because she experienced little that was not 'unearthly'. If she found a toadstool that she didn't recognize, it had beamed in from Mars. Rebecca Marks had called him the Wandering Jew: the stranger everywhere, martyred but gifted with the right to exist outside ethics. Roth had been prey to women's animus projections. That happened to artists.

He had appeared on 'the art scene' at the time when another distasteful word, 'charisma', was also over- and misused. Anybody who got into the newspapers as dangerous or mysterious had 'charisma'.

Charisma was like a newly fallen apple to a wasp. The problem was that men with charisma were, ipso facto, supposedly strong and they attracted women who needed someone to lean upon, and someone through whom they could express themselves. Roth, big, muscularly strong and possessing charisma, attracted neurotic women.

Problems followed when they realized that Roth was as pliable and lost as all other men who become husbands, inspiring wives with the reflection that men are but children.

7

Roth finished in the bathroom. It was now half past nine of that decisive June day.

Although reconciliation was on his mind, he knew how dangerous it would be to go to Leeds. For himself, drugged up to the eyeballs on a bike – an addiction to bikes was in itself a form of drug – but most frightening for her, who had told him many times that she had seen enough of his going out drunk, playing Russian roulette by tearing round blind corners on the wrong side of the road, or getting the pilot to skim too close to a mountain slope so that he could memorize it, as if he wanted to count the bloody flowers.

How could he have done such things, risking lives? There was nothing admirable about that. At his age! (For she was still saying it to him at sixty-five; at seventy.) He was a madman. Who might be waiting around the corner when he drove the Laverda like that? A child walking home from school, perhaps? Playing with other people's grief as if they were paints on a palette! How indeed could she be expected to live with such a person as he could turn into – one eschewing all that was kind in his nature, becoming murderous as soon as he stopped painting?

As soon as he arrived staggering on her doorstep, she would believe that it was the savage half of him, the gentle half having been left inside his studio.

And if she let him in? The moment that a conversation threatened, she would anticipate being drawn down again into his mad maelstrom of feelings.

Why was he thus? Was destructiveness necessarily involved in the practice of art?

Dorothy often spoke of the wolfish destructiveness of Picasso. In the Picasso Museum in Paris you could see how with each style of painting a new woman came. The women follow one another through the Picasso galleries as the dominating icons of different rooms. For a time, the artist was possessed by a particular woman, because of her beauty or, as in the 1940s with Dora Maar, her tragic air which personified the times.

After the infatuation, there followed a period requiring expression – a new style. For its sake, a woman was discarded as totally as a worn-out way of painting.

'*I* don't want to be one in a series of your women!' Dorothy had exclaimed. 'Tina, Rebecca, Joan Kilburn, me, then who else, who comes after me when you have wrung everything from me? *I know you!*'

There was nothing more desperate for her to say. Or scream; for by this stage, he had got this quiet woman to scream at him from time to time. It was not natural to her and it left her quaking, flushed, and even more angry with herself.

Soon she would calm down into an icy bitterness.

'The danger of life with an artist is that there's always something else, some new interest for him running underneath, and no one else can see it! *Yet!*'

Roth realized what a menace he was. What a tigress was his anima. Was it worth it?

Maybe, if you believe that art 'justifies the human condition', 'transcends the confines of material existence', makes life worthwhile, and has to do with God. But what if art is no more than a game? The evidence of Picasso's last paintings is that he died staring out of preposterous wealth and fame with unflinching horror into nothingness. He was certain there was only extinction awaiting Pablo Ruiz Picasso. So what was all the pain and the money worth?

When it is admitted that there is no eternal life, then art *is* a game. To see it in any other way is to be merely sentimental.

Yet atavistic magic still lay at its root, persistent under what was reasonable. It fed the illusion that the artist does not merely create metaphors to illustrate life, but transcends and ennobles it.

Also surviving among our superstitions was that other primitive notion of the artist as the victim, cultivated and fattened for sacrifice, burning himself out in forms of expression on behalf of others. Because of it, the artist is indulged in his predatoriness and destructiveness. Hence the magnificence of those otherwise sordid deaths of Pollock and Rothko.

Meanwhile those close to the artist could not help themselves from paying their tithes; from being used, burned up with nothing left for themselves afterwards.

Picasso's widow, Jacqueline, the last one of these sufferers, as his wives and mistresses often regarded themselves, was so much in thrall to his creativity, a sacrificial victim herself, that she killed herself after he died. There was nothing else left for her. She was lonely for her torturer.

Roth was horrifed by what he might do to Dorothy, unintentionally, just because of what he was. Even at his age he was still a danger to her.

Was art worth that? Was it worth so much for the sake of a game?

Again the telephone rang. Roth waited. Hovered. Ran. Sweated.

That awful silence, before someone speaks. The whole world stops.

As usual, Roth did not give his name or number. A woman with an Irish voice asked for 'Kevin'.

'Sorry, wrong number.'

His heartbeat increased again. It was the pounding that frightened him most.

'What number are you calling?'

The woman put down her phone.

Heart still hammering . . . the taste of sweat . . . and then the coolness; the shivers as it turned into droplets.

Did Dorothy have Irish friends? He couldn't think of any, but she, or someone, was spying.

Those mamzers at the Station, to see what he was painting?

He dreaded their finding out, as he hated anyone looking over his shoulder while he worked.

Any strange car in Ashby, and he imagined a private detective. Especially if someone sat there for a long time. Detectives could as easily be women as men, these days.

A bizarre possibility entered his mind: Dorothy was in cahoots with his busybody sister, Hannah, to 'do something about' him. He knew full well how they talked, the women. Oh, yes. (The sweat again; the pounding.) They had already conspired – Hannah, Dorothy, Fall, even his gallery – to get him to see Dr Kaplan. First Roth visited his surgery in Golders Green, in that street of little shops, where lay in wait together the deconstructers of his life: Krupnik the lawyer, Kaplan the psychiatrist, Medwin the estate agent specializing in unusual country properties.

No, that was not right. Of course not Dorothy. It was the others. He was getting her muddled with the others.

But the unfolding possibilities had filled him with terror, making him load the little black case with pills and sketch-book, and memorize the combination number with nervous concentration. It only needed two doctors to agree, for you to disappear for ever.

8

At ten a.m., Roth opened the kitchen door for a breath of air. Someone had been sick. Who?

He remembered. Fuck it; I have. Meshugener!

Last night, he'd gone out to the pub with gourmet ideas on his mind for supper later.

The advantage of having money was that you could do whatever you wanted, whether cheap or expensive. Executive class on an aeroplane one day; take a crowded bus on the next. Change your residence without having to sell or even think about moving the gear. At one time he'd possessed a flat and studio in London, another in New York, a third in Paris. He'd owned cottages, a railway station and patches of an Italian olive grove so that he could paint the wild flowers in their pools of light and shadow. He couldn't even remember some of the properties he'd possessed.

Roth, to relieve his squalor, sometimes had food delivered from Harrods. Sixty miles up the M1 came a van. Yesterday's intended medley of pleasure had involved lobster, cream, Welsh lamb, honey and a sauce he'd read up that day in his cookbook.

The Peddlars had changed his plans. Though nowadays he avoided talking to people, this time upon finding the ear of the young man whom he called his 'disciple', Adam, he had grown garrulous. 'Young Adam', Roth called him. An old chap can get bloody sentimental.

Roth was already drunk on the brandy consumed during the afternoon when he arrived at the pub. Out of nowhere, and as so often, the thought burrowed into his head that Dorothy and he

had no child. It combined with an irrational anxiety because he
had not been able to get through to her on the telephone, neither
in the morning, nor the afternoon, nor in the evening. Roth had
wept into his beer, drunk too much yet again, stumbled home
to rush the ingredients of his planned meal into the oven while
he re-watched one of his old videos over his shoulder, burned
his fingers, and burned his food.

The kitchen, with hackings of meat and carapace, scattered
herbs, bits of lamb floating in cooked honey the colour and
texture of darkened blood, had looked like the aftermath of a
Viking raid on the Orkneys. He ended up swallowing something
inedible before retching the lot up on the step. After his sleep
in a well of vivid dreams, he might have forgotten about last
evening.

There was something else he had almost forgotten. Ashes
reminded him that he had spent yesterday morning burning two
of his paintings which he had re-purchased. Landscapes painted
in the mid-Forties, they embodied what he saw as unsatisfactory
attitudes to nature. He called them his 'optical' pictures, in which
he had attempted the enumeration of nature's details that it is
impossible to enumerate: leaves, blades of grass and waves
upon the sea. These were the pictures that Mrs Kilburn had
so much liked, whose favourite painting in the whole world
was Richard Dadd's 'The Fairy Feller's Master-Stroke' – that
canvas, once neglected but in the hippy era fashionable again,
in the Tate Gallery's Victorian collection, filled with microscopic
detail which had been the obsession of a patricidal artist while
in the criminal lunatic asylum.

Even Roth's postwar landscapes had not been sentimental. He
had delivered up a lucidity like Van Eyck's, yet such canvases
did not now seem a worthy thing for a man. This particular
pair were views of northern Italy. Vineyards and hill towns
were painted under a too scrutinizing eye. A crystalline light
was focused, as if a lens of dew hung upon every object. They
were *tours de force* of looking, inspired by the early masters of oil
painting who had been in love with the detail one could wring
from the new medium.

And they were painted from a standpoint outside of the

picture, framing the view as if the onlooker were a spectator before a stage. They were executed before he had thought about child art, Islamic art and the sand paintings of American Indians, in all of which the artist appears to be looking around him from the centre; he himself is in the Garden of Eden.

Today, Roth repudiated standing separate and aloof. It was incredible that there were so many painters still imprisoned in the pastoral ideal and painting from the point of view of a redundant cosmology. They arranged their scenic props on the canvas, groups of trees on the left, bridge off centre to the right, horizon cutting the frame according to classical ideas of proportion, as if they still lived in the eighteenth century. They refused to take into account that man has escaped the gentleman's park and now floats in space capsules. When he crashes back into the atmosphere, 'landscape' looks more like a Rothko. The curved black form of space, balanced upon a band of brown bleeding into white, in a block over the earth's curve. It did not mean that one could no longer paint flowers and trees, but one had to look at even a primrose from the point of view of an altered cosmology. Traditional landscapes were an anachronism.

Since Roth had flown, and made rapid earth travels, he had tried to buy up his early pictures. He had hunted down a collector in Cheltenham and, after negotiations kept secret from his accountant and his dealer, he had bought these two back for £3,000 each; ten times what the collector had originally paid.

It was an expensive indulgence but Roth wanted them back because they represented a failure of nerve, the evidence of which he did not wish to survive in his oeuvre. 'Weeding out my siblings,' he called it.

From the kitchen doorstep, Roth saw a calming view. Thatched cottages, a crumbling limestone church, old ash and oak trees, slender-ankled horses in a paddock, roses up a wall, and the sign of the Peddlars. It was a view that he could never understand. Against his will, it threw him out and made him merely a spectator.

Partly, it was so alien because his parents had been born

inside the Pale of Settlement. Relatives there had been massacred through cycles of pogroms, and finally wiped out in Hitler's war.

Images of the Pale haunted Roth still. His parents had possessed a few photographs, some framed, others preserved in folds of tissue paper. In most, the original sepia had merged into yellow blotches that were like the thick smoke of burning corn, but they remained distinguishable. Roth imagined the unsmiling groups – with bushy beards, in peaked hats like those of modern railway porters, and with ubiquitously doleful expressions on faces drawn back tight on the skull by middle age – assembled in a thousand miles of burnt debris, forest, marsh and cornfield. They seemed stiff with permanent fear; it was not only because of the long poses.

One of Roth's great-grandfathers had been a *shokhet* – a ritual slaughterer. Another had been a mohel – a ritual circumciser. Other relatives had been without profession, drifters, *luftmenschen* – 'people of the air'. Roth believed that his ancestry, a mixture of butchery and flight, partly explained his art. And his birthplace in Prospect Terrace, Leeds, was where Jewish textile workers had lived under the shadow of smoke and factory walls.

Naturally, the myths of English country life baffled him. It was hardly even a joke. Ever heard a Jewish joke about English country life? Vicars and fox-hunting and hayseed farmers?

His present neighbours pretended theirs was an idyll of tradition, that they had struck the good and peaceful vein, but Roth could see nothing either idyllic or intrinsically and historically peaceful about it. The history of the countryside was a bloody one and when the landowning set rode massive horses with abandon across miles of farmland to hunt a fox that was not much bigger than a cat, then allowed a pack of dogs to tear the exhausted creature to bits, he believed they would as happily have hunted unruly peasants or Jews, had they been allowed to. It was said that in certain hunts they mutilated foxes, cutting their tendons before releasing them to dogs, and that they filmed them being torn apart. Were their natures different from those of the cossacks and landowners who had tormented his grandfather in Lodz and driven his father away? He doubted it.

Most of the erstwhile rural poor had been driven from Ashby already, as effectively as his father when a boy had been chased from Lodz. Ashby no longer held indigenous villagers. Mr Sandbach, the farmer, commuted by helicopter from Northumbria. His workers lived in a council-house ghetto on the edge of the next village. Roth had taken over the local school for his studio and, apart from his making money, it was the only thing he did of which they approved; for the place had been empty when Roth arrived, since the present-day village children were all at public schools.

Ashby now housed professional men and successful salesmen who indulged their taste for country life at the weekend but for the remainder of the week hardly saw the place during daylight, for they commuted to London so early and returned so late. They occupied hall and vicarage, two ex-farms, one ex-pub, an ex-shop and a dozen cottages done up in the style that Roth termed 'commuter eyesore' – massive windows, fake Georgian doors, and old orchards cleared for gravelled parking lots. It was a two-car, two-freezer, in fact two-of-everything village. What Roth observed most prominently in his neighbours was their division from one another. So why did they hold up the ideal of the family and dare to pity Leonard Roth for living alone?

How could he feel himself to be part of *their* landscape? That was one reason (there were others, too) why in his year here he had not painted one local subject.

His neighbours knew his reputation as a 'landscape artist'. They had soon discovered that he was not such according to their own ideas of village scenes and pretty woodland glades, but that he was a painter of wild, exotic places, executed in a manner so savage that 'you couldn't tell which way up to hang them'. His wild lifestyle was also not what they expected of a landscape painter.

They were wary of the isolated, manic artist. They pitied him. They wanted to mother and father him; especially, he suspected, because eminent painters had large bank balances. From the way he'd had the old school done up, and from the occasional chauffeur-driven limousine of a picture buyer that slunk into the village, they judged he had both money and influence, despite the fact that he himself tore around on a motorbike. He was definitely 'touched'.

For his part, Roth felt sorry for them, particularly for the men. So far as he could grasp, they lived in Ashby to serve their wives and children, commuting to and fro in the dark, packing motorways and trains, but flattered to be considered good providers. Because of this, their wives would not leave them. Thus through their lifetimes they endured their muted, genteel versions of the sex war.

As a further reason for not painting landscapes any more, a sinister veil had grown over the light. The seasons were dead ones. It was June but many leaves were still clenched, baby-hand-like, and trees were dead at their tops or remained bare. The ash and oak trees had a look of midwinter. From time to time there was a hot breeze as if from the opening of an oven door, then a cold wind would follow. It felt evil.

Perhaps there was some unknown nuclear disaster on the planet. Over the icecaps, maybe.

As a Jew, Roth supposed he was good at forecasting doom and apocalypse, just as his father had been. Mankind had felt thus many times before, for instance before the Armageddon 'promised' by the Bible in AD 1000; and when the West was threatened by Islam pouring through North Africa and Spain. But now hanging, literally in the air, was the real end.

If the trees were not dying of air pollution, the farmer's herbicides were killing them. The chemicals were burning the leaves. Would everyone choke to death before the nuclear holocaust arrived? Starve and get cancer because we've killed off other living things, except for plagues of minute flies? Wrecked the ozone layer?

Would the end come with a single nuclear disaster or through the poisoning of earth and water?

Roth enjoyed a pretty view because his cottage was on the right side of the church on its ancient mound. But hidden behind the crumbling limestone building and a Queen Anne farmhouse were Sandbach's helicopter pad and his massive asbestos sheds that soon would be humming with grain-drying machinery.

From such farming, on this scale, the villages of this genteel countryside were increasingly marooned in prairies of wheat, rape or bare soil.

They were spiritual wastelands. A walk through the massive fields of England and northern Europe, where Roth no longer looked for his painting subjects, was like an expedition through the world's penultimate phase. His throat was irritated by the dust of nitrates and depleted soil drifting in clouds from the prairies. Rising in the wakes of tractors the size of Boeings, the soil dust loaded with chemicals blew across the sites of demolished hedgerows and copses. Doctors were reporting numerous patients with sore or cancerous throats. Tractors had cut so close to many villages that the roots of garden and churchyard trees were cut or eroded. Bridleways, pathways, lines of trees, hedgerows and pools for miles had disappeared, allowing the apocalypse to blow.

He had thought of the earth and its covering as the mother who could not die. Old myths told him so. But now landscapes were dying.

As Roth's art had always been a celebration, how could he paint now?

Roth was fond of walking. He would spend days following a coastal path or hill route. Yesterday, he had taken a short walk. He had felt *luftmenschen*, trying to exorcise one of his moods of grief, longing and dissatisfaction with he-knew-not-what, which were more appropriate to an adolescent. Perhaps such longings return in old age, as rites of passage towards that other awesomeness of death. He called it his 'Slavic despair' and he took rambles to keep it from others. It had been his attempts to phone his wife, several times and failing, that had thrown him into this mood; so frail was his balance.

He had avoided villages and other walkers because of what might be written upon his face. Eventually he had sat down, uncorked the half-bottle of brandy from his pocket, and wept. When the sensible question intruded – What am I weeping for? – he realized that he did not exactly know. It was only partly because of his personal problems.

But he had been sitting, as it happened, on the banks of a stream, or what had once been a stream. He had put himself there because the short, curved bank down to it was the only patch of grass to be found, the farmers having ploughed and sown so close to the few remaining hedgerows. The stream was reduced to a foul-smelling ditch, its water black because nitrates and pesticides leaking out of the fields had killed all living things, watercress, fish and molluscs, so that the water flow had simply stirred up mud.

He had suddenly thought: I am Roth, the worshipper of nature, weeping into a polluted stream.

9

The seed of the Station Gallery had been sown in Auschwitz. There a Jew named Behrens, whose fingerbones still showed he had been a pianist, told Rosblum about a hen shed in Auxerre where Soutine had left paintings.

They conversed in mongrel French and Americanized English.

'Who's Soutine? I don't know anything about art. I've always had to work for my living,' Rosblum said.

Behrens explained that Soutine was an artist born inside the Pale, once living in Paris, poor and drunk but prolific. Just before the war, the tide had turned for him. Americans and Madame Castaing, who had a château near Paris, had collected his work. When the Germans arrived, Soutine fled southwards, making for Ceret where once he had been happy. He slept and painted in barns and sheds, then returned to Paris to look for a hospital because he was ill.

'And stupid,' Rosblum said.

'So what's so wise about you? You got rounded up.'

'I didn't go looking for it. Alois Brunner had to come looking for me. I hid in the crypt of the oldest Orthodox church in Christendom, dressed as a chorister. So what's this Soutine's pictures like?'

'Carcasses. Hens hanging. Page boys. Cooks. Suffering humanity.'

'Suffering humanity ain't worth a dime. Look at us. These pictures worth anything, then?'

'A fortune.'

'I can get my hands on sugar cubes. Two sugar cubes if you tell me where this hen shed is.'

Even two sugar cubes wouldn't keep Behrens alive, but he told. And didn't get the sugar cubes.

If Pericles Rosblum hadn't been as he was, he might not have survived, either. If he had a virtue, it was that his was a driven personality – driven towards what, he did not yet know; at the moment it was focused upon using any means to stay alive.

The Soutine story stayed in his mind. Stupid hopes kept people alive in a camp, even if it was like warming chapped hands at a lighted match. It was memories that sunk them; thinking of the harbour-front cafés in Salonika, of meeting a dame beneath that archway built by that Roman general. Thinking of your mother, of family life, of the smell of souvlakia, grilled fish and oregano. You gave up living when you thought of past happiness. But when you conjured up something you might do after the war, you could still get out of your bunk.

In 1947 Rosblum was in Auxerre labouring on a roadworks project. He found twenty pictures – twelve in reasonable condition, three restorable, the other five containing mere ghosts of images; one of them was entirely obliterated, threadbare from having been used to block a window.

Rosblum, disappointed, at first neither knew nor cared which was hen shit and which was paint on the canvases, but he kept them. He recalled the extraordinary flukes of fortune that did occur, because of the war, and because you could kid even the experts with modern art – you read that in the papers all the time. He took a chance and scrubbed the pictures in the back yard of his *pension*, putting his foot through one in the process. It was a nude, his landlady was hovering nearby, and he was afraid of her seeing it. He borrowed money to buy a truck and he transported the pictures to Paris. There he began to show his real talents.

Rosblum did not rush into decisions, and when he had made them, he kept them close to his chest. He learned that from too hastily selling his first strangled, dangling cockerel. Though the sum amazed him, later he saw the picture offered for sale in a dealer's window for ten times as much. He was more circumspect with the next canvas.

From offering the Soutines around he learned two more

lessons. First, that what he had discovered by trading in shoes, sugar cubes and nails in Auschwitz was true of picture dealing too: the rarer they were, the more valuable they were.

Second, that art dealing, involving naive artists and massive sums of money in an area full of mysteries, was an ideal field for crooks.

Being what later would be termed 'streetwise' gave Rosblum an advantage among the Parisian aesthetes into whose company he was introduced through his cache of pictures. His crude manners, plebeian mores, mysterious background and pragmatic morality made him fashionable among Left Bank philosophers. Sartre introduced him to Genet and Rosblum claimed that Sartre contemplated sanctifying him in a monograph, similar to his *St Genet*.

In the cafés, Rosblum met the first of those whose know-how he learned to milk. He developed his talent for bribing, flattering and bullying gentle art experts. Most of them were a pushover. Some of them could put their hands on venture capital.

Rosblum first went into a business partnership in the Rue des Beaux Arts. In 1948 he moved to London, as he had a better grasp of the language there. Also, he had a hunch that something exciting would be stirring.

In England he discovered that art dealing was a gentleman's profession and, unlike others in the business, Rosblum ran the Station as if he were a German gauleiter. He always knew what he wanted, so meetings were brief.

No lingering over long lunches for his staff. In his boardroom he cured old Etonians of indulgence by having the chairs removed. When everyone had to stand, matters that might have been discussed until an early lunch were dealt with in half an hour.

It was only Rosblum who chewed matters over slowly, if it suited him to. When he'd made up his mind, he talked about his 'intewition'.

In Notting Hill Gate, in a terraced house that had once been a middle-class family residence, then a slum and was now upmarket again, Victoria Voyce rose at seven. After, sometimes, a brief twinge of hangover, her life became characteristically busy. But first she spent an hour in the bathroom. Her two school-age sons said it was an hour, although perhaps it was less.

Victoria had now turned forty. As mid-life crept up she had crowded more sprays, creams and perfumes into her bathroom cabinet, then bought another cupboard so that she could fill that, too. The paste upon her face was striking. It was high-class punk. Some of her 'young artists', as she described newcomers who started their careers in mixed exhibitions at the Station, lived for a whole month on what she spent in one visit to Harrods; though, to be fair, nearly all her income derived from divorce alimony and the Station paid her a relative pittance.

The minute Victoria left the bathroom, fully attired in her business clothes, her life was busy with people. People to be lunched, entertained or interviewed; seen in the gallery, communed with over the telephone.

After getting her sons off to Holland Park Comprehensive School, Victoria psyched up to face her engagement diary. She spent evenings at exhibition openings full of businessmen and their wives; she sat on arts committees; she went to conferences of dealers and experts. *Artists* were as welcome at her meetings and conferences as, in the words of Leonard Roth, 'cows in a dairy'.

A little after ten o'clock, with Roth on her mind and in her Filofax, Victoria took the quietened Central Line, changed to the Jubilee Line at Bond Street, and eventually was blown by a warm, dark, unhealthy, dirty wind out of Baker Street Underground Station. It was like being expelled from a vacuum cleaner. Walking in the direction of Lisson Grove, then taking a few turnings to the right in the area of Marylebone Station, a quarter of an hour later Victoria entered the Station Gallery.

Rosblum had established himself in early days in this area, shocking his cultured advisers with the banality of his gallery's name as well as of the district he chose (one had wanted to call it 'the Balmoral'), though now he amazed them with his 'foresight': time had made 'the Station' sound like a hip gallery in New York. His intewition again. He settled here to afford the space for *big* pictures. As he became a pariah among the Bond Street and off-Bond Street dealers, he felt most comfortable staying and expanding where he was. He owned half a street and an abandoned chapel by now. He boasted that, with the space he had, he was one of the few who could exhibit Anselm Kiefer or Anthony Caro. Space was 'impoitent', these days. Being away from the West End, he could also boast that people came to him, and for him.

Victoria's shoes tapped on a vast, polished floor made of Welsh slate. It covered the ground of three original houses. This expensively empty area in central London served to emphasize both the value of the pictures and the general wealth of the Station, which could afford to be so generous with space. At the moment, small canvases by Ivon Hitchens hung there and it was as unnerving as viewing them across an empty football field. A girl who had been educated at Cheltenham Ladies' College was answering the telephone, making notes of the conversation, and typing a letter. From her diligence it didn't look as though she were there merely for the marriage market.

Leonard Roth was of prime importance in the Station's stable. He was of such significance that his pictures were kept upstairs or in the basement and only occasionally exhibited. Clients knew that they were privileged if they were even allowed to see them, let alone offered them for sale.

The attitude of the Station staff to its clients was not syco-phantic; rather it was the other way round. Clients were looked upon as people in need, like beggars knocking at the door of a monastery; only, these were the overwealthy, humbled in their search for spiritual values, which was all that was left for them to buy. The Station knew its clients as people for whom a work of art was the ultimate status acquisition after mink coats, yachts and country houses. They could not acquire a painting without the aid of dealers who knew where the work was to be found, had the knowledge of what was valuable, and claimed to be able to persuade the artist, or a previous collector, to part with it. As Victoria put it: 'The Station is not interested in starting with new collectors at a low level. We address ourselves to sophisticated clients who have established their credibility and have built up, or are in the process of building up, substantial collections.' The gallery insisted upon knowing a great deal about prospective purchasers before even showing pictures to them. They wanted to know who was in their circle of friends, and where they would display what they might acquire.

A collector admitted to the upper floor of the Station felt let into a holy room. Bells rang. Security was checked as doors of glass or mahogany were opened. Video cameras kept watch. The client found himself in an all-white space, including floor and ceiling, with two black leather armchairs, a low glass-topped table, a telephone, black velvet curtains to draw across the north-facing, heavily barred windows, and adjustable lights. Not a picture to be seen, until Mr Rosblum or Victoria Voyce, the two chief executives, telephoned for it to be brought in from store and set against the wall on a viewing platform. Victoria Voyce was an overpowering guide, and the viewing room was like a medieval shrine. Rooms, even houses, would be expected to be built around the pictures, as churches were once erected over the relics of saints.

But first there were murmurs of praise. In came, say, a middle-period Roth. (Early and late works were the rarest.) The warm-up began. 'This is a picture that releases itself slowly, I feel, after one becomes acclimatized . . .' Then followed the hard sell. Clients were reminded that there weren't likely to be many more Roths available. The artist was in his seventies and not in the best of health. There were advantages in acquiring at the moment. The market was fairly stable. With the life-output in view, one knew just how many pictures one was dealing with, but, it was pointed out, 'in the unfortunate event of Mr Roth's dying or becoming unable to work' – 'there were rumours' – prices would rocket. Wonderful, of course, for the present owners!

The proposed sale was ridden with hypotheses.

'Let's not jump around on this one, it's a very special work we're considering today. Most Roths of this quality have found their way into major public collections by now – the Tate, the Art Institute of Chicago, the Pompidou Centre, the Museum of Modern Art in New York. If you acquired this picture, I don't think we could let it go for less than thirty thousand. Would that be any problem, do you think? No? Then I must ask you, where would you place it in your collection, should we consider your acquiring it?'

'I guess I'd have to reconsider my space and make some modifications, Miss Voyce. May I hang anything near to it, do you think?'

'I really don't believe we could contemplate such a move. Mr Roth is very sensitive about that, and possibly would not consider dealing through us, should we allow such a thing.'

'I'd really like to meet him myself, a man with that kind of integrity.'

'Nowadays we don't have a lot of connection with him ourselves, he's such a recluse. Incredibly difficult to deal with, and always has been, as you will see if you look through our cuttings book. Highly gifted people can be like that, can't they? Mr Rosblum has been helping him out with doctors, and so forth.'

'Can we have any chairs in the room?'

'With difficulty, I might feel. It depends what they are like. We could advise you over this.'

'Well, if I put it in my dining room, where do we eat? And if it goes into the bedroom, where do we sleep?'

This way, Victoria could 'release' as many Roths as she judged fit.

The gallery had always had problems with Roth. For instance, when he was dragging around with the awful hippy Mrs Kilburn, the West Country dream merchant, whose husband was a plumber, or something to do with water. She explained that 'water was very important to the Celts'. No doubt Roth had been seducing her with his 'nature goddess'. It's amazing how a certain kind of woman perks up when a man talks to her about the 'goddess'. She gained a lot of influence over him. He became a member of Crumbly Van-Dwellers Against the Bomb, or some such organization. She wanted him to put fairies or extraterrestrial beings in his landscapes, and to return to his hyper-real mode. She nearly succeeded, too. It would have ruined his career.

Or when he was with that child, Rebecca Marks, who made the spoons disappear and 'by accident' set off the alarm bells in the gallery.

Now Roth was giving real trouble, and not just embarrassment. It was over his contract. He had been suggesting terminating it for a year or two, and so far the Station had managed to put him off. Fortunately, he had only muttered about it, without making a formal declaration.

If, or when, he succeeded in cancelling the contract, what claims did the gallery still have? For example, were works commenced, but not finished at the time of termination, the property of Rosblum? What about the earliest works, which they had assumed the right to deal in but which Roth had started to work on before his contract, and completed after it had been signed? Wouldn't Roth's lawyer point out an inconsistency? Can pictures be dated accurately, if Roth chose to alter the dates on the canvases? Did the gallery have an entitlement to his notes and sketches?

And then there were the perennial difficulties and the games that could be played with inventories. The usual method was that with each consignment of pictures, the artist sent in a list, to be co-signed by both parties. Usually, an artist scrupulously followed the system in his early years, but when his career was established, he grew careless. Two months after sending work in, Roth or, more likely, Dorothy would phone to ask for another copy because the original inventory was lost. The new one, too, would become mislaid. When fresh lists were drawn up, a few pictures might be overlooked.

To Victoria, artists seemed unbelievably careless, but the tricky element was that old lists just might turn up among Roth's drawers, or be discovered by somebody going through his studio after his death.

Everyone knew that was an imminent event. Even more pressing, then: what could the Station do about the stuff that he was surely hiding, or selling secretly?

10

When Roth signed his first contract with the Station in 1951, an exciting period of British painting was beginning. Roth had been forty-one years old. Not young, but young enough to have plenty of painting life left in him, and six years hadn't much diminished the energy with which he came out of the war. He was also a veteran of what he regarded as the 'Third World War'. This was the sex war and he had lost his first wife, Tina, to a fireman while he was in France and Germany.

There were many men who had come out so finely attuned to be killers that they turned into murderous psychopaths during peace. Roth became an artistic version of one. When he made his breakthrough from calm, optical landscapes, it was said he did it through painting 'with the disregard and energy of a mass killer'.

It was 'the boundless savagery of his appetite' that saved him from being a camp follower, a mere wet Brit version of American abstract expressionism. His maverick nature and his travels also saved his work from the cosiness that might have crept in had he settled in Cornwall, or with the Welsh hippies 'and their earth cult'. It was the war that had made him turn to nature as his prime subject. This was not from nostalgia for country life, but because seeing nature devastated taught him that man's relationship to it mattered fundamentally.

That relationship was art's function. It took Roth from the war's end to his signing with the Station to resolve the gap between how he felt and what he painted; to get over his 'optical' phase of quietly observed landscapes and begin to paint like a man who had experienced the war and the twentieth century.

Eventually, he saw the possibility of a perspective that would not imply he was a detached observer. Rather than an act of quiet worship, his painting became an expression of unity with nature. Thus Roth found himself expressing his inner life, as well as what he found 'out there'. Painting became not a contemplation, but a relationship with nature.

And the nature he found was also within. Storms, deserts and calm, pastoral landscapes of the spirit.

The 1955 Tate Gallery show of 'Modern Art in the USA' had thrilled him with its huge Rothkos and Pollocks. He was not so different from many others. Strangers are normally too polite to communicate in the precincts of galleries, but at this show they forgot their embarrassment and stared at one another, whispering their expressions of awe as if they had arrived at Eleusis together, and had been flung into a numinous experience.

As American abstract expressionism hit Britain, Roth's way of attacking canvases, risking everything, made him famous; but it also encouraged him to live in the same manner.

There were others who gained a frisson from this. Dealers, critics, lecturers were fascinated. It offered no danger to themselves, but they could turn it into a myth. All encouraged him to press the self-destruct button. It got him into the newspapers and on television when he rode his bike recklessly drunk, beat up someone in a restaurant, held a public quarrel with Dorothy, abused a critic – all with the tacit approval of the Station, which hedged its bets. If his risk-taking proved fatal, their contract ensured a claim on his legacy; and as soon as he died, the value of his stock would shoot up. Especially if his pictures had been scarce during the recent years, if they were not released too rapidly, and if no one knew quite how many Roths there were in existence – in the racks of the Station Gallery or in their warehouse in Slough.

Nowadays, the finer details of what their policy was to be following Roth's demise occupied much of the time at Station meetings. They discussed obituaries: who would write them, what they were to say and where they would be placed.

Roth's carelessness was formed in early years when his work had not been valuable. When money had struck, it had come in such a shower that it had seemed churlish and boring to scrutinize. He had been plunged into a world of 'investment potentials' that didn't interest him and that he didn't understand. Trusting Sam Fall in business matters, he followed his need to paint. That was what he wanted money for, so that was what he'd do with it. Also, it was painting, not the counting of cash, that produced more money.

If Van Gogh had lived for only another three or four years, the dealers would have turned him into a wealthy man, but can one imagine a Van Gogh who was not poor? What would he have done with wealth? He might have bought himself a modest house and studio. Apart from that, he would have gone on living in the same way, painting in the fields and eating in the café, leaving the money to his brother Theo and his family, but relying upon him to send generous supplies of paints. To have behaved in any other fashion would have devalued those bare rooms, those poverty-scoured peasants, those hands grubbing for potatoes that he had depicted.

Artists such as Roth were so accustomed to being poor that they didn't know how to handle prosperity when it hit them. Beside, it struck the galleries first, and they *did* know what to do with it.

Although Roth had his suspicions, if he'd known just how many of his paintings were stored by the Station, he would have been amazed. His only defence against their ability to twist him around their little fingers was what they called his 'truculence' – a little bit of his true character that he could fit into the myth. Victoria believed it had to do with his coming from the north of England. Once in a catalogue she had described him, in a phrase that made him squirm, as a 'gritty Yorkshireman'. Leonard Roth, a Jew whose father came from Lodz! But it continued to suit him to live up to his reputation.

It was a little after half past ten, by which time Roth had digested his regular coffee, toast and honey, that Victoria, to get unpleasant business over at the beginning of her day, asked for a call to be put through.

11

Roth grabbed the phone in his usual yanking-out-a-bad-tooth fashion.

'Victoria speaking. How are you, Len?'

Knowing, as with Fall, that she hadn't phoned to enquire about his health, he answered irritably.

'Please don't call me Len! Okay? What can I do for you, Victoria?'

'Look, Roth! We need to know what work you've been doing. Also, to be candid, all of us here feel we can't go on wrangling with you about the work you owe us according to your contract. I know you value bluntness.'

'I'm doing nothing much these days, Victoria. Too much on my mind.'

'Sam Fall mentioned that you have some interesting canvases. We'd like to come and see.'

'When did he say that?'

'Shortly after you moved to Ashby. He simply mentioned it in passing.'

'They were all false starts. Experiments. I've done nothing since then. What I did do wasn't worth keeping.'

'We'd like to come and see,' Victoria repeated.

'No! Why don't you sell some of my stuff that you have already?'

'Roth, it's terribly painful to have to tell you this, but we feel that this isn't quite the time to exhibit you. We have to take so much into account before we sell. Tomorrow there could be war somewhere, or a stock-exchange collapse. We don't operate in a vacuum, as you know.'

'Kvetch, kvetch, kvetch!'

Victoria ignored Roth's muttering.

'At the moment everyone's expecting a dip in the London stock market, perhaps a recession. You know how sensitive the art world is. In the present climate, our clients are not spending. If they do, they are buying cheerful stuff. You can hardly say that your recent work is that. Such a contrast to the past. The market isn't entirely personal to you. Bacon's taken a drop, but so has Hockney, just a little. And, I might add, the situation isn't helped by you flouting your contract and selling works directly from the studio. We do know that is happening and they turn up in surprising places. One obviously recent work was seen in a House of Commons office. Anyone could tell it was recent because of how dark it is. What has happened to you? We ourselves have had hardly any canvases for over a year. Hardly anything from your last trip, nor since. Yes, you did let us see a couple of self-portraits. Very gloomy, I hope you realize, not typical works, and not easy to sell. Why do you have to be so secretive? It's no good for your sales for you to be hiding away as you do. Things are changing in art behind your back. You can't afford to be out of the arena for so long. People forget you, and you yourself lose the knack of gauging the market temperature.'

Knowing that Victoria, breathless now, was waiting for a response, Roth teased her by remaining silent. He wanted her to fear that she had overplayed her hand. It did the trick.

'To look on the optimistic side,' Victoria continued, more quietly, 'you're a wonderful painter when you get going, and we want to do our very best for your work. But when times are difficult, everyone from the government downwards stresses the pretence that life is fun. This is the "Beryl Cooke season", as one might say.'

Victoria lingered over *Ber-yl*, then triumphantly snapped *Cuk*, like someone first savouring, and then swallowing, something delicious, freshly brought out of the oven.

'Ironically, I think that we'd do better with a show of your earlier work, the less contentious landscapes if we could get our hands on some, but they hardly ever emerge. Your more recent, introspective stuff is temporarily out of fashion and it makes commercial sense to hold it back. What little we have of it.'

'Francis Bacon? Sidney Nolan?'

'Francis is a law unto himself.'

'So's anyone who's any good.'

'Anyway, I told you, Bacon too has been falling, temporarily. If your paintings were more cheerful . . . if you could turn in some of your energetic, brightly coloured landscapes again – '

'It's the light's fault, not mine! It *is* gloomy. The light this year has a sickness. If people noticed it, they wouldn't expect cheerful landscapes. How can people not notice the light?'

'One doesn't, you know, in London. If one were to look at the sky one would fall under a bus.'

'You can't sell my work because you've got too many Cheltenham Ladies' College girls handling it. Schnorrers out of country houses. And they don't understand what they're selling!'

'If you're talking about me, I'm Harvard.'

'That fucking convent you run at the Station . . .'

'Don't you think you've got a bit of a chip on your shoulders?'

'Yes!'

'*Len!* Leonard! Roth!'

'Dorothy's holding a party tonight, Victoria.'

'Well? You've already told us, as a matter of fact.'

'In Leeds.'

'Your address is another problem we're having. Nobody seems to know where you live. We do have some cheques for you. Where do you want your mail sent? To Hertfordshire? To Leeds? We're not at all sure of your movements.'

'Send it wherever you want! Whatever you want! Okay? You don't understand a fucking thing! Nebbish!'

'Oh dear. Do you have to be such a bear? We'll send them to Leeds, then.'

'No!'

'Well, give me a ring when you've made up your mind. I must go. Have a meeting. Bye, Leonard! Have a good day!'

——Fucking adding machine. Bloody calculator with nail varnish, trying to pass me off with lies about the market. I'm too old a dog for that.

Losing accounts, too. Losing addresses. Losing pictures.

The ploy of the deliberate mistake: wear the artist out with worry, confuse him, concentrate his attention on petty things so that the big manoeuvres slide through unnoticed, unchecked. I'm an old dog and I know that one, too. It's a sign that something else is going on.——

12

Dorothy would sleep with her back to him, and he would wake her with his erection resting between her buttocks. He had been asleep, he told her, and it had happened involuntarily. Small, electric pulses came from the tip of his penis. 'Oh, what a lovely way to be woken up,' she whispered, turning to assist him into her. Even though already love-weary and love-aching, she would flow against his flesh, among his limbs, under his hands. Their words, their words were of clay, unable to rise to the happiness.

Give us a drink.

No. He resisted the temptation. At eleven in the morning, it was too early. He had always been scrupulous about not eroding the pace and concentration of a working day by taking alcohol. Once he lost that, he would lose his last hold on life.

The temptation to drink earlier and earlier in the day, to take more in the evening and to tolerate morning hangovers, had been growing for a month. This was the first sign of one of the old, cathartic, month-long binges. But they used to be followed through with companions. Today, the course would have to be pursued dangerously alone. He knew that if he plunged into one now, it would be his last. At the moment, he felt that he was steady. He saw light on the way to recovery from last night. He was overcoming the morning queasiness.

He deliberated for half an hour, hardly stirring from his chair, then decided to phone Dorothy.

Over a further half-hour, he tried three times. Yesterday, he had not been able to get her at all. Today, the number seemed permanently engaged.

There was no reason why this should depress him. But he felt worse than if he'd not attempted to get through at all.

Looking through the window, Roth could see his neighbour, Spender. He was a retired military man who had inherited a chain of fishmonger's shops in London and the southeast. East End origins, but you'd never guess. Roth realized from his manner that his wife must be away – visiting their fucking awful kid at school, probably. Roth knew it from Spender's stroll, pausing to look at the flowers, a glass in his hand. If his wife had been at home he would have felt urged to mow the lawn or weed in brisk, military manner. His manliness would be at stake.

They were a funny pair, these apparent gentlefolk, communicating in the rudimentary calls of their species. And Roth did think of them as a different species. 'Jolly nice morning!' and 'Darling, where's the oil for the mower?' Roth imagined that this was how they talked in bed. 'Darling, where are the condoms?' 'Oh, do you really have to?' If Roth passed by, he knew how Spender would greet him. 'All well?' he would say in clipped fashion, not showing any feeling other than a smile; not pausing in his flight, in truth not caring a damn.

'As a matter of fact, my sister has died and I've had cancer diagnosed,' he felt like responding sometimes, sure that Spender would answer: 'Oh, bad luck! Must dash. Well, keep your pecker up.'

In the nearby, tangled graveyard, Roth saw Mr Sandbach, dressed in 'thorn-proof' tweeds and polished, twinkling brogues as he waded through the grass and the mildewed graves. Roth knew that his darting eyes were trying to detect some untidiness: yes, indeed, he bent down and removed a twig that had blown on to an urn. You would expect a farmer who commuted between his farms by helicopter to show a pan-European smartness, but Sandbach remained a small-minded villager, who picked up straws in the wake of his baler and who went through his sheds looking for lights to switch off. Now he was on his way to ring the church bell where his ancestors were buried. Ashby had but one bell, which would clatter for an hour. Roth was sure it was Sandbach's way of laying claim to the countryside, where he had gobbled up half the farms in sight.

Sandbach had decided that his recent neighbour was mad, his art a 'joke at the expense of the public'. Roth thought that Sandbach's farming was insane and criminal.

Roth wanted to speak to him, and he went to the door. Each caught the other's eye.

'Those bird-scarers!' Roth shouted.

'Hullo?'

'They've been at it all night! Can't you turn the buggers off?'

The burly Mr Sandbach rolled towards him with a landowner's firmness of one possessing the earth. The truth was that behind Sandbach were the banks and finance houses that owned the land. None the less Sandbach was smiling and condescending, prepared to humour the one *he* thought was the idiot. As he came close, his shoulders were squared for confrontation with a maniac.

'We have to do it for the pigeons, Mr Roth. They're like the Chinese. No matter how many you shoot, there'll always be some more.'

'Not all night! Pigeons don't feed then. Pop! Pop! You could turn them off at sunset. I can't sleep, for fuck's sake! They give me nightmares.'

Roth made exaggerated, springing gestures with his hands that alarmed Mr Sandbach. Then the farmer smiled.

'My wife tells me you were making enough noise yourself last night with that motorbike of yours. What were you doing with it in the middle of the night? It's happened before. She wanted to call the police. The whole village must have been woken up.'

'Practising.'

'What?'

Roth kept his Laverda in the hallway and after he had stumbled from the pub, too drunk to take her out, he had first thought of phoning Dorothy once again, thankfully had discarded that idea, and next had mounted the bike for a quarter of an hour. He had revved her in flushes of pure joy, filling the house with blue fume and the village with noise. A scream of pain, was it? A howl for attention? When he had finished and was exhausted, he had covered her again, tenderly, with a white sheet.

The farmer was still leering, his head on one side, refusing to take a madman seriously. Playing with a motorbike at his age! This bullet-headed yeoman saw Roth's rumpled clothes, the unironed shirt that had merely been soaked overnight in the bath, as signs of his having no secure material links with the world and, in particular, no woman.

'I was forced to make excuses for you when I arrived this morning, Mr Roth. Mrs Sandbach could hardly get a wink of sleep after that performance last night. Are you feeling better now?'

'I haven't been ill.'

Roth wasn't going to whinge to Sandbach or anyone else. Look towards your end as a private man. He was determined: no blubbering consolations and hypocrisy about death.

'If ever there's anything you want, you'll find us a very friendly community in Ashby Green,' Sandbach said in a conciliatory tone. 'There's no need for you to stand aloof. I'm sure I can speak for all when I say, none of us is too toffee-nosed to help someone who has fallen by the wayside.'

'Pardon?'

'Divorce must be a very unpleasant business.'

Roth was startled. He must have told more of his fears than he had realized in the pub, and the gossip had got around. Had young Adam, who had lent him a sympathetic ear in the Peddlars last night, been talking?

'I'm not surprised it makes you ill, Mr Roth. If we had some better weather for a change, it might cheer us all up. I've not been so good myself. Throat.' Mr Sandbach touched his throat. 'And all these damned flies everywhere. They get in your throat, too. I was covered in them the other day. Had to take a bath. The sink, the toilet, everything was full. My clothes were alive.'

'They're out of your *rape*.'

Roth laughed, but the pun went over Mr Sandbach's head.

'Your hands are shaking, Mr Roth! Mrs Spender told us at the vestry meeting that you weren't what yer might call "yourself". I hope you don't mind us talking about you, but none of us

wants to play the Pharisee to the stranger in our midst. So
don't be afraid to knock on any door in Ashby Green if you
need something. We talked it over.'

'Thank you, Mr Sandbach.'

Nebbish. Mamzer. Fucking dickhead. You condescending
shit'ouse.

'That's all right, then.' Sandbach continued to smile, amiably
but threateningly. 'I'm glad I've got that off my chest. Mrs
Spender said she heard you talking to yourself. I hope you
don't mind us knowing about it? I do it myself sometimes when
I'm ploughing all day and I've had enough of listening to the
wireless in my cab. I suppose you can easily go a bit funny,
doing your sort of work. You must have to concentrate until
you go a bit – I'm glad I have Mrs Sandbach, myself. I can't
imagine how I'd do without her. Her and my boys. Especially
as I get older. There aren't any children involved in your case,
are there, Mr Roth?'

'No.'

Arse'ole.

'That's unusual, but it must seem fortunate now. Except that
I expect you're lonely. Why don't you join us in the church?
We're a friendly crowd. Vicars aren't like they used to be.
They're more what yer might call "professional" these days.'

'Because humankind has a conception of good higher than
any god has yet shown. It isn't to be found in the church but
in the human mind, Mr Sandbach. We're better than our gods,
if we did but listen to ourselves.'

Fucking toad.

Mr Sandbach looked as if he'd caught Roth swearing.

'I don't understand that sort of talk, Mr Roth. Is that what you
Jews think? I'd rather pretend I haven't heard it. I think perhaps
you spend too much time alone.'

'The telephone . . . You must excuse me.'

13

It was Hannah, Roth's elder sister.

Roth could always see the caller, and isolation had intensified his imagination. He visualized Hannah looking and behaving more obviously Jewish than himself, despite her lifelong effort to hide it. With her round face and frizzed hair, she took after their mother. Their mother's big brooch would be pinning her dress. Ruby and silver brooch; black, loose dress.

Her telephone was in an unheated hall, and today, only weakly dappled with light from the stained glass in the front door (a fan of sunrise), Hannah would be standing there, despite her varicose veins. She believed it was disrespectful to sit at such an august invention as the telephone.

Hannah thought that her brother was 'something'. This was not because he had exhibited pictures, but because he made money and was living in the south, 'mixing with the county nobs'. Now that she had three successful children (one boy was a teacher, another son was a bank manager, and her daughter was the wife of a barrister) and her husband employed six women manufacturing handbags, she would have taken a subscription to a hunt herself. She, sister of a Jew who found English country life baffling, was the only Jewish person he'd met who admired it seriously.

Only, apart from being Jewish, she lived in Leeds. Though moving house every few years further into the increasingly rural suburbs along Harrogate Road, she was still not far enough into the country to join the fox-hunting set.

At each removal she rediscovered the objects that she had adoringly collected. Roth's early pictures and drawings;

newspaper articles, particularly if they were either in highly
glossy magazines or in the local paper; a couple of books written
about him; grocery boxes filled with exhibition catalogues, cards
and letters. Evidence of the career which she admired but found
incomprehensible. She would fuss over these as a substitute for
mothering him.

She loved her younger brother. As if reality were a gradable
condition, to her he seemed more real than anyone else. She
would not have admitted it, but her brother was more real to
her than her husband. She had often said that Leonard was a
big man in every sense of the word; big in body and in spirit.
She remembered how, as a child, he had been more extreme in
his feelings than anyone she knew. If he was angry, he was more
angry than anyone else. If he was silent, his silence solidified and
set around the household. If he was happy, he appeared to light
up the world.

What lay heaviest between them in their later years was their
differing experiences of Hitler's war. Roth had either seen the
worst for himself, or men whose hollowed eyes and gaunt
cheeks aged them by fifty years gave him accounts hot from
the scenes of atrocities. Eight thousand Jews driven in naked
and walled up in a mine in the Ukraine. Jewish victims cut in
half or having nails driven into their heads by Einsatzgruppen
officers – intellectual Germans, many of them: physician, opera
singer, philosopher, Protestant minister. Children asking their
mothers why they were being undressed in a January frost at
the edge of a pit. The ground in Minsk heaving with the bodies
of those who were buried before they were dead.

Hannah and Leonard both still mourned Rachel, the youngest
member of their family. At the age of twenty-three she had
left Leeds to return with her new husband to 'the homeland',
Poland, where they were caught in the Nazi invasion.

For Hannah, in Leeds throughout the war, all that happened
in the Pale was a distant nightmare which could be muffled in
private tears and wailing. She had got over even that now. If
anyone asked about her family's suffering, she passed it off,
bravely. 'Oh, it was a great many people's story, no use going
on about it.'

Leonard could not even paint it. Not directly. But Hannah saw that her brother's harrowing showed in his art.

'Men are more sensitive than women,' she would declare, not reasonably, but nevertheless protectively.

'Lenny, how are you? I've not heard from you for a week! Your own sister! We're all worried about you. The children. You forget you've got nephews and a niece. Dorothy's worried, too. I've not heard from you since you were released from the clinic last week. My Jacob and I have been discussing it, Lenny. There's no stigma attached to it these days, if that's why you don't talk to people, even to your own sister. Why don't you contact me?'

'Why don't you sit down?'

'How do you know I'm standing, meshugener?'

'Because you always do. It's time you put a chair in the hall. How are you?'

'I'm all right. Jacob still has his heart, poor man. And his gland trouble. We're all getting older, aren't we? How are *you*?'

'I'm all right. I was just on my way out to the studio, Hannah.'

There was a silence. Although she was worried about his psychological state, he did not like to talk about psychiatry with her, because her faith in doctors was total, whereas he got into their hands despite himself. He looked upon psychiatry as sceptically as he looked upon religion and its leaders: although we are all in fear of death and are confused by life, that does not mean we must accept being led by those who claim to be qualified to know the answers.

'Is that all, Lenny? How's that nice Mr Spender?'

'I hardly see him.'

'Why not? You should talk to him a bit. Make friends. Are you still taking your pills?'

'How is Dorothy?'

'I think she's all right. You know the gallery's been round to her place claiming your pictures?'

This news razed other thoughts from his mind. Roth felt hot. His heart beat heavily. The sweat again. He shouldn't get excited.

'Those from last year in Greece? She hasn't let any go?'

'I don't understand your business, Leonard, but apparently they said they had a right to them, because they pay you a retainer. Dorothy tried to ring you but you weren't in. She got on the phone to your accountant to make sure and he told her the same thing, that the pictures do really belong to the gallery.'

'Not until *I* release them, they don't!'

'Well, I can't comment, but she had no choice.'

'When did this happen?'

'A couple of days ago.'

Had Dorothy gone out yesterday to escape talking to him about this?

'How many of my children did she let go?'

'Your children! Don't get so serious about nothing but pictures, Lenny. Meshugener! That was always your trouble. I don't know how many they took. Not many. They were mostly those mad pictures you painted in Greece, yes, that Dorothy had . You sent them to Leeds, after you stayed on in Greece. I don't like them much, anyway. But how are *you* doing, Lenny?'

'She mustn't let them take away my pictures! The whole point of sending them to her in Leeds was so that the gallery wouldn't have them. They *are* my children.'

'I know, I know, and it's a pity you didn't have any real children, Leonard. Mrs Ginsburg next door gave her husband twelve, to make up for his family lost in the Holocaust. "Never mind the quality, feel the width", that's a case of. They run wild over the neighbourhood. Is that you laughing, Lenny? He's a tailor. The Station men were very forceful, I believe. They wouldn't take no for an answer.'

'How many came?'

'A couple of big men. They were like bouncers from a night club, she told me, and they came when it was dark. You can't blame her for being frightened.'

'She should have called the police.'

'Mr Fall said they were within their rights.'

Sam hadn't said a word about it. Was he dealing with it and not wanting to upset him?

'But how are *you*, Lenny? How *are* you, Lenny? Tell me!'

'I think I'm much better. I'm all right. Please leave me alone. I must get to my work. I must speak to the Station about this.'

'I knew a stay in the clinic would settle your mind. There's no stigma attached to it these days, Lenny.'

Roth fell silent again.

'Leonard, are you still there? You don't seem so right. Are you there?'

'I'm here. Still in the land of the living, Hannah, don't worry. But I must settle this business of my pictures and then get into the studio. I've some bits and pieces to tidy up.'

'You went quiet. I wish you wouldn't do that, it gives me the pip. I thought you'd rung off. You had me frightened. I feel as though my heart's stopped when you do that and you've been doing it since you were a child, making us all suffer with your silences. Just like when you run off and hide, the way you used to have a habit of doing . . . Lenny, where are you? Are you there? Have you heard any more from Dr Kaplan, Lenny? Speak to me!'

'Who's Dr Kaplan?'

'Lenny! Don't have me on!'

'I've never heard of him.'

'He has the clinic, Lenny!'

'What clinic?'

'In Kings Langley, of course! What clinic, the boy says! Do you hear him! Where you stayed. Don't fool me, Lenny, it's too darned serious. Where do you think I mean? Lenny, are you sure you're all right? You're still taking the pills?'

Silence.

'*Lenny, are you there?*'

'Yes, I'm fine. Who's been telling lies about me being in the funny farm, Hannah? Was it Dorothy?'

'Lenny! What are you talking about to me, your own sister? You were there for two weeks.' Her voice fell and was resigned. 'I think we've been here before. You're kidding me, aren't you, Lenny?'

Silence again.

'What's *wrong* with you, Leonard?'

Roth thought hard for a minute, despite feeling his sister

hanging on to the silence as if her heart might break, and then
he confided quietly: 'What's wrong with me is that I miss the
place. That's the pain.'

'What place?'

'Yorkshire. My roots.'

'But you don't come and stay with me! You could do, so easily.
There's always a bed for my own brother. What sort of people do
you think we've become? Do you think we're snobs because my
Jacob's doing well?'

'I mean, Prospect Terrace.'

'That's only a heap of stones, Lenny! Surely you could buy
a dozen of them now, just with one of your pictures? It's no
more than a slum, these days. The Pakis are all over the district.
The West Indians. You can't walk in Roundhay Park any more.
There's all sorts of trouble going on. There always is where
there's foreigners. It's the worst place in Leeds for muggings and
violence. Gangs go around and it's never out of the newspapers.
There's no decent British people left there. Decent people have
moved out. We had to go up Harrogate Road.'

Hannah suddenly added: 'There are even some Jewish people
causing trouble. You remember that model you used to have,
Rebecca Marks? She was in the paper the other day. She's
changed her name to Marx, silly cow – him! Worse than Hitler!
I wouldn't have known her except for her photo. She's part of
an organization calling itself Scumbags, making what they call
a "revolution" by setting fire to garages and throwing bricks at
policemen.'

At the mention of Rebecca Marx, a barbed dart struck Roth
somewhere in the region between liver and lungs. He would
not have said 'heart', for his feeling was something other than
love: conscience, intrigue and the wonder of suddenly unburied
memory.

Rebecca must be thirty-eight now. Was she still stealing? Had
she settled her differences with her father; if he was still alive?
Did Hannah really think that Rebecca had been his 'model' only?
Hannah was good at being blind, and also at pretending for the
sake of 'appearances'.

Roth did not refer to it.

'If you want to be in Prospect Terrace so much, why don't you make things up with Dorothy? She's there because she's got to have somewhere to live, and she knows just as I do that you'd never live there alone. Too many ghosts, too many memories. I know you. You'd go ma– She'll have you back, Lenny, I know she will! She'll be glad to. She loves you, Lenny! You can't go on making changes as if you're a young man. At your age you've got to settle down.'

'I can't. It's impossible.'

'*Can't* you ever settle down? At seventy-one!'

'I can't start quarrelling over again, and she wouldn't do it, anyway. She doesn't want to live with me. Where does that leave me? As you say, if I found her somewhere else, I couldn't live in that morgue alone. I guess I'm just a bad case of yearning for the Garden of Eden, Hannah. That's the truth of it. That's probably why I paint landscapes.'

'Come again?'

Roth heard a faint, blowing sound. He imagined Hannah blowing a strand of hair from her eyes.

'All men suffer the longing for the womb, imagining there's some original paradise from which they've been expelled. That's why I've gone chasing all over the world, if the truth were told. Looking for the original garden, the first womb. Painting my way into identification with it. I suppose it's a madness.'

'And you think you don't need a psychiatrist! Listen to me, Lenny. Everyone's talking about the Yorkshire Ripper trial. After he'd stabbed his victim in the lungs with a screwdriver, he gouged out her eye, because she was staring at him, it said in the *Sun*, and she must have been alive when he did it, because the postmortem showed that she died slowly. He committed thirteen murders like that, all so horrible and obscene. Do you know what he said at his trial? That an angel spoke to him from a gravestone. That God told him to eliminate as many women as he could. Don't you think that if you're going to start talking about God and the Garden of Eden, Lenny, you'd better see your psychiatrist before it's too late?'

'I both love it and hate it.'

'What?'

'Yorkshire.'

'Why don't you come and see us, then?'

Silence.

'Speak to me! Why don't you come and see us?'

After another moment of silence, Roth answered: 'Why don't you put a chair in the hall, Hannah, then you can sit down?'

'Because I'm not always having to talk for hours on the telephone to a brother who doesn't come to see me. Why don't you come?'

'Because I – can't bear the place, either. It's soaked in murders. Brady's and Hindley's, burying they still don't know how many murdered children in the peat of Saddleworth Moor. There were legendary killings in the nineteenth century. All that suffering in the factories of West Yorkshire in the past has soaked into the buildings and into the psyche. It haunts the moors and it finds its expression in violent, obscene killings. The place has a sinister spirit, its own *duende* – '

'Come again?'

He didn't pause to tell her what the word meant.

'I'm better away from there. I'm afraid of it, too. It must have entered me also. Perhaps it's why I paint as I do.'

'I ought to come down and see you, Lenny, before it's too late. Afraid of the place, loving the place. What a complex you've got!'

'No, please don't, Hannah.'

'Why not? I'm your sister! Perhaps I can do some good where Dorothy couldn't. I thought at first she was bad for you, a goy wife, then I changed my mind.'

'I'll come up there.'

'You've said that before. You'll come, you won't come! You don't call, though. I'll come and see you.'

'No!'

'Why not?'

Silence.

'Why not?'

'You want to cure me with doctors, that's why. Like all the rest do.'

'The rest? Who are you talking about, Lenny?'

'They're *all* spying on me and would like to put me away. The Spenders. The farmer, Sandbach. I can tell by the way he looks at me and treats me like a child or an idiot. When I complain about his bird-scarers and pesticides, he humours me. If it wasn't that I know he's sick, I'd stick one on him. He snoops around at peculiar times.'

'What sort of times?'

'He hangs around at dawn watching the windows.'

'You've seen him?'

'Yes. At other times I can tell someone's out there in the dark. They say at the vestry committee that I'm going bonkers in my old age. That I need "looking after", and "who's going to do it?" They have nothing else to talk about. The whole church committee's spying. I've seen the way they look at me. Everyone wants to put me away in the funny farm, Hannah, including you. Including even my own accountant. I know it! That's why I don't want you to come here. I'm *not going into the funny farm!* Once you're in, you can't get out.'

'I hope you're not drinking at the pub, Lenny. With the pills, that's fatal.'

'Well, I am. That's what I like doing. I know what I need, and it isn't doctors. It only needs two doctors to get you locked away. I know what it's like, my God! Lunatics wandering the wards muttering all night, nurses padding about asking if you "want a cup of tea, Mr Roth", the minute you fall asleep, or "It's time for your pills, Mr Roth", and the patients watching television all day long. It's the last place for a rest, and *there's no legal way you can get out again! You're incarcerated for life, Hannah! You have no rights any more! It would kill me – I'd kill myself!'*

'So you remember where you've been, after all? You've been kidding me!'

'All I want is to be left alone!'

'Please don't shout, Lenny. We all mean you no harm.'

'Didn't they do it to one of the royal family whom they wanted out of the way? I still read the newspapers and watch the telly. I'm not completely out of touch. Wasn't a cousin of the Queen discovered recently, rotting in some institution in Surrey? And you think it couldn't happen to me?'

'Medicine's changed since your young days, Lenny.'
'*There's nothing in life I fear more! Leave me alone, Hannah!*'

He had escaped that dreadful sequestration in the clinic only a
week ago. They had not allowed him to paint, saying 'it would
make a mess'. They believed that painting would worsen his
condition, as painting had brought it on. Therefore, in his bed
he had gone over compositions in his head, accepting or rejecting
ideas, developing or discarding colour areas, tones and forms,
in a series that was entirely mental, without once putting pencil
or brush to paper. Because he could not express them, his ideas
had pursued him through the night, like butterflies on a dark
path, through an impenetrable wood. It had always been like
that: if he could not paint, he was haunted.

Therefore he stockpiled the pills and cherished his reliance on
Sam to bring in the whisky, should they put him away again.

One night he would burst into a dream. He would imagine a
painting and disperse himself through it, flying.

14

In earlier days, Roth kept his drawing up to scratch by attending life-drawing sessions. He sought the discipline of objective drawing, especially at times of strain between Dorothy and himself. The concentration helped to hold him together.

When he was fifty-two he had discovered the twenty-year-old Rebecca Marks modelling in Bath. Roth, then living in a Wiltshire village, hadn't found it easy to obtain models. He enjoyed the change and conviviality of going to Bath on his bike for one day per week, and of staying overnight after drinking with friends.

Rebecca was what is called 'sculptural', with a form that would have appealed to Maillol and Moore. What had struck Roth most forcefully was her naturalness on the rostrum. She had not been doing the job for long, yet she had the ease of a professional, understanding by instinct how to relax and to adapt what had been chosen for her to do, unnoticeably distributing her weight so that she could hold the pose for an hour at a stretch with little strain. Rebecca had the confidence to hum and sing to herself while on show. During breaks, instead of scuttling for the shelter of the screens, she would walk unguardedly among the artists and students with her dressing gown flapping carelessly open, or she would wash at the sink where they cleaned their brushes. Northerners easily form bonds with one another when they're away from home, and at the first break, Roth learned that Rebecca also came from Leeds.

Roth hired himself an attic room, stayed for longer periods in Bath, and offered her private sessions. Developments followed quickly. She told him that her father had thrown her out of his house. According to Rebecca, he actually used the phrase 'and never darken my door again!' She moved her belongings (one old suitcase and a huge ex-army rucksack, leaking a trail of cosmetics) into the attic. There Roth learned that Rebecca's father had not been able to put up with her persistent thieving.

Neither could Roth, eventually, although he found it exciting at first. She helped herself to shops' and supermarkets' goods as if the world were a department store in which she owned all the shares. She had learned, she said, that no one notices so long as one acts boldly and as if having a right to what one has stolen.

One day they were travelling in a friend's car, discussing, as so often, Rebecca's lifestyle. Roth's intellectual friends made excuses for Rebecca as an existentialist. Roth had got her to read Genet, whom she called 'a great poofter', so these discussions irked her. Rebecca was silent until the car pulled up at traffic lights. 'Wait here for a moment,' she demanded and got out. She crossed the road to a hardware store outside which brushes, dustbins, ladders and buckets were displayed. She helped herself to two plastic buckets and a yardbrush, and carried them back to the car, swinging them happily. 'Open the boot – fast!' she ordered. 'You see how easy it is?' she said as they sped down the road.

Rebecca and Roth, one a refugee from a father and the other from a wife, shacked up together in the attic. She was very beautiful and Roth painted her obsessively.

The girl appeared gentle and excited about her first home-making. She stole the five-litre tins of emulsion paint with which they decorated the walls; also four unmatching dining chairs from outside antique and junk shops. In the attic, valuable objects nudged with tawdry ones.

In some stores, she would pay for an item, then, wagging her till receipt, she would get a fresh store attendant, a young man whose brain was obviously melted by her good looks, to carry to a waiting taxi an assortment of unpaid-for goods that she had also assembled.

She would do her 'shopping' either early in the morning when store staff were not properly awake, or at the end of the afternoon when they were tired and busy. She detected who was the most bored and indifferent girl in attendance at a checkout and took her groceries and toiletries out that way.

The couple wandered on the bike around the West Country, laughing and pillaging stores of small items that could be fitted into pannier bags: soap, perfume, tubes of oil paint.

Roth had no need to steal. They both did it for the excitement. Half the things that Rebecca took, she gave away. She had only to overhear of some need, even from a casual acquaintance, for her to satisfy it by thieving. Her innocence was almost saintly.

She was also a prophet. In the 1960s it was Rebecca Marks who had described to Roth the coming breakdown of urban England. She gave this armageddon that was waiting upon the horizon as her reason for immorality. 'Nothing matters, anyway,' she said.

Roth indulged her, he reflected, because the excitement dulled his thoughts of what Dorothy must be feeling.

Rebecca described social collapse, not theoretically and vaguely but with accurate, apocalyptic visions. Working-class riots, black people creating mayhem, nights of wholesale destruction and fires erupting simultaneously in various cities; the rioting being spread by that very organ, the 'capitalist television news', whose greatest interest, you would think, would be to stop the spread.

In those days, Rebecca had not been a Marxist. She had been that extraordinary phenomenon, a Jewish fascist. She described it mystically as 'esotericism', 'the central truth' and 'the true religion', but at bottom this was the mysticism that inspired a side of Hitlerism. Rebecca was obtusely thrilled to adopt the philosophy of her racial enemy.

Roth, realizing that she was merely playing, accepting also that theirs was a purely physical relationship, ignored her views. Looking back he also saw that, on the rebound from Dorothy, he too was drawn to the reverse of what he truly believed in. He never took Rebecca's 'fascism' seriously, any more than he took seriously her worship of 'evil'. Like himself she was exploring the exciting underbelly of life.

Elegantly dressed in stolen clothes, she spat: 'English people are such slobs. Especially my generation. You can see by looking at them that they're going to be tearing Britain apart in a few years. That's why I want to be different. But I can't afford to buy what I need, can I?'

The problem was that Roth, when he grew more serious about her, could cure her of neither her ideas nor her thieving.

He threatened that their relationship would have to end if she didn't stop stealing; if only because, after the first exciting weeks, he could not bear his tension every time she went out. She promised many times to stop. The result was that she started lying, too, and they had terrible rows.

Once, for instance, in Marlborough, Rebecca left him in a pub to which she promised to return after half an hour. An hour later, he walked down the street looking for her. Passing by a shop selling handbags he saw Rebecca within, and a store attendant standing at the door with her arms folded. He had to pretend not to guess what was going on. For a moment he even wondered whether to acknowledge Rebecca. However, he went into the shop. 'What's wrong?' he asked, in apparent amazement.

'I'm just paying for a new bag,' she answered. 'I'll meet you in the café next door.'

Apprehensively Roth sat in the café. When Rebecca joined him, she had a new handbag of crocodile leather. He was relieved that she had somehow got them to let her off. However, she would not admit that she had been thieving, no matter how angrily he charged her.

They walked through the town, arguing. They mounted the bike. The bag was in the pannier. He was still shouting at her, over his shoulder.

Rebecca pulled out the bag. Yelling, 'I don't want the fucking thing, anyway!' she flung it over the heads of the crowd.

15

3 February 1963

My Dear, My Dearest, Roth, Leonard, Len, Leonardo, Leo, whoever you are! At any rate, always my Darling.

Here is your Dorothy, writing to you at four in the morning. Yes, the dreaded drink. It sends me to sleep, but then I wake up in the middle of the night. As you know so well.

I thought that through our being apart for a while, both of us might be able to see what has been happening to us. Whenever we are happy, sooner or later a cloud comes over your face. That is the first sign of a tide turning, when your destructive side is about to surface. And your unfaithful side. (Don't they go together?) I am so used to that hell swamping us that I become nervous at the first signs, and probably I make it worse. I hoped that through your being left, without criticism, to follow your own course of infidelity and rage around the West Country for a short time, you would see what that side of you is doing to our love.

When we have talked about ways we might move forward, my dearest, deepest hope has been that somehow the two sides of you might merge once more into the difficult, complex man whom I love so much.

You remind me that, when we first met, I wanted you to share all of yourself with me, the dark as well as the light. That I wanted you warts and all. Of course I did not really want to encourage you to turn into a destroyer, wrecking bars, beating people up for no good reason, being unfaithful to me. I hated it. I pretended not to mind. But I *lied*.

I lied because it made you sexually very powerful and I

could not resist that. But it got out of control. It became something far stronger than either of us. When that part of you is suppressed, you are very difficult to live with. I believe it is because you try to suppress it totally, so that you become unstable.

You become anxious, too, because your work is weakened, like your personality. You were putting the gentle, sensitive, 'feminine' side of yourself, that you drew upon for your painting, into your day-to-day existence instead, for my sake, and your art suffered. You can't stand *that* – can you?

So then I wanted my wild old Roth back. But I didn't really. I wanted my lover back, complicatedly two-sided, yes, but both in one. I cannot tell you how often I have mourned him.

Now you 'set up home', as you call it, with Rebecca Marks. Oh, Roth!

To start with, I wonder if you realize what your using that word 'home' does to me? We who have never, really, in just over a decade together, had one, have we?

Only a series of stations. Amid travels, two years of seeming to settle in London, the same period here in Wiltshire, and now you are off again. Is all our life to continue like this?

So much for my thinking that being without me you would miss the companionship, fun, friendship, our shared life, travel – yes, that too, despite its pain – painting, music. You exchange that for a girl who could (forgive the cliché – or forgive yourself the cliché) be your daughter. No doubt she has all sorts of qualities. I wonder! But also, as you so well know, it especially hurts a woman of my age that you go off with a youngster. Call that an older woman's point of view, if you like. Only because, generally speaking, older women don't go off with young men.

How would you feel if I did?

Suppose I had said that I wanted children more than I wanted you, and was going to find a man who could give them to me? How could you hurt me so?

I can hardly see or feel for the blinding love for you that is all through my body. I cannot bear to think that you can throw me into this hell. I am forty-eight years of age. You have your fruits, your children, in your paintings. It is too late for *my* children now! The only 'child' I have is you, you bastard! And now you've gone off with a *baby*!

I scream with pain for my lost love . . . my lost lover. Music we listened to, your paintings, your paintings in catalogues that I have, that new book with the photographs of the painters on the lawn here, and I wearing the dress you liked so much, remember? They mock me with my own stupidity in thinking I could balance you up, hold you tight with my love.

But I know that I am responsible for unbalancing you as well, by my swings between the constructive and destructive sides of your personality. Usually they were because I had been lying to you about my need for that demonic side. I don't need it. I deceived you because I was afraid to lose you. Well, you have left me, anyway. It amounted to nothing, all that struggle and pain.

Please, Roth, don't go down that road of using drugs to give you the highs and the lows that you seem to need. Are drugs an alternative to the highs and lows of Paradise and Hell that we have shared together? To get into 'transcendent states', as you call them? Please don't do it. *It will kill you*.

I am trying to arrange for your clothes that you left and some of your pictures to be forwarded to Bath.

Your (always your) 'Dora-thea', 'gift of God'. As you so often reminded me.

9 March 1963

My Darling,

I don't know what to write that will bring comfort to either of us. No new discussion or arrangement or proposal can alter the fact that we come round in circles, and that we have both of us tried to change things but failed.

I must leave here. If I stay waiting for you in Wiltshire, at what you so aptly call 'the Old Rec', I will despise myself for learning nothing from the past and I might come to hate you.

Your bitter daemon is much stronger than anything I can

offer to balance it. The effort has wiped me out. I can think
of no new thing to help you towards contentment. There is
always something else. Something *else*.

I cannot keep it up. I have neither the physical stamina to
offset you, nor the desire to be so trapped again.

The relief, now that I have put you out of my mind! I can
set forth without first looking out for the pretty woman who
might be your anima projection and who has dogged me,
whoever she is, wherever she is, maybe around the next
corner, ever since we met.

And I do not have to live, hour by hour, with *your* painting,
judging, helping, using my own talent for that.

You will say that I offered. I say that you kept asking, or
saying that you felt you shouldn't ask. A subtler sadism but
the same thing in the end.

I can even think of painting again, myself. Today I have
cleared those attic rooms we never went into, wiped the
windows to let in a little more light, and primed some
boards. Oddly, I couldn't bring myself to make use of any
of those primed canvases you left behind, nor work in your
studio where everything is to hand. It's all there, as you left
it, should you come back. But I won't be here. I've had a
good day and found that preparing to do some painting was
the only thing, *the only thing* that would stop me thinking of
Rebecca Marks.

Now I am the one who looks at women in the street, because
I am looking out for her type, and wondering why you chose
it. I know that most men look at pretty women, but no one
with your intensity. The devouring voyeur.

Whatever else hurtful, I am saying that I love you as much
as ever, perhaps more –

One week after receiving this letter, Roth was back in the Old
Rec – with Dorothy, who did not leave.

The circumstances seemed fortuitous. Were they?

Rebecca disappeared after a quarrel. He realized that, such had
been their criminal secrecy, he did not know the address of her
family nor of any of her friends. There was no way to contact

her except through the police, but that might provoke other problems. He realized, too, that the classic Freudian explanation of thieving applied to Rebecca; she was stealing love, and he had failed her.

He waited for three days, left a note and returned to Wiltshire.

He called back in Bath a week later and found a letter from Rebecca.

She had 'seen the light'. She had realized that he was a 'crud', and she had joined a Marxist squat.

16

In time before Victoria went out for her long lunch break at one o'clock, Roth rang the Station. He must find out which ones of the Greek pictures they had taken from Leeds. Dorothy had sent some of the canvases on to Hertfordshire, but not all, and he was unsure what was still stored in Prospect Terrace.

The number was engaged. He phoned again. He asked for Victoria. 'Who is speaking, please?' 'This is Leonard Roth.' 'She's in a meeting, Mr Roth.' I'll bet she fucking is. 'Would you like to leave a message, Mr Roth?' 'May I speak to Mr Rosblum, please?' Don't tell me: Rosblum is fucking out today. 'Mr Rosblum is out today. Would you like Miss Voyce to call you later?'

Roth put the phone down.

No fucking thank you. I'll get her, in time. I'll get her. Okay? Now he was angry, and that was dangerous.

He was so accustomed to the sweating that by now he could feel it finding its way through his skin, like juice squeezed out of an orange.

To throw off the nagging temptation to drive a hundred and fifty miles to Leeds, he locked the cottage and, in the clanging of the church bell, a packet of Tofranil bulging from the left breast pocket and Valium from the right pocket of his shirt, he walked, or rather staggered a little, clinging to the fence from time to time, sweating, heart pounding – why won't it stop? I know it's the fucking pills – around 'the Green' (it had been fenced in by the Sandbachs during the war) and unlocked his studio.

The old schoolroom was the last in his sequence of retreats that had begun in boyhood when, in the damp brick shed at the bottom of the yard, or in the attic his mother had provided, he sought a hiding place from family lunches, family visits, his parents' quarrels, and especially from his mad father's rages.

Ever since childhood he had tried to keep his refuges secret. He got his mother to lie to the rest of the family on his behalf:

'Where's our Len again? I'll skin the nebbish alive!'

'I sent him on an errand, Saul.'

'An errand? *Now*? With the meal on the table?'

Meanwhile, at ten years of age he was hiding in the shed among the spiders and the washday tubs. If the door happened to blow open he could be seen from the dining-room window. Drawing. There he first cultivated that precious mood of being secret, and of dwelling in a fantasy: secrecy and fantasy, madness and argument, were the essences of painting, so far as Roth was concerned.

As time had gone by, the family and its quarrels had simply grown bigger until it embraced the pool of the whole world. Dealers, accountants, doctors, the 'Arts Police' (as Roth called all officials who dealt with the arts), psychiatrists, the Nazis, and even much of womankind were part of that family he had to hide from. Their incomprehensible concerns, their angers, their loves and pleasures were parallel to those of that first, claustrophobic family which didn't know why he painted pictures.

That horrible moment when, as a teenage boy, he had found his father hanged by his braces from a beam in his bedroom, had cancerously enlarged itself into the deaths that every family in the world watched, with astounding equanimity, in the corners of their living rooms every night: the televised shots of wars, accidents and starvation. One bit of the world was killing another, and all of the rest was watching it, nightly. Today, Roth hid in his studio from the massive world of death, as once he had hidden in a brick shed, then in an attic from his father's suicide.

He recognized that the impotence of age, with its accompanying remoteness, was also a refuge, to replace the shed and the Dream Room.

It was within his studio that he went into a refuge within a refuge: the recesses of his mind. He imagined his mind as like the cave at Delphi where the oracle hid. Like your father, you could kill yourself, the oracle whispered at the back of his brain in the quiet hours of the night.

Roth would often come out of the studio soaked, sweating, exhausted, limping like a boxer out of the ring.

He entered through a Gothic porch which had carved over its lintel, in nineteenth-century Gothic script, Socrates' saying: 'KNOW THYSELF'. It was like entering a stone womb. Old wooden benches set into this cavity were scratched and initialled by generations of children. Beyond were the awesome cloakrooms and passageways, which Roth had crowded with picture racks. Further racks were erected in the teachers' room.

The big school room was full of light from the high, arched windows and from the extra ones that Roth had set on the north side of the roof. Jars of pigment along a shelf were ranged from cool to warm, prussian blue to cadmium red, like the long bars of a bright sunrise. These pigments, which he ground in a pestle and mortar for studio work (he used tubes out of doors), poured like light itself over the paintings. Even the stained jars, the stiffened brushes, the huddle of discarded tins and paint rags provided specklings of colour, though they had grown increasingly sombre. The floor was splattered with colour, for sometimes he laid canvases down and leaned over them.

Some of last year's Greek landscapes, four feet by five feet, executed in oils out of doors, were stacked against the walls. Sunrises crashed on to mountains that were as eruptive with red, viridian, chrome yellow and orange as the sky was with the slabs of light that touched the slopes. Bleached towns poured over ravines or over cliffs above the sea. There were seismic collections of wild spring flowers which Roth had caught last year in the ancient theatre in Dodona.

Good painting had the power to restore memories more strongly than photographs or a diary could. The concentration imprinted so much on the mind: the scent of blossoms, a passing cart. He remembered it all. He had been achieving something in Greece. It had been cut short.

From this last year in Ashby were the self-portraits, mostly in oils, sometimes executed in acrylic or watercolour. They were growing steadily darker. Light was increasingly painful and perhaps he wouldn't be able to bear the harsh light of the Mediterranean any more. In one year, after enlarging the windows, he was thinking of introducing curtains and screens.

Through the self-portraits he was trying to understand and take a grip of himself by means of the only medium he had faith in. For it was as if there were an invisible pane of glass keeping him from reality, and he was like a fly trapped against a window pane. The screen was that of his own nature. Despite his efforts, for example pouncing upon mirrors to take his image by surprise when he shaved in the morning, life was crushing him against something he could not grasp.

Dozens of these new works were scattered around. They showed his face pulled into those grimaces in which he hoped to take himself by surprise. In one his mouth was open, in another it was slumped to one side. In a third his tongue was hanging, or a finger pulled down the corner of his eye. One face held an expression that had begun as a laugh but had turned into a scream.

As whatever does not add to the image on the canvas dilutes it, he obliterated elements that did not contribute positively. In some only a mouth or an eye had survived his attacks. Many showed wiped-out, blank faces, preserving the disturbing memory of an expression in the oval of a face, smeared with a rag. The hair in this one, and in another maybe an ear survived, painted *trompe l'oeil* after days of patient labour with sable brushes; details that contrasted with square feet of smearings. The small areas of heightened realism owed much to Dorothy's way of working.

No one else had yet seen more than one or two of the most conventional self-portraits, the brightest and earliest, which he had sent in to the Station. Beginning them in Greece, he'd intended a brief turning-aside from landscapes. It was when he had been at the nadir of exhaustion, impotence and grief; when he felt he could neither leave with Dorothy, nor live on alone, hardly knowing the language, in a remote place where children threw stones and the women in black cackled when he set off on painting expeditions.

Worrying over the irreconcilability of his need to stay, pursuing what he had found, and Dorothy's need, for her health and sanity's sake, to get away from him and the place, had produced a tension in his stomach that had told him he might be cultivating a cancer. Roth had thought: What would Rembrandt and Van Gogh do? His answer had been to prop up a mirror and paint a self-portrait.

One with this difference: he determined to stop the moment he realized he had ceased actually looking and had fallen into habit, repeating preconceptions. He would discard 'art'. He would not try to improve or rescue the work according to an aesthetic standard. Instead he would paint entirely for himself, to see what he would find.

That first one had led him to a series of suspended mouths and eyes. No more filling in, no more cheating with what came easily; with what had been seen and formulated already.

This process of leaving out rather than putting in had been hard work. At first he had not been able to concentrate for more than a few minutes without being distracted by design, placing, styles of drawing, colours that would look well together, and means of expressing moods or feelings which he already knew how to do. All that was easier than setting down quite simply what he saw, altering only to get closer to the truth.

With every oil on canvas, he found himself in greater isolation; with every drawing executed with charcoal and washes of dilute ink, using a brush and then a pen, or a soft pencil which he rubbed with his finger; with every watercolour. There was a tickling sensation in his brain.

Thus he had found himself stranded on the raft of a painting, first in an apartment in Greece and now in Hertfordshire. His desert islands.

Often he turned back to the first self-portrait. The oil paint was so diluted with turpentine that it was as thin as watercolour and tentative, for he had found that he could not manage more than half an hour at a time of such painting. At first he had thought it a failure, and had put it away. When he looked at it again after months, it had chilled him. He had produced a painting of a dead man.

No: sometimes the dead have an expression of being caught in equipoise, holding the secret of life as well as of death. His own face was not like that. It was of a man decomposed. It was flesh that would smell. The eyes were dead, in a way that the eyes of the real dead are not; it was not dead, it was merely without life. The expression was of a yearning without sparkle. He had the look of a prisoner; of one taken away from life. The mouth was slumped, not in repose but in despair. It was a face from the gulag of the emotions.

17

It was half past one. Roth put on the stereo a recording of Bruckner's Fourth Symphony.

He set his chair fifteen feet from his easel and stared at his latest work. The cadmium-red scar of a mouth defined on an otherwise misty canvas. An eye wiped off and painted again.

Behind the easel was erected a full-length mirror, and at either side his face squinted at him from two other mirrors. He looked a scarecrow.

He would begin a work by keeping everything loose and general. Once a part was defined, especially if it was an eye or a mouth, everything new would have to be related to it and the course of the painting was fixed. Eventually, he would concentrate his drawing upon the most telling detail.

With the present four foot by three foot canvas he was at the point when he must take a risk. Upon the horizontal limb of the easel, a scumble of old paint, scraped with a palette knife from this and other paintings, had been deposited, to solidify and betray his indecisiveness.

He knew that he made false starts when his eye did not grasp what his mind envisaged and that it was a strain he went through before a new way of painting was born. His mind outraced his eye. He must be patient. Or he must *do* something. Time and again in the past when a canvas had threatened to collapse into muddy chaos he had pulled it back by taking a desperate chance, risking everything.

He had made up his mind what mark to make when he heard behind him a polite cough, piercing one of Bruckner's silences. There are moments in the work of Bruckner and of other death-haunted composers – Mahler, Beethoven – when the music pauses and leaves the listener suspended for a period which is like the heart stopping, before loud, apocalyptic chords; chords in which Roth saw those shadows, like great wings, that were cutting out the light. It was at such a moment that he was disturbed.

As the music thundered into life again, Roth turned and flushed. At one time he had been able to paint while guests sipped coffee or whisky in his studio. He had shared space with Dorothy, and it was she who had insisted on having her private place because his presence crushed her. Now, he hated anyone to see him at work. As Hannah would have said, it 'gave him the pip'.

In his second month in Ashby, for instance, he had come into his studio and found Sam Fall hovering among his canvases, compiling an inventory. To do with the Roth trusteeship, Fall explained. A dark figure in a business suit, he had given Roth a shock disproportionate to the visit. It was the hovering; as if hovering not to wait, but to hunt. Was he a friend? Ever since, Roth had wondered about letting Fall have a key. Sam was the only person he had ever trusted with one. Shouldn't he have the locks changed? There were three elaborate locks, plus alarms, and it would be time-consuming to explain them to a locksmith. Having him around for a day would also be a nuisance. Finally, Roth had done nothing about it.

Having worries on his mind, today Roth had neglected to shut his door as usual and Sandbach, with normally acceptable country manners, had followed him in. Roth, absorbed, had not even noticed that the church bell had stopped ringing. How long had the farmer been silently spying on him – the first person to see so many of the self-portraits? It was an ill omen.

The farmer was not looking at the pictures but at the artist, searching the face that had been so startlingly turned to him. His own aghast features showed what he read there and in the mirrors repeating profiles of the face.

Roth rose and stopped the symphony, not because he wanted to speak to Sandbach, but because the farmer's presence polluted the music.

'Nothing's higher than God,' Sandbach croaked. 'That's what I was always taught and I'm surprised at you, an artist, talking the way you did. I was always told that an artist loves what's beautiful and right.'

Sandbach invoking God!

Part of his business consisted of dealing in second-hand farm machinery. He sold tractors and combine harvesters to trade missions from desperate Third World countries. They were bought as they were inspected, seemingly in good condition, but before they were shipped out to be the 'salvation' of some near-starving community, Sandbach got his lads to change new tractor tyres for old ones, and the working gearboxes for faulty ones.

'Mr Sandbach, I have to work!'

'I wouldn't like to meet any o' them on a dark night,' Sandbach remarked, chuckling, when he had taken a look at the portraits. 'A bit garish, aren't they? Though it's none of my business, so long as they make you a living. It's the bottom line that counts.'

Roth started to turn the portraits to the walls.

'My offer still stands for you to join us at church, Mr Roth. It'd do you more good than swallowing all those pills,' Sandbach blustered, perturbed by the painter who was trying to block the view of his paintings.

Perhaps Sandbach thought that the madman might cut his throat. Maybe he had seen some idiotic film about Van Gogh.

'Come to Sunday dinner with us, then we can talk about everything,' Sandbach offered as he backed out.

Roth could not recover after this invasion. People felt like this after they had been burgled. He was sullied.

He struggled to recover by staring at the depiction of his grimacing mouth.

I could go north today on my bike.

His Laverda lay back in the cottage hallway, under her sheet. He could visualize her looking embalmed as if for the grave, but don't be deceived! She was poised for flight. Underneath the bedsheet, gleaming red muscles rippled; an arrow potent with feline volition, already pointed towards the north and facing the front door. Which he could open . . . which he could open.

Meanwhile, another intruder was hovering at the door of his studio: Adam, his young disciple.

18

Adam was not a pretty sight. Careless over food and health, he was leaner than was natural, not clean, and he smoked heavily. About his person there was a faint odour of urine. He showed a lack of essential pride, even though he sported signs of vanity in the shape of an earring and a pigtail.

These were marks of belonging to a different world and time from Roth, whose own vanity, of the old-fashioned variety, was tickled by Adam's considerate attitudes. His hand open, held forward, or first to put money on the bar for a drink. His readiness with solicitous enquiries.

Adam was one of those who adapt themselves to whomever they admire or depend upon, which was flattering. Also, because his own features were ruined and his tolerance widened by the cozy haze of drug-taking, he did not stare at Roth with the usual alarmed look.

Roth's only friend here was this London art student who claimed that, like Roth seeking 'peace' and a cure, he had been sent to stay with his parents in a village near Ashby. He had been 'amazed to find that the Leonard Roth is still alive'.

They had met two months ago by coincidence in the Peddlars and soon Adam was using the inter-loan system of the local lending library to look up monographs and reviews of exhibitions. He began to talk like Roth and tried to look like him, even acquiring an expensive leather jacket. Roth had found himself relaxing into old, vain feelings of supporting and flattering the sycophants and the young; pleasures that he thought he had forgotten and no longer desired.

He had long ago realized that there was a voyeuristic element in the attention he attracted. Young painters wanted to be near him and to follow the same beam that his eye followed when staring at a bunch of flowers or through a window. They wished to touch, to receive or give a hand upon the shoulder, because there was magic in the association. Roth's pictures had taken the risks for them in advance and some of his power might be transferred to their own generation.

A further reason for Roth's sympathy was that he did not have a son. Roth was swayed by the return of old flatteries into thinking he had come far enough towards being a human being again to be able to help Adam into the self-discipline of recovery. He imagined that he could do something for someone else. The painter had the idea that he was forming a mutually creative relationship. In giving one might be given to, and Adam had the touchstone of his youth to donate. Roth was moved to overlook Adam's scrofulous appearance and wearisome opinions; to hand over gifts of money, some drawings and his only copy of a bibliography of articles compiled by a PhD student in 1975.

They had got into the habit of meeting three or four times a week in the Peddlars, still pretending to be casual about the arrangement. Adam was too respectful to try to pin the older man down and Roth liked it that way.

All over the county indigenous villagers, descendants of those labourers whose backs and spirits had been broken in working the land during the eighteenth and nineteenth centuries, huddled like castaways in the rear rooms of public houses isolated among the new prairies. The Peddlars was a meeting place for Sandbach's farmworkers and a few ex-Ashby inhabitants who nostalgically returned from distant housing estates. Roth and Adam were encircled by alienating conversations about family life and its amusements which were a thousand removes from their own experiences. It encouraged intimacy between these two, who were isolated by their interest in art. Drink further made it possible for Roth to be kind about Adam's opinionated, impressionistic ideas.

Roth would remember little of his night's drinking. He had difficulty in recalling where he had visited, or his steps to and from there, but inexplicable, burning lights of memory would penetrate this murk. They arose like images in dreams, arbitrarily, giving him no clues to why this moment should remain vivid. Yet he might recall everything; the look of room or person, the surrounding odours, and details of what he had been thinking, usually with the memory of a blurred pain in his head. What he could never recall was how long this moment might have lasted; whether it was ten minutes or an hour.

Surprised by Adam this morning, Roth was flushed with strobelike visions of last night, for instance of the boy weaving through the room with pints of ale. Even he, though he had done much to wreck himself, exhibited the inevitable walk of those his age who so calmly, beautifully, drift through the present because it belongs to them. Roth had therefore written Adam a cheque for £300 to enable him to visit Paris.

'Everyone will give you anything you want when you are young. It's a good job the young don't realize it!' Roth joked. Kaplan would have explained that Roth was trying to recover his own youth in France by proxy. Kaplan would have been wrong.

Today Roth had forgotten about the cheque until Adam reminded him, saying that he had come to thank him.

Roth had steadily resisted Adam's requests to visit the studio. No amount of flattery and drink could weaken this resolve. Instinct made him even more apprehensive than he normally was about visitors. However, now that the boy was on the doorstep, a bottle of wine in his hand and offering thanks, Roth had to invite him in. Hunched with misgivings, Roth led him between the racks of paintings.

The effect was like an ancient preparation for a numinous experience: a preparatory passage through dark, confusing tunnels before bursting into space and radiance. Adam was not too dulled to be unaffected. He put down the tissue-wrapped bottle of Yugoslavian plonk with the reverent attitude of one lighting a candle in a church. His stooped body straightened. His careless, inattentive stance became alert and tense like a confronted animal. His face, normally grey, brightened and almost flushed.

Roth turned his back in order to reverse more of the self-portraits to face the wall. He was growing tense from these unwanted visitors.

'Fuckin' great!' he heard spoken softly from behind him. 'Fuckin' great stuff!'

Roth sprang round, searching for signs of sincerity and discernment in Adam's face, as a painter does when his work is surveyed. He was flattered to find them. Adam's eyes were on the landscapes of Greece and several earlier, favourite canvases that Roth kept by him. Adam was pacing with a significant tension in his body between the boards, canvases and watercolours. For a time his nature was changed by the pictures.

'They're so fucking lyrical!'

That had taken Adam by surprise. These late landscapes were purified. They were made up of embryos of colour that emitted the energies of light from within. Adam saw, indeed, in mountain, sky and meadow, soft curved shapes and rose colours with a foetal energy to uncurl, bursting to live and dance. The pictures were so contrary to the man whom people were allowed to see. The paintings were not angry at all; they were energetic, but their inner content was peaceful. The thought crossed Adam's mind that perhaps Roth behaved as he did in public houses because he was saving his alternative self for his studio.

'Is that one of the studies you did from the air?'

Adam was looking at a large acrylic on canvas from the 1970s. Roth remembered the day on which it had been painted. The blue, deepening to a stronger tone above, had been so powerful that it burned his eyes. It grew paler but more luminous below, where it reached a level plain of clouds that shone like a snowfield. It was these stacked tones and colours that Roth had set out to capture, and the movement. Being up there was not like sitting in a chair or standing still, a spectator before a landscape.

'It was done in the studio after being in the air. I relied on my memory.'

'What a great fucking idea, to paint from the air! To change the perspective.'

'Peter Lanyon was up there before me,' Roth said, disparagingly. 'The real break was to put myself in the middle of the picture and spread it around me. A new feeling of space. That's a sensation you get from being in the air.'

'And what a fucking wonderful space this fucking room is! I wish I had this kind of space to work in. I'd probably be able to do something myself, then.'

Was Adam hinting that he would like to occupy this studio? Roth flushed. Should he tell the presumptuous boy that he'd never get down to a day's work no matter what wonderful space and time he was granted? He had all the time in the world, but all he'd been able to show Roth was some hazily observed sketches.

Roth remembered in time not to tell him the blunt truth. It wasn't worth the trouble. In the past he had found that it only incited envy and hostile criticism in return. He had never found anyone able to admit that they were too lazy to work and pay the price of creativity. That was the problem Roth had with teaching, years ago. The kids wanted luxury in order to paint and felt that they could do nothing without the circumstances that Roth had earned for himself, forgetting that he hadn't always enjoyed them and they'd come as a consequence of his work. Except in the financial sense, Roth had always laboured with insecurity. He had always painted as if he were shipwrecked and clinging to a raft. Painting was Roth's only means of survival and that was his reason for doing it. These kids wanted to be sure they were already surviving extremely well before they'd think about painting. Roth hadn't chosen the life. It had just turned out that way.

Adam's pictures stayed locked in his head. That was easier than the labours and troubles of handling paint. He was not on antidepressants, like Roth, but on psychedelic drugs. The sort that, like the flattery of 'self-expression' encouraged in 'creative' classes, gave the illusion of removing the barriers of craft, experience, objectivity and labour. They provided the illusion of having produced something which was in truth no more than a cloud in the brain.

'I've not always had the space,' Roth said with a shrug. 'You don't always need it. You can work on a desktop. Fra Angelico painted in a monk's cell. William Blake lived and worked in two cramped rooms in London. When he died, he said: "I but go into another room." Perhaps that was his idea of heaven: no more than another room for him to glow in, to paint in. In a tiny room, you can lead a big life. Or be in a great place like this and lead a small life, like I fucking – '

Finding himself drifting into pub habits of intimacy, Roth pulled back. Now that he was sober, he didn't want to reveal so much.

Swallowing his broken sentence, he hovered indecisively over a group of the self-portraits and selected a few of the least revealing, but brightest, earliest, most 'painterly' ones.

After a few minutes' silence, Adam whispered: 'I don't know how you do it.'

'It's just something seen clearly, suddenly,' Roth murmured to himself, while keeping his back to the boy; still turning pictures and returning the ones that he judged had been viewed for long enough back to the wall. Adam wanted to help turn the canvases but Roth shrugged him away.

'The light through a window or over a landscape, through the trees, or in your own eyes as you stare into them in a mirror . . . but always anyway light giving its blessing and benediction in colour, expressing something that lies behind . . . beyond. Then the excitement . . . the flush in the blood . . . It's fucking wonderful when it happens.'

Roth pulled himself together to be more articulate.

'It's all in the seeing. There's an anecdote about Turner as an old man at some sort of posh fucking soirée in Cheyne Walk, an honoured guest but barely speaking to anyone and remembered only for staring out of the window at the river, watching the light die. I can't understand why people were so baffled by him, thought him uncouth, uncivilized, a barbarian not fit for their fucking drawing rooms. What else should a painter be doing but staring at the river and the light, for what else was there? What fucking else is there?'

'*We* understand that, Mr Roth, but others don't.'

'And on the canvas it comes back to you,' Roth continued, still sifting his pictures, talking to himself in fact. 'Not in a literal fashion, not as fields and trees, but, when you're working well, when it is all truly exciting and relentless, paint and images working directly on the soul, there appear marks and tones and patches of colour which are equivalents of those excitements of the light upon the hills – not representations, but equivalents, expressing what lies behind the light. Paint and images working directly, in their own language, straight on to the fucking eye, *bang*! and not wandering, filtered and thinning through the mind. That's what painting is . . . that's what I'm after . . . that's the thirst that's never satisfied until it reaches its bourne. Colour and tone and texture of paint and canvas. Materials giving rise to sensations that are not material and imprisoned by "the senses five". You know Blake's phrase? Amazing things can happen. One can be swept away, carried on a painting as on unseen wings . . . but one needs energy . . . flight.'

Adam watched Roth's hands waving over the surfaces. It was as if he were reshaping the images. Adam recalled the first time that he had shaken that hand. It was an old man's and yet unlike one. There was a destructive power in that lean, big gorilla's paw and Adam hoped that the dangerous game he was secretly playing would not land him in its grip. The bloody old fool was not just paranoid and gabbling away because he was on antidepressants. He had instincts.

'But the later pictures are so dark,' Adam repeated.

'They're not dark,' Roth remarked, simply.

It struck Adam that the old artist did see them as bright paintings.

Roth was staring at him with frightening eyes. 'You don't know what I'm fucking talking about, do you?'

'I do, Mr Roth, I do!'

Roth shrugged, left Adam to study the array along the wall, and went to put away the wine. It would be a lesson to Adam that this was his working, not his drinking, time. Pub friendships are better kept as such. They do not flourish in the cold light of day.

He retreated into what had been the teacher's staffroom, now a kitchen, there to smother his anger by grinding coffee.

Returning ten minutes later with a metal tray on which were

two mugs, milk and sugar, he caught sight of Adam riffling through a stack of letters. Some were from Dorothy. Some were from lawyers and from his accountant. There were bills for materials from Winsor & Newton. There was some of his own, unfinished correspondence to his wife, scrawled in the pit of one night or other, often accompanied with drawings, stained with drink or tears.

The boy let go quickly and was fumbling for his matches.

Roth asked him not to smoke. Adam, the more afraid because of Roth's mild reaction, thinking he'd been caught out but not knowing for sure, responded as to the stroke of a whip.

Roth continued to say nothing about Adam's spying. That would be crueller. He watched contemptuously as his visitor, disgustingly to Roth's epicurean mind, polluted fresh, good coffee with milk and sugar, while he sat in his chair with his own strong black stuff. He tried to appear calm, but he was seething. He had therefore put himself where he could not be looked at. Adam surveyed more of the self-portraits, holding his cup in a hand that was distinctly trembling.

Having images of himself surveyed aggravated Roth's feeling of age, nakedness and being out of step with the young. Roth felt as dead as Rembrandt or Van Gogh. Age was in itself a feeling of being half invisible. People no longer wanted to look at you, feel for you or talk to you, in case you raised problems. Being with the young was like travelling in a strange country and finding that the expected landmarks have vanished; searching hopelessly for what one recognizes, and fearing impatience with one's fumbling incapacities. The young search for the new beyond the old, while the old are looking for a few familiar signs surviving from the past. The old see the young, but the young do not see the old. They might as well be dead and already peeping out at them from that boring old heaven, with the harps and the goody-goody people. As well as being angry at his spying, Roth envied Adam's youth.

Meanwhile, Adam paced quietly and respectfully, as if he were in a church. He stared for pious, long periods at canvases. Murmuringly he asked permission before he sifted gently through a stack of watercolours and drawings.

Roth didn't explain his work any more. He regretted having spoken and realized that nothing had sunk in. In time, he could rely on Adam to offer explanations of his own. That's how youngsters are.

Adam indeed soon commenced to hold forth, talking of tones and colour in art-school jargon.

Despite his elder wisdom, Roth felt a restless tiger of irritation stirring. Uncomfortably, he crossed and uncrossed his knees, spilled his coffee, rose and prowled, expressing that other prowling beast of anger inside him. After the first shock of amazement at the quantity, the light, the size, he was not understood. After all that he had tried to say, he had conveyed nothing that mattered. There was merely a spy in his studio.

'It doesn't matter what one paints, so long as it's well done,' Adam said, with arrogance and gravity. 'A good painter can as happily paint a dustbin or a kipper as a fucking Venus.'

'Who taught you that? That attitude is the essence of academicism!' Roth snarled. 'You've no right to be even looking at my pictures. You are fouling them with your eyes.' He commenced to turn his canvases back to the walls. 'Schnorrer! I'm wasting my time!'

'I'm sorry,' Adam stuttered, embarrassed, guilty, taken aback and not able to deal with the menace that had sprung out at him. 'I only mean, a crappily painted Venus ain't improved by being a Venus, and the contents of some fucker's dustbin – '

'They teach that in all the art schools, because that's what an academic who has nothing more to offer than technique *has* to believe in.'

Roth was pacing his studio with long, angry strides, and shouting.

'But I tell you, there is no such thing as a good painting of cleverly painted nothingness! I don't know what you've read in my catalogues, but you've never read anything I have said to agree with that. The subject matter is crucial to a painting! I'm interested in painting human emotions, joy, grief, pain, loss. All that lies behind what we are, what we seem, what we do . . .'

'Loss?' Adam repeated.

Roth wished he hadn't said that. It was too revealing. It made him more angry with himself.

Adam, if he'd been wise, would have made for the door. He knew enough about the person whom he had roused. He had seen Roth's ire from time to time in the pub. He had read and heard about him.

Instead, Adam hid by looking even more intently at canvases and talking extravagantly, rapidly, about 'smothering purples', 'shrieking yellows' and 'doorways to darkness'. Words that he imagined were similar to Roth's own. Not to Roth, they weren't. He felt more boxed in by meaningless language than he had been before.

'Though I realize that I'm unfashionably spiritual,' Roth apologized quietly, bitterly sarcastic.

It caused Adam to turn round. Roth was white with anger and beaded with sweat. Terrifying.

'I'm sorry, Mr Roth.' Adam backed off. 'I really am. I admire your work, it's fantastic – and people think that you're not working! I know there has to be a lot of input to produce that fantastic output. I didn't mean to upset you.'

'I'm upset about Dorothy,' Roth tried to apologize. 'My nerves are ragged.'

Adam merely shrugged, with an irritating gesture that made Roth grit his teeth. Clearly, Adam could not understand why this was so important. Marriage was another subject that Roth was unable to talk about, because his views were old-fashioned. He believed in the sacredness of marriage, not because of vows and morality, but because two people's experience of being one was so intense, it could not be broken without the following half-life seeming a shadow.

There and then in the studio, memories poured in. They were moments of superhuman ecstasies, those of gods or saints who had entered mortal life. Although he ached for them to be restored, now they possessed a power that at the time they did not have, for they were blissful then precisely because he had not realized that they were so. Today they were in an intenser form within the framework of loss – as medieval church glass is the stronger for the black surround of leading and walls.

'Dorothy's holding a party today,' Roth said.

'You told me that last night.' Adam smiled again. 'And the night before.'

'I'm going up to see her. I think we can restore our past . . . it's a good time . . . have some fun again . . . surprise her.'

'You said all that before, too, but I thought it was only because you were drunk. How are you getting there?'

'On the bike.'

'Didn't you tell me that the drugs make you dizzy?' Adam's eyes were focused on those two bulges at Roth's breast, and the tips of the packets protruding out of the pockets. 'You're mad to go on a bike, Mr Roth. You'll kill yourself. Or someone else. You should stay here.' Adam grinned. 'You just want to get your leg over.'

He had no idea why Roth had turned white again and was towering over him with rapidly clenched and unclenched fists, with all staggering and weakness caused by Tofranil, Valium or alcohol overcome.

'I didn't mean anything, Mr Roth!'

'Nebbish! Schnorrer!'

Roth's painting table tumbled over as he moved. This maddened him, too.

'Get out! Nebbish!'

Roth could hardly force the words between his teeth. He was close enough to smell Adam's staleness.

'Fucking spy!'

Instead of having the good sense to retreat, Adam stood and grinned.

'Get out,' Roth repeated, quietly.

'I didn't mean – ' Adam began again.

Roth had him by the shoulders and was shaking him, like a dog with a rat. He was looking around for somewhere to throw him. He peered as if he did not know where the door was, but perhaps he could find a window that would do. As if his own studio had become a strange place.

'Mr Roth! You're fucking mad!'

Adam was being pushed down the passage. Out through the porch.

'You're fucking lucky I don't kill you!'

The boy was partway down the path, rubbing at his collar, before he dared to turn. He glimpsed a white face, beaded with sweat, in the porch before he fled.

——I'm getting out of this hell. I'm going to Prospect Terrace; I'm going home.——

19

'You're through.'

'Mr Rosblum? Is that Mr Rosblum? Mr Rosblum!'

Adam phoned at two thirty. Pericles Rosblum only rarely went out for long lunches.

'Go on, kid. I'm listening.'

'This is Adam, Mr Rosblum.'

'I know. Gerron with it. I haven' a lorra time. I'm in a meet'n'.'

'Mr Rosblum, he's painting like a dream but he's out of his mind.'

'This is Roth you're talk'n' about?'

'Yes, Mr Rosblum.'

'Go on.'

'He tried to attack me.'

'What did you do to deserve that? You shouldn't upset him. He's fragile. He's a valuable property.'

'Nothing, Mr Rosblum. I got in to see his pictures.'

'You did? How many are there? Are they good? What are they like?'

'They're wonderful, Mr Rosblum, and the studio's chockfull.'

'I guess I'll have to get up there myself, then. Describe 'em to me. What sizes are they? Wharra the colours?'

'Some are very bright. Very luminous. Very clear. The recent stuff is getting darker and darker. There's some big stuff and there's lots of small. Landscapes. And lots of dark self-portraits.'

'He's doing more o' that shit?'

'Mr Rosblum, the man himself's a wreck. His face . . . I've never seen anything like it. He can't put two sentences together and make sense, but his painting . . . it's not just good. It has that quality that some great artists have when they're old. He's creating a whole new language of painting, Mr Rosblum. Artists'll be imitating it for a century.'

'You're doin' some good work up there, kid. You sound like you could be one to write his ob-it-u-ary. Stay wirrit, kid. Your cheque come through?'

'Yes, Mr Rosblum. Another thing: he's setting off north today. On his bike. He's out of his mind, drugged up to the eyes, mad as they come. He'll kill himself, for sure.'

20

Prospect Terrace was in the Harehills district of Leeds. Among high-rise offices and flats, Harehills was almost the only old housing remaining in the area originally settled by the Jews. There had been 25,000 when Roth was born, in 1910, and now there were hardly any. They had moved out to developments over the villages and fields.

Roth's was a traditional working-class family – they did little to influence their own lives, and nothing to affect state affairs, although they imagined that they tried. The nearest they came to heroism was in having their lives wasted for them.

Roth's father, Saul, had come from a village outside Lodz, in 1895 escaping one of the pogroms inspired by the assassination of Tsar Alexander II on 1 March 1881. Saul had been fifteen but wise beyond his years, naturally enough. He read any book or dog-eared pamphlet he could get hold of, as an escape from the drifting smoke of burning cornfields which meant there'd be no bread for the winter.

Saul was the lucky one. His parents, knowing that they had not the resources to rescue the whole family, sacrificed themselves and their three 'useless' daughters to fortune. This meant going into hiding while cossacks burned their village to the ground. Meanwhile Saul's mother sewed most of their savings into the lining of her son's coat and sent him forth with instructions on how to bribe his way along an escape route out of Poland.

Leonard and his sisters absorbed this epic in their childhood. How, when the flames of the burning village were still brighter than the dawn over the smoke-scented plain, Saul slipped forth;

the uncles and aunts at points on the way who sheltered him; how, when he came to the river Oder, at that time the border between Poland and Germany, he paid to be carried across on the shoulders of a peasant, who seemed massive in Saul's memory, as he waded and swam the river; how Saul made his way to Rotterdam, where he bought a ticket to New York.

He had never seen the sea before. The first part of his journey was by ship to Hull, on a rainy deck that was crowded with other frightened but optimistic Jews. From there, he caught a train, supposedly to take him to Liverpool to board a steamer for the USA. Saul, with hundreds more, was turned off at Leeds, which was as far as the ticket that he had purchased, but could not read, would take him. This little cheat was one of the main reasons why so many, who like Saul could speak only Yiddish and Russian, settled in the West Yorkshire city.

They first colonized the Leylands, on the east side of the city, to the north of Leeds Bridge. Like Jews everywhere, they were engaged in the clothing trade as cap-makers, hosiers, furriers, slipper-makers and tailors. Saul, having learned to work in leather, found employment in making ladies' patent slippers, a bizarrely gentle occupation for so brusque and erratically tempered a man as he grew to be. Between the 1890s and 1910, the glut of refugees caused further wage reductions for the already sweated labour, whether gentile or Jew, and Saul stunted soul and body in work from seven in the morning until midnight.

But he found nourishment for his soul in the cellar kitchen of Mrs Berman. All the Leeds ghetto knew her. *Mrs Berman? Why, yes, of course!* You descended a flight of steps from a yard, being careful not to slip on the grease of rain, leaves and dog's dirt, and at the foot of a four-storeyed house, jammed between the Zionist synagogue and, of all places, the Society for the Conversion of the Jews to Christianity, flourished an intellectual coterie under the care of a noisy, extrovert, fat little lady. Dr Weizman, among other famous figures, let me tell you (Saul announced at a later date), paid a visit to Mrs Berman's – what would you call it? – hardly a salon, but nevertheless its equivalent.

They discussed literature, poetry, music and the theatre. The *pièce de résistance*, Saul said, was Mrs Berman herself giving readings of Yiddish stories, especially Shalom Aleichem's 'If I Were Rothschild'.

Saul also learned about Karl Marx. Ironing out the 'laws' of life and history, Saul grew determined to educate his son, when he had one, in those same laws.

What surer way could there be to bring him up an anarchist?

When Saul looked for a mother of his planned son, she also turned out to be small and plump. Leonard's mother's maiden name was Martha Ferguson. She acquired her unlikely surname when her father landed. Asked questions that he did not understand, he tried to answer: 'Forgotten, forgotten.'

Martha Ferguson soon spotted her resemblance to her sweetheart's idol. Thus Mrs Berman, unknown to herself, figured for ever as a rival in Martha's life. Martha, too, had a round face, with an Asiatic look of the steppes. To differentiate her features from those of her 'opponent', she emphasized the roundness, which it was impossible to diminish, by wearing her hair in two bundles at the sides of her head. The effect was sumptuous and grand. At least, her son thought so. Martha carried it off because of the beauty of her bearing. She also had those heavy-lidded, thoughtful eyes that impart a look of wistful, sybilline dignity to studio photographs of the period, when poses were held for a very long time. In real life Martha rarely looked like a sybil because she was always laughing, shouting or waving her podgy hands, making her rings flash.

You would never describe Leonard's father as sumptuous. He was a tall, thin man who had glaring, darting eyes. Behind metal-rimmed spectacles, they were for ever alert against being cheated, though cheated he often was. He sported an aggressive black moustache and beard, and there was a forceful neatness about him in general, but especially in his black suits.

His facial expression, though, which could not be neatened and clothed, was a great contrast. It was stretched from holding in all his unassimilated knowledge. This was not so much stored as smouldering in dangerously lit fuses. His face was tortured by a relationship to the world and to his wife that he could not understand nor come to terms with, in spite of Karl Marx.

Roth believed that his parents had originally suited each other because Martha seemed passive, while Saul appeared active and ambitious. As is often the case, the undercurrent of truth, emerging when it was too late to revoke the marriage vows, was the opposite of this.

It was Martha's, not Saul's, forceful diligence that kept the family together. It was Saul who was spendthrift, without foresight to plan, therefore developing a weakness for clinging to rules and laws, blaming the World and Dialectic and History and Capitalism for his misfortune.

In the frequent pattern of marriages, Martha changed from respecting to despising her husband; Saul altered from lovingly offering a lead, as he had seemed to do during their courtship, to dominating his wife in patriarchal fashion because he feared her. Even more did he fear showing it, though she probably understood him all along.

By the time Leonard was old enough to form impressions, both his parents were in their forties and therefore almost geriatric, according to the standards of those days. Certainly they were set in their ways.

They fought like two cats sewn in a bag.

But they had prospered sufficiently to have moved to number 11 Prospect Terrace, further out from the Leylands. The terrace consisted of lower-middle-class houses that seemed grand because they had bay windows. 'Proper bay window' was the working-class goy phrase for someone who had done well.

First they had a daughter, Hannah. Then Leonard (initially named Leonid). Doomed Rachel got her purchase on the world just in time before the marital relationship ceased and the father was banished.

No matter what it looked like, it was Martha who was the tough one, who got her own way and did the banishing. No matter what rules Saul discerned in the universe and sought to bring home, it was his wife who ruled and disposed there. It was the image of his mother, with his two sisters, that Roth, all through his life, saw in the home. Leonard was spoiled by the females, who believed that he was their true future and the purpose of their lives. *That boy, he's another Michelangelo.*

Was this an act of faith? To the disinterested, Leonard did not seem so very talented. When Saul consulted those who he supposed were able to judge his son's aspirations – the rabbi and, once, a goy art teacher – he was told that the boy had a little talent, but not 'genius'; not something worth sacrificing for.

His lack of describable 'promise' was a help to Roth. He could be more at ease if not too much was expected of him, and it might all be his mother's delusion. This left him room to pull his surprises, which was what he enjoyed, in art as in life. In any case, genius is often less an innate ability than a powerhouse, a drive, a compulsion, a motor: there is Mozart who could compose from the cradle, and there is also Beethoven, who struggled.

Part of Leonard's fight was that he had to develop in the face of his iconophobic father's terrible opposition. The mention of art was one of the things that inspired Saul's fits.

He had two consuming reasons for his detestation. The first was that the creation of images was against the law of Moses. The second was that Marxist laws explained art as something useless or merely anodyne, created with 'surplus wealth', something that it was wrong to indulge while people were suffering. The fact that people always had suffered, and that therefore by his argument no art should ever have existed, cut no ice with him.

'What's the matter with you, Saul Roth? Kvetch, kvetch, kvetch!' Martha exploded in the days when she still believed she could calm her husband's rages. 'Your son's a genius, and you aren't proud of it? You can see it with your own eyes. He never stops drawing till drawing comes out of his ears. You can't even get him to leave off for meals. Is it because you are jealous of him, you nebbish? If you had half the talent and a quarter of the energy, you'd have your own workshop by now and then you'd have use for an attic. Now the empty place tells you that you're a failure. What do you want the attic for? Give it to the boy!'

Thus she won her battles by energetic nagging, and when Leonard was fifteen, the attic became his studio, his Dream Room at the top of the house. His mother or sisters came up respectfully, sometimes leaving a plate of food outside his door. His father, pretending that the studio didn't exist, never invaded it.

Leonard spent there all the days he could and half the nights also, right through his youth and during many of the subsequent years when he was not abroad. After the brick shed in the yard, he made his first alternative world of marks and images there. No matter how little he used it, he still felt it to be his main studio to this day.

21

His parents' quarrels singed the air. They brought a hush over the neighbourhood, and Leonard learned from the evenings at home the basic techniques of how married adults torment one another and create pain. The neighbours, though engaged in their own warfares, broke off to eavesdrop on the Roths'. There were kitchens full of it, yards, streets, towns, clamorous, oozing with its racket, all over Leeds and all over the world.

Martha conceived it her duty to protect her brood from her husband, when with incalculable rages and iron beliefs in 'judgements' and 'laws' he taught Leonard, Hannah and Rachel the cosmologies of Moses and Marx.

The parents took different sides on every subject. Among the children, Leonard and Hannah followed their mother. Rachel was her father's child, devoted to socialism and the Russian Revolution.

Especially they disagreed about Zionism, his mother opposing it mainly because she associated it with Mrs Berman, to whose kitchen Saul never took her because, so she believed, he felt ashamed of her. She also thought that he had 'something going' with Mrs Berman, whose own, shy husband was busy all the time with a sewing machine in his attic. Her opposition to Saul's ideas was an outer wall of defence, while she sheltered her brood under her wide skirts.

Blame was the important thing, from both sides of the marital fence. Saul poured on to his ignorant wife his blame for all that sheer ignorance warped and tortured in the world. At home, in synagogue and at school, Leonard had it hammered into him that there wasn't anything on earth, in heaven or in hell, that wasn't someone's fault or responsibility. He was taught it both by Moses and by Marx. Everything was accountable as either good or bad, deserving praise or blame.

The first art collection that Leonard saw, in Leeds City Art Gallery, was filled with moralizing paintings and moralizing, he eventually realized, was at the root of their being bad art.

A huge spoil heap of moral pretentiousness and judgements overhung Roth's youth. This detritus of a past era created a shadow, as the spoil heap of a depleted coal pit overhangs a mining village. He had to dig himself out in order to paint and draw simply, honestly, before his subjects; as Van Gogh had to abandon his moral, Protestant, northern attitudes before he could paint freely in the sun.

Eventually, Leonard perceived that art should show its faith by celebrating its energies – not by illustrating moral tales.

Cézanne could have told him this a quarter of a century before, but Cézanne did not live in Leeds.

Martha would shake with laughter at her own anarchic humour and she never stopped making jokes, sometimes even tormenting her husband by making light of the misery of the Jews. '"Sammy," the teacher asked, "what is the name of the longest river in Africa?" "Miss, you should have my problems."'

It was Saul who laid down the iron laws of Jewry. He also quoted Moses against the depictions of living forms, particularly human ones, and the turning of Jewish shoemakers' attics into Dream Rooms.

'Why don't you just enjoy your food and shut up, instead of giving reasons for everything, Saul Roth?' Martha asked him. 'Why don't you? I know why!'

'What do you know, Martha Roth, who is too lazy to study even the Torah?'

'Well, I'm not saying!' She banged the back of the grate with a poker. This he might take to be a threat that she would summon the neighbours, if he flipped his lid and became violent without reason.

'*I* know why, Saul Roth! You think I'm a stupid woman. But I'm not saying!'

She associated that sort of thing (explanations) with Mrs Berman, for it was in her kitchen that the men learned to *explain* everything. 'Mrs Berman this, Mrs Berman that!' was Martha's answer to Marxism, Shavianism, Fabian socialism and Zionism, while she threw pots around the kitchen, frightening the children. As a way of rebutting Marx's attack on capitalism, it struck Saul as irrational. He told Mrs Berman so. But, being unanswerable, it drove him mad.

Literally. He had terrible fits that frightened his family, and the children became in full need of their mother's skirts. One of Leonard's earliest memories was of running under them.

Once, Saul attempted to cut his wrists, but only succeeded in mauling his palm. He threatened to leave the house and never return. He said he would throw himself under a tram. He said he would jump out of the window. The family took no notice. Hannah kept on reading her English schoolgirls' tales of boarding school, hockey field and life in the dorm. Rachel played the piano or helped her mother to make bread.

But one day when Saul vanished upstairs and could be heard flinging windows open, the terrified family believed that this time he was going to do what he promised. 'Golly!' Hannah exclaimed. 'Golly, gosh!'

The children bravely chased their father up the stairs and down, from room to room, back up the stairs and down once more, arguing and restraining him as well as they could. Martha was pulling at her hair and banging at the pots. She did not know where she was.

Neither did her husband. The children could not hold him back as Saul leaped. But the window was in the back scullery and he fell only four feet, scraping his elbow on a bucket; a grazing about which he complained for a week.

It was from his father that Leonard inherited his pugnacious and erratic attitudes. Also, the madness in his art, without which it would have been nothing.

When Saul was not mad and angry, he might imperturbably explain life away with gloomy aphorisms.

'Life begins at fifty,' he would say, drily. 'And so does arthritis.' And: 'There are more important things in life than money. The trouble is, they're all too expensive.'

But one evening when he felt he had made enough jokes and laid down sufficient laws, he went into his lonely bedroom, the expulsion to which his angry wife had consigned him, and hung himself by his braces. It was Leonard, sixteen years old, who discovered his father.

22

Perhaps it was Leonard's revolt that had brought about his father's death. He had started to move out of the Leeds *shtetl* and shockingly drink in goy company. The thought that his ambitions might have driven his father to suicide haunted Roth.

Yet how could the father have understood Leonard's love affair with the light and the sun?

Staring at pieces of leather all day, Saul had been bent over in a sweatshop, the small windows cloudy with dust and cobwebs. Above the streets, smoke further cut out the light and everyone was so used to it, they thought it normal. The smoke, the dirt, the poisonous sulphur of northern towns could previously have been imagined only by a Hieronymous Bosch, while it seemed beyond the power of later memory to quite recall it.

Unless Saul had a glimpse of light reflected on wet cobblestones on his way home, he plunged straight into the further black hole of a terraced house. Later, he visited a dimly lit Jewish Working Men's Club, or Mrs Berman's cellar, or the equally dark premises of the Leeds Hebrew Literary Society in a basement in Byron Street. There and at home he articulated the seething memories that were now half folk tales, of pogroms, crowded transports and the bellies of refugee ships. That was another darkness which he laid at the bottom of his children's minds. Saul clung to these gloomy stories as to the sodden, black, cold logs of a sinking raft.

Leonard acquired the other side of his inheritance from his mother, even though the typical Jewish mother is supposed to be weighed down with pessimistic darkness, the darkness of the

womb that refuses to retreat from its offspring. Her humour was
the light and the sun.

Roth left school at thirteen and went to work cleaning up the inks
in a textile studio where they designed waistcoats and ties.

At fifteen, he won a small scholarship under Jewish patronage
to Leeds Art School. He was supposedly studying textile design,
but wangled his way into the classes run by the painting school.
Despite the gratitude he owed and felt to his parents and his
patrons, he changed his name from Leonid to Leonard. As
always, he began his rebellion in his art, signing his pictures
with his new name and leaving them around the house.

As a further stab at his father during his first term, Leonard
allowed himself to be seduced into the terrible premises of the
Society for the Conversion of the Jews to Christianity. There he
heard the Sermon on the Mount.

Apart from the relief from his father's Mosaic ravings, what
moved him was the illustration in a child's guide that he was
given to peruse. To the text 'Consider the lilies of the field . . .
Solomon in all his glory was not arrayed as one of these' was a
shiny, coloured lithograph of a king walking through a field such
as was unimaginable in sooty Leeds, where most flowers were
funereal, municipal, sickly, stuffy. Here was what he had not yet
seen: the spring flowers of the Mediterranean basin, sprinkling
the rocky ground in a brilliant, clean light. Leonard saw a world
covered in bright robes.

To interpret the world through colour became his obsession.
One day, he summoned his courage and walked the street
wearing a canary-yellow pullover. By this stage Roth had grown
lanky and awkward. Like many tall boys at puberty, he had not
yet gained control of his body and his limbs acted independently
of his brain. He was for ever stumbling and knocking things
over. In embarrassed, awkward fashion, he strolled for a mile
among dark-suited, black-hatted, black-bearded Jews. He sat
in a café, and came home when others were returning from
work. A few people looked at him. At one corner, a whistle
followed, most likely not because of his pullover but because
of the self-consciousness of his saunter. When people took no

notice, it embarrassed him more than a snatch of laughter did. If they were silent behind his back, he thought they were talking about him.

Leonard could not have explained why he had to walk the street with a yellow chest, one that was the braver for the remainder of his ensemble consisting of black suit, black shiny shoes, black fedora and a black fuzz around his chin intended as an artist's beard. He knew only, intuitively, that colour would dynamite his father's world.

Picasso said that Matisse painted as he did 'because of the sun in his belly'. Young Leonard Roth walked the street wearing the sun in order to declare himself a colourist. Roth had been protesting against the darkness of his father, and bearing the sign of his mother's bright world.

His father's death meant that he had to return to work, but he did actually do some designing now, in the textile studios. The bright ties and waistcoats worn by the rich through the Depression years were part of Roth's education in colour.

So were his first ventures on to the hills outside Leeds. Before he left for Paris at the age of twenty-one, Roth had saved up for his first motorcycle, an Ariel Square Four, 500-cc, four-cylinder machine that was new on the market. It had a massive headlamp, a long, snaking exhaust, and upon it he made the first of the impulsive flights that were to typify his life.

It had taken him until his late teens to realize that such open spaces existed near Leeds, and now he haunted the hills. He went to exercise his cramped lungs, but even more for the pleasure of seeing clearer light and colours; a sky tinted with blues and pinks that were more than the result of the fumes, chemicals and massive pools of smoke permanently filling the valleys.

Leeds Art School had trained him to search out with his sketchbook local incident and 'character'; to bring back pictorial anecdotes to be worked up in the composition class. It was upon the hills that he discovered for himself how to put at the centre of his artistic desires not anecdote but his response to light, space and the movement of atmospheric colour.

But even on the highest, remotest hills, the skies weren't entirely clean. He ran his fingers up the sides of a blade of grass and they were blackened by it. Down in the valleys, the town-hall parthenons, banks and mills were layered over with a funereal velvet of soot, a deep patina which had, indeed, a beauty of its own.

There had existed a couple of nineteenth-century painters in the north of England who, if given only cursory attention, seemed to merge with the general, anecdotal moralizing of the period. However, looked at more carefully, it was clear that they had grasped the character of the fiery, chemically induced light and the sooty tones of buildings and trees against it, apparently unique to the north. These were the Leeds painter Atkinson Grimshaw and L. S. Lowry's teacher, the impressionist-inspired Manchester artist Adolphe Valette. They might have been models for Roth, but he turned away from them.

Leonard observed that, apart from L. S. Lowry, the best northern artists bolted for the sun, and the move made many of them great. Mathew Smith, although he had the nature and the appearance of a timid clerk in a wool emporium, yet fled that fate which his wool-merchant father planned, met Matisse in Paris and became a fauve, a 'wild beast', and a sensualist. Henry Moore never ceased to depend upon northern memories – the eroded millstone-grit outcrops on the hills, or the shoulders and back of his mother whom as a child he massaged for her rheumatism – yet he united these images with the spirit of the south, with Mexican art and with Michelangelo. The crippling, colour-hating, work-ethic, chapel-going Protestantism of the industrial north drove David Hockney to become a playboy in colour and line who fled to California. Ted Hughes went to live in Devon. Even the amiable J. B. Priestley left. The north of England showed great capacity to exile its artistic spirits, but such artists were especially forceful when they got to the sun, because greatest darkness can be the womb of greatest light.

It had happened in other northern regions. D. H. Lawrence fled Nottingham, but couldn't forget. Van Gogh shed his burden of northern Protestant responsibility, guilt and preaching for the hedonism of southern colour.

In the colours of Leeds sunsets Leonard Roth first saw darkness and light, the two sides of his inheritance and his temperament, pictorially fused. Those massive piles and towers of crimson, chrome orange and yellow, as the sunsets crumbled through layers of smoke, were his peephole into the world that would eventually be his.

The southern life already drew him like the memory of something that he could not quite recall. Like his predecessors, he followed through the gap.

23

20 August 1980

My Dear Roth,

Yes, I am sorry I had to leave you in Greece. But I did have to do it. I have reached Florence, staying in Maria's flat where we have been so often before. I found some of your drawings left in a cupboard! So many memories. So much emotion. I'm saturated. I had to soak the place with tears before I could sleep in it. A purification with salt.

But I don't, I can't, believe it all comes to an end like this. Here.

I miss you so much. Where is Roth? Why is he not painting blue skies, blue flowers, blue me?

So much to say. And so much said already.

Please make it all better. You are the only man in the world. Please remember. Find a way. Look after yourself.

I'm all cried out. I hope. Your face. You.

But then there's your ego. Your ego. You. Why? Proof of artistic aristocracy? Bullshit.

Goodnight, whoever you are.

——Okay, okay! The fact that Dorothy and I have never been able to resolve a fucking thing doesn't mean that we can't ever . . . does it? Well, anyway, it's worth a try, okay? I have to do something, I can't stay here, eating my heart out, twiddling my thumbs, gringeing, waiting for the trap to close. (But what trap? There *was* one somewhere, its jaws hovering in the air.) Speaking only on the telephone, not meeting a soul other than the fucking awful Adam. No. And not sleeping, but only absorbing the nausea which lonely rooms inspire, their objects turning ghoulish. The worlds of Van Gogh's *Night Café*, Munch's *Self-Portrait Between Bed and Clock*, Francis Bacon's naked light bulbs swinging over lonely, naked flesh.——

Roth knew only too well what lonely people did. They talked to Adam, regretted what they had said and ended by beating them up.

If they could not paint, as for instance when they were confined in the fucking loony bin, they filled notebooks and they wrote letters. Letters vivid with loneliness, burning to articulate what had been said to no one all day, begging, pleading, but trying to be restrained and not let the madness show, the dirty underwear; misunderstanding what was so far away, at their destination.

Roth's hand trembled when he wrote things down. He had much to say, but the words tumbled over one another. He resorted to them mostly when he was drunk and they induced his reckless traits. It was no use writing to Dorothy any more. There were dozens of letters already, many never sent and now mouldering in drawers. No more!

He saw himself hesitating on a road in Greece with one. I can still throw it away; fling it on the fire. But at last, unable to resist temptation, I slide it between the lips of the letter box. A thrill in that. Gone. My heart stands still, as after an orgasm. In Greece the letter boxes were made of grey tin, usually rusty, and had a flap on them.

Roth remembered the epiphany of first reading the letters of Van Gogh; the letter as the eyes and lips of loneliness. You walk around knowing that you are not seeing the world as everyone else sees it; ycu in your comical straw hat. It isn't God, church and priest that matter to you any more. You have come through that tunnel and, although you will be seen as a religious painter, yet you leave the church-going and the priests'-hand-kissing to the peasants. That is one of the reasons why they resent you: you do not go to Mass or church. Yellow, blue, green are what you worship. These speak with the voice of the numinous, while to others they are merely colours which hardly matter except to indicate, in a crop, that it is ripe, or in a sky, that it will be fine or rainy weather. The children threw stones at the painter of Arles, as they had at Roth in Greece.

——Think about this, then: had Van Gogh been destructive, or had he merely been *self*-destructive? Following his manic fucking vision, yes, but in his relationship to others did he not sacrifice himself to succour them; as with the prostitute, Sien? When he realized that his brother Theo could no longer support him, that he was a destructive element in the wings of Theo's marriage, Vincent withdrew to kill himself rather than go on being a parasite.

How different from Picasso, telling his mistress Françoise Gilot that she should wear a kerchief over her head so that no one could see her face. 'In that way you'll belong even less to the others. They won't even have you with their eyes.' The Old Magician wanted to obliterate her and then recreate her in his own terms, as if she were a canvas he had begun again.

Is there any greater destructiveness and possessiveness? You could describe a tradition of such artists. Rembrandt, for example, who was cruel and neglectful of wife and mistress whom he so lovingly painted. Van Gogh was at one extreme; Rembrandt and Picasso were at the other.

Picasso was knee-high to a sparrow; yet the way he stood when I met him, he might as well have had his destructive dick in his hand. He was utterly masculine; his ranging and forceful creativity was its expression. He was *masterly*, in fact. His whole method consisted in tearing nature apart. His eyes were fangs.

Then he reassembled it.

Picasso talked to me of his love for Perpignan. When I went there myself, I fucking guessed why. Was it not the special chaos of that city where the slums of poor blacks and Algerians around the castle nudge the stylish apartments of the bourgeoisie? Chaos is creative. Therefore Picasso chose, or made, chaos.

Our generation of artists, following Picasso, is one that takes the canvas to be not a mirror held up to nature but a theatre of action. This is as commonplace to art now as religious subject matter was in early medieval times; as oil paint applied with brush upon a canvas, eventually to be framed like a stage show, was for nineteenth-century painters. But so many of my generation proved simple-minded enough not to realize that you can have your fantasies on the stage, but not in life.

However, Jackson Pollock had to make of his life an action painting, throwing himself and others in a car against a tree. He tried reckless driving more than once, until at last he succeeded.

Mine was a generation that made of risk and suicide an art form.

That's been said before.

Wasn't suicide, among other things, a revenge upon others?

Then what, after all, was to be made of Van Gogh killing himself? Was he bowing out? Or was he getting his own back on Theo?

Destructiveness and self-destructiveness are tangled. I cannot separate them. No fucking way.

I know that I'm self-destructive. Attacking myself provokes the energy in my art. But I'm destructive of others, also. In Greece, before Dorothy left, it had reached its limits.

If I go to see her in the right frame of mind, if nothing tempts me to shout, lose my temper, and if I explain to her, *explain* –

After he threw Adam out of the studio at around two o'clock, Roth turned most of his pictures back to the walls or restored them to their racks. He cleared up the materials of the painting day he had intended to begin. Picked up paints and brushes spilled over the floor.

He laid tablets of Valium and Tofranil out on the table – one, two, three; one, two, three – first in straight lines:

. . .

. . .

then in a pyramid:

.

. .

. . .

and swallowed them, starting from the top of the pyramid, after careful consideration.

He counted what was left, making a mental note to remember how many he had taken so far today, but forgot the number almost instantly, and slipped the packets back into the breast pockets of his shirt.

24

Action at last. Roth started to hum. He began to sing a scrap of Mozart.

He locked the studio. He did lock it. His heart was beating fast. The prickly heat was upon his brow and on the back of his neck. It would go. Once he *did* something, he would grow steady.

Roth returned across the village, still singing and optimistic. Taking the key for 11 Prospect Terrace from the drawer where he religiously (religiously; that was indeed the word) kept it, he prepared to leave. He slipped his motorbike leathers over his studio clothes. He removed the sheet from the Laverda. Soft cloths waited and he caressed a little dust off the petrol tank. He did the same for the instrument dials, blew them and wiped them.

When she was not in action, she was remarkably cowlike, a lumbering sack. It made him want to love her into life again. The day would come soon enough when he really would be too old and she would become a relic. He had seen old men, before they took finally to their beds, polish up and service vehicles they had loved in order to store them in garages or at the ends of gardens, thinking perhaps that they would chariot them to heaven; though they were only waiting for vintage-car collectors hunting a bargain . . .

Roth pulled on his gauntlets, smothered his head with a helmet, and rocked her off her stand. The chrome glittered on her adornments; the nuts and bolts he'd had plated at Mellin-Griffith's works in Cardiff. Two hundred quid's worth of jewels (it would cost three times as much today), as some might buy diamonds for a woman.

Roth opened the front door. Grey and dull air. The bird-scarers were still exploding pop-pop in the fields, as he wheeled her down the path.

On the road, he mounted and balanced himself. Switched on the ignition. Roar.

Slowly, by the churchyard, along the lane; then head down under the fairing to reach sixty, the end of the petrol tank in his ribs.

Again he was making one of his impulsive, homesick returns, a hundred and fifty miles. Sometimes, unknown to Dorothy, he had gone there to do no more than stare at his home, without trying to enter. He had noticed the cardboard boxes filled with empty champagne and wine bottles stacked outside. Had said hullo at the nearby newsagent's. Wandered through battered Roundhay Park, which had been grand in his parents' days. With a lump in his throat, he had watched the children on the swings. The fact that Dorothy and he had no children had been her sadness. Now, at the sight of a child, his heart, too, might turn over. He had thought of sending Dorothy a drawing of the house, or of the park where the children played, but it broke his heart the second he brought out his sketchbook.

Sometimes he had sat in the pub at the corner of the terrace. It was filled with a damp cloud that had seeped in from the streets. It had tobacco-stained walls and no decorations, and it reminded Roth of the final cell in the Necromanteion at Parga in northern Greece, where the dead had waited for Charon to ferry them over. The last time he had called at the pub, he had sat around an unvarnished table with half a dozen other walking wounded from the sex war, in what seemed like the aftermath of a battle. Every person was broken by a lost marriage or relationship, but hardly anything was said, beyond muttering in common grief. Nothing could console them or ever come right, and they were uninterested to hear of its possibility. The only animation in an hour was when a couple slagged each other across a table and no one attempted to put a brake upon their acid, fated words.

Sometimes Roth made a detour over the hills to the west, trying to restore his youth, to refresh himself with the steep falls of moorland and douse himself with the spaces of light.

He could not help these journeys, though they tore him to pieces. Thoughts of his childhood home would arise not out of his mind but from his stomach, like the gobs of blood of a consumptive, up to his throat where the cords tightened.

The Laverda had been designed as a racing bike and adapted to the highway by adding lights; with twin cylinders and eight valve heads, she was sluggish until she reached 6,000 revs, so he built up speed as quickly as possible. Flying through country lanes in the afternoon, he was struck by what was normal as if it were a strange spectacle. Men rolling barrels into the cellar of a pub. Girls on horses. Flowers of pimpernel; specks of scarlet dotting the border of a field, as if the thorns of the hedge had pricked blood from the earth. A wood lying on a hilltop; a blue, light feather.

He got on to the M1.

An hour on his way, he realized that he hadn't eaten, his mind too crowded with other thoughts.

He hated to sit alone in good restaurants, so today it was to be the Cholesterol Café. There he approached the kind of meal that, in the old epicurean days, he would not have been able to bear the smell of, let alone eat. He took one bite, but could touch no more.

It wasn't only because the food was disgusting that he couldn't eat it. He hit the motorway again with the familiar feelings of going north: that tension again. There returned the coil in his chest that he had been able mostly to forget during the past year, and his stomach felt full of razor blades.

Powering up the motorway, he could recall every knob and bump of Dorothy's body, every characteristic of her soul and detail of her life. He went over them again and again. It was difficult to remember that she was, indeed, only a woman, when she loomed so large, dominating his mind.

25

——So Roth's living in a country village again, in a place called Ashby or, sometimes, Ashby Green. Once when I phoned I heard a bell tolling in the background and I realized he was in a cottage by a church.

Yet another one! Apart from in London, the only settled home we've shared (we don't share Prospect Terrace – in spirit that's entirely his) was the Old Rectory in Wiltshire in the 1960s, and that naturally had a church outside the window. Isn't it an odd fate for someone with such a big chip on his shoulder about God? An artist possessed of such rage against the divine, whether Christian or Jewish? I think he sees Him as a rival, the alternative world champ; someone to knock down. It's an attitude he picked up from sparring with his father's Moses. Living in these villages, it's as if he has to seek the actual battleground. Yet that in itself – settling in a village and taking on God – is enough to drive him crazy.

Beyond the garden wall of the Wiltshire rectory was a huge rotting building the size of a cathedral, sheltering its minute congregation. They used to say 'it was built on wool'. Isn't that a silly expression? Those people were full of silly phrases.

Though I had to admit that *I* liked them, finding them kindly and comforting. They were refugees from what terrified them in the newspapers. They lived in a haven of gentility where they supposed that nothing had changed in the world for a hundred years; nothing that they couldn't alleviate by contributing pence to a famine fund.

They had babies, too, babies, making me sick with jealousy, for babydom was a very conspicuous part of village life. Some of my female neighbours had let go of careers that they'd never imagined they'd abandon, yet they looked out at me from their happy, milk-and-nappy-smelling, toy-littered nests pityingly, as if they understood that my career, too, was slipping from me, but without their compensations. There was *something wrong* with Roth and me, and they longed to draw me into the chthonic world of womanly wisdom. They wanted me to confide in them. Perhaps it was my paranoia, but my middle-class neighbours seemed smug.

Can you imagine Roth boxed in by such a place? Now there he is in one again. Why is he not here with me?

The wall of the Rectory had a small gate into the churchyard, with mock orange all around it. The poor old vicar was for ever popping through to ask favours: of Roth!

It started on the day we arrived. Behind the removal van came a bike and a black-clad biker. Roth had a Harley-Davidson then.

All the vicar knew was that his new parishioner was well-heeled, and he could overlook even the bike and the biker's gear for that. He was in the kitchen with no more than a 'May I?'; you know how they can be. As soon as he started asking for a contribution to the Death-Watch Beetle Appeal, Roth attacked him for 'whingeing after old ladies' twopences when the Church had a billion-pound investment portfolio'.

'A totally different fund, I'm afraid,' the vicar explained, blandly.

'Then change the funding, instead of using it as an excuse to invest in multinationals that exploit Third World countries.'

'That's out of my hands.' The vicar smiled.

'I suppose it's in God's,' Roth snapped.

'Certainly it is.' The vicar was not used to disrespectful and sarcastic parishioners.

'Roth!' I rushed in, recognizing the signs of his coming to the boil. Already I knew he was going to instruct the vicar that it was a hypocritical God who directed the Christian Church to spend millions indirectly on exploiting Africans, while screwing from humble Christian individuals their few pounds to alleviate the damage . . . et cetera, et cetera.

It was only our first day.

'Twas a delight for sore eyes when the Jehovah's Witnesses called. You know how they knock at one's door in pairs, dressed in nondescript, tailored suits so as to give no offence, and with small children in tow to demonstrate their family values and to inhibit one from insulting them? It didn't put a brake upon Roth.

As everyone knows, once a Jehovah's Witness has started to quote the Bible there's no stopping him. Nobody remembers the Bible so well, and to every answer made, they quote another passage. It's a cheap trick, because one can find a quotation to support any idea whatsoever. Roth hated the way they 'tricked ignorant, polite people'.

His approach to God's door-to-door salesmen was firstly to ask them, politely but icily, to go away. He didn't lack respect for their right to a point of view. He knew that Jehovah's Witnesses as well as Jews had been massacred in Hitler's camps. Although, unlike Jews, the JWs had been given the opportunity to change their religion, most had refused to do so, preferring to wear a purple star next to the Jews' yellow one. So Roth admired their tenacity, bravery and conviction. All he wanted was that they should not persecute others with it. Especially him.

How could those who so genuinely put the value of this world at nought understand a hedonist like Roth whose spirituality (if I may put it that way) depends upon his delight in this world?

So when they would not leave, he surprised them by yelling, fast and furious like some demonic Hitler, blaming them for every ill. He knew that, once they had him listening to their Bible quotes, they would never stop until they had smugly sold him a *Watchtower*, so he wouldn't let them have a word in edgeways.

'Shall I tell you how the world will end?' he'd yell. 'It'll be one of your people who'll press the button, starting some holy war against what you call "evil", communists or blacks or Jews . . .'

Towering over them, he'd rage until they folded their Bibles and backed off down the street. Even *I* was afraid of Roth, most of the time, though I knew he'd never hurt me. I felt sorry for these inept little families, stiff with their illusions. In case they thought of making another assault, Roth would carry on yelling after them.

There was a road on either side of the Rectory. Once, half an hour after JWs had been to the front door, they came to the kitchen from the back lane, thinking it was a different house – there to face the same raging lunatic.

'Do you approve of incest?'

By this stage your average Jehovah's Witness would be numbed. Only Christ Himself could face the Devil incarnate. I have sometimes seen Roth's face smeared with crimson or blue paint.

'I asked you, *do you approve of incest?*'

Heads, backing away, were dumbly shaken. The family man in his weary pilgrim's suit bravely sheltered his brood.

'You don't? Then why does the book of Genesis tell us we're all descended from the same two parents?'

Roth would return trembling from this performance. The first time I witnessed it, I thought he'd gone mad.

Eventually, the JWs learned the lesson I have learned and gave up trying to change him. We discovered this when a group of strangers was hovering outside the gate, so Roth went out to them. Not yet guessing who they were, he asked if he could help them; asking as politely as Roth is able. The man was anxiously consulting a notebook. 'Mr Roth?' he enquired. JWs being truth-tellers, it was then admitted that Roth was officially marked as beyond redemption, not to be visited any more.

Is anything more absurd, then, than to think of this agnostic Jew from the industrial north accommodating himself to the twittering sparrows who ran the church in our village?

The vicar rarely knew where to put himself when he met us or our friends. If we'd been poor and lived in a council house, he would have ignored us. But we had one of the largest houses in the village. Roth was well off and was sometimes seen on television. Large cars visited us. Famous strangers, some of them beautiful, some rich, another who read the television news, slipped into the post office and the pub.

Roth tried to be polite and accommodating, for the sake of my peace of mind in the village. He gave money for the church roof in the end, though not neglecting to remind the vicar that he did so for the sake of the architecture. (He liked the gargoyles.) He was very happy for them to use our garden for parties and to let them set up their canteen in our kitchen. He donated watercolours for them to sell, and as much as they wanted of our fruit and flowers to the harvest festival. Then he spoiled it by looking at the displays, the stuffed birds and the garden gnomes, and being overheard remarking that it looked like Disneyland. I honestly think he meant that it would delight the children. But his words dropped like lead.

And then he found out that our vicar was one of those English rural gentry who had offered hospitality to the Nazis before the outbreak of war. The country-house parties, the grouse-shooting, the fishing weekends for the fascist hierarchy, and Goering deciding which country mansion would become his English hunting lodge: all these became a forgotten cupboardful of history after Churchill took charge. However, we learned that in the 1930s Hitler's chief henchmen had cavorted in our rectory garden. That was where our vicar learned some of the potty ideas about Jews that leaked through to us; how 'there's no such thing as a Jew who doesn't make trouble' and all the other sickening anti-Semitic slurs that everyone knows only too well by now.

Is it any wonder Roth felt himself a stranger with a loose grip on the world? He couldn't even feel safe in an English country village where the pretence was kept up that *everyone* was safe.

He was a frontiersman, even in Wiltshire. He'll be a frontiersman in Ashby. He's not able to be otherwise. I believe it's because of those Jewish ancestors and relatives, crossing Europe without a penny in their pockets or a useful language in their mouths; driven from their burning homes in the Pale.

That's why the only equals to his energy are American: the painters who work believing their life depends upon it. They have a hostile continent, not a piddling island, to conquer. The expatriate Jew is their equivalent in Europe.

As if being the wife of a crazy cowboy isn't enough: I tell you this.

I did just about the worst thing that a woman who is an artist can do for herself: I married another artist.

What was it Henry Moore's wife said? 'You can't be married to a man like Henry and do anything else.'

I've met only one case of artists married to one another and both continuing to practise. That was the American painter Georgia O'Keeffe, who was the wife of the photographer Alfred Stieglitz, happily linked through their creativity. According to legend.

I don't believe it.——

26

Dorothy got up early these days. On this June morning, she was up at six – even though she had also been awake during the night. Although Roth had exhausted her, yet, having nothing better to go to bed with than a reading lamp and an electric blanket, she did not sleep well.

As soon as she rose, she acted purposefully, whatever the time. The need to become absorbed had got her painting again, and she as often painted in the night as during the day.

All her activities were in order to buoy herself up in an unending river of negative self-reflections. Her present picture was a satirical attack upon woman as victim, executed to help exorcise self-pity and masochism, and to teach others. In the rear bedroom stood a five foot by four foot acrylic on canvas. Because of the detail, a picture normally took her a month to complete, and she was two weeks into this one. It was entitled *The Bridal Chamber*. On the bed was a waiting virgin. Satirizing the manner in which men had depicted women as if they were glad to be raped, it copied the pose of Titian's *Venus of Urbino*, though it could as easily have been a naked woman by Matisse, Gauguin, Rembrandt, Picasso or any male artist one cared to nominate. She wore only a crown of roses and she smiled invitingly. Stalking into the room came a man, encased protectively in a business suit, but he had a ferocious wolf's head. There were various symbolic props, such as a broken doll on the carpet. Even the fall of the silk sheets invited entrance; let alone the virgin's sprawled legs, her fingers invitingly parting her hymen. Through the window could be seen a formal eighteenth-century park, symbol of man's conquest of nature.

Dorothy had chosen her studio deliberately for its symbolism, too. It symbolized woman as victim. It was the back bedroom; the one that she had been told was Rachel's, Roth's sister who was murdered by the Nazis.

Dorothy had tried working during the night, but had soon abandoned it, to read and reread the small print of that ghastly medical book from the university. She had spent the whole of the previous day hunting through the library, being worried ever since her meetings with Mr Parker in the housing-association building around the corner. The book she had borrowed now lay, in its blue library binding, hypnotizing as a ticking bomb on a table before her.

At around three o'clock in the morning she had taken it off to bed. There she lay awake, uncertain what to do about what she had read. This was not because she couldn't see what needed to be done, nor because she was afraid of speaking to the demons overshadowing her life – Kaplan, Victoria Voyce, Rosblum, Fall – but because of whatever had happened when she had interfered in the past.

It was a strange sensation to be exhausted yet with eyelids that would not close, as if the muscles that controlled them had died or frozen. Dorothy had fallen asleep over the book only an hour before dawn. Yet, no matter how often she was restless in this way, regularly she would get up at around six, impatient for the day of the greater world to start, the first sound outside, a car, a voice.

The first drink, always. Drink was on her mind instantly, as a battle in which she ought to resist.

But early rising was one compensation for living alone. When they had been together, they had spent so many of their mornings cosseting one another in bed. She used to joke that the reason there were so many afternoon and evening scenes in her husband's oeuvre was because he rarely got up in the mornings. Then he spent hours preparing himself for work. He had to go through what he called his 'rituals', focusing his mind. This meant drinking half a dozen cups of coffee, getting under her feet, mooching around. She could still see him doing it. Missed him doing it; even though it was adapting herself to his rhythms that had frustrated her own.

She used to tell Roth that they didn't rise in the morning because they were unable to face reality. Nowadays, though Dorothy hurried into activity, it wasn't from a concern with any more reality.

For instance, she hardly ever paused to look into a mirror; the last person she wished to see was herself. It intrigued her that Roth was painting self-portraits. Sometimes, catching sight of herself by accident, she thought: a week has gone by since I took a proper look at that face. At my age one knows only too well what there is to see.

At last, the day had arrived when she accepted that she was sixty, without having sensed the process of ageing. So, today, she took no steps to flatter herself. This morning she wore baggy trousers, an old green jersey that had belonged to Roth and swamped her, and tattered sneakers. For the first time in her life, not clothes to please him.

On the other hand, since she was dressing so deliberately to *dis*please Roth, and as if he were present to see her, she was still chained to the post. Couldn't win.

The house at Prospect Terrace was musty with furniture that never ceased to seem strange to Dorothy. It was not antique, it was merely old-fashioned, coloured dark brown or grey, with threadbare, smelly upholstery. It reminded her that she did not belong here. Roth hung on to the house as a mausoleum to his parents, so it was filled with their furniture. There was still his father's mezuzah in its glass box in the hallway. Added to the furniture was more old-fashioned stuff which Roth had collected in the Fifties and Sixties, when junk shops had thrived on the mania for 'modernization'.

Roth had a taste, inherited from his mother but required for his bulk, for large, comfortable, homely items. Dorothy felt uncomfortable, like a dwarf, among it, and was never able to fill the sofas and chairs. She didn't dream of throwing any out. She saw herself as a guardian of this collection, as preserver of some part of Leonard Roth's life for posterity.

While living here, she also had a need to defend herself against him, his ancestry and the ghosts. The room where his father had hung himself was not much different now from how it had been when the event occurred. Dorothy slept in Roth's mother's bed, which had originally been Martha's marital bed. If Dorothy did look into a mirror, that also had been Martha Roth's. The brick shed at the end of the yard was still cluttered with the implements of an old-fashioned washday, as it had been when Roth used to hide there as a boy.

Dorothy had reached a point when the ghosts were too much for her. She was holding a party as a desperate device to keep them at bay, and by half past nine her preparations were complete. She had covered with cellophane the salads, quiches, cheese and bread. She had laid out the wine: cheap boxes on display, better-quality bottles hidden in the background for the good friends, later. Yesterday, someone had come round from the pub to set up a small barrel of beer.

Sam Fall had sent her a crate of champagne and she put two bottles to chill in the fridge. Fall knew about her struggle with alcohol. At the worst moments of their marriage, Roth and she had been hiding bottles of whisky and champagne from each other. She wondered why Fall had sent the present.

Drink was most tempting when bad news slugged her. As when she had got wind that they were trying to cut her out of the trusteeship to Roth's estate. She hadn't been told openly. She had winkled it out of Sam Fall that Roth was 'thinking about it' and she had then phoned Roth, but he was high at the time and evasive. Afraid to 'interfere', she had really hit the champagne then. Champagne was her greatest temptation, so Fall's was a double-edged gift. What was he thinking of? Never mind. Enjoy it while it lasts.

Soon. Later. For the moment, there were serious matters to deal with.

For the time being, instead of being tempted by the alcohol, Dorothy made herself a mug of coffee *au lait*. She spilled the first cup. That was typical of her these days – her nerves gone; age creeping up. She was for ever fumbling and stumbling.

Was she apprehensive of the phone call she had to make because she was afraid she'd make a mess of it – again?

She used to be a calm and practical woman. Now her difficulties in catching trains, making phone calls, or cooking meals without spilling hot pans, rendered her apprehensive. It intensified the fear of being alone, despite having chosen to be solitary.

She and Roth could hardly do a damn thing properly for themselves any more. Having spent their lives wrapped up in each other, they had left themselves dependent upon others to manage their business affairs. At least she recognized it, and had grown suspicious of Fall, Rosblum and Kaplan.

Why wasn't Roth suspicious? Did his lack of guardedness on that front have to do with why he could give his energies and time to painting? She couldn't paint committedly, because of worrying about this, that and the other. Was that the truth behind the myth that real artists were innocent and naive?

Dorothy, instead of being single-minded about painting now that she had a chance to do it, twisted and turned. She had left Roth partly with the intention of picking up the remnants of her career. The memory of their rows over her frustrated ambitions rang in her head like the memory of a noisy carnival. She had blamed her failure on the time spent supporting him, so she ought to be proving herself now. Yet, even without Roth, here she was finding other tasks to preoccupy her and largely, as in the past, they had to do with him. Either positively, as yesterday, trying to track down his condition and symptoms; or negatively, as today, when instead of painting she was planning the party that was necessary in order to keep his spirit at bay.

The worry left her feeling slack and tired, and the best Dorothy could do with herself while waiting for ten o'clock was to switch on the TV. It was a big old set in a cabinet, and she constantly feared that it would either blow up or fuse. Because it was Roth's, she would not exchange it. She was relieved when, after a few hitches, it came on channel. She did not care which one, so long as she didn't have to make attempts at adjusting it. Neither was she interested in the trashy magazine programme. She put it on because it caused a bright flicker in the dark house, and because she needed distraction from the blows received from the book.

'Television is the herbicide of the soul' – that was what Roth said; and, despite her own thoughts, what she heard was his voice, drowning everything else; just as she saw the world as he would have seen it. After she left him, she had even looked at Florence with his eyes. She often felt his hands on her body when she awoke in the night. She saw his outline at the ends of certain streets that held memories. Often she thought she saw him coming towards her. She could hardly hear herself any more. She still listened to him talking to her, in her head. Nothing could drown him out.

At long last the old clock chimed ten, which was the earliest time at which she could phone Dr Kaplan. She tried him at his clinic in Kings Langley, where his receptionist must be at her desk by now. This was it.

'May I speak to Dr Kaplan, please? This is Dorothy Roth.'

'I'm sorry, Mrs Roth. He's with a patient. Are you in Leeds? Can he call you back? It's about your husband, I presume?'

'Yes. Look – '

'I'm afraid that I just can't interrupt Dr Kaplan now, Mrs Roth. The earliest time he's free is at eleven fifteen.'

Dorothy tried another number.

'Mr Fall?'

'Mr Fall is with a client. Who is that, please?'

'This is Dorothy Roth speaking. I must speak to Mr Fall.'

'If I can get hold of him, he'll call you back in a moment.'

Dorothy sank on to the old sofa. It smelled of dust; even, she imagined, of old bagels, matzos and gefilte fish.

Have a drink?

No.

From time to time, Dorothy looked at those pages in her book which were marked with slips of paper.

The phone rang at last.

'Mr Fall? Sam, I've been reading – '

'This is his secretary again, Mrs Roth. Please hold a moment and I'll put you on to him.'

'Hullo?'

'Hullo!'

'Sam! It's Dorothy Roth speaking.'

'Dorothy! How are you! Did you get my champagne?'

'Yes, thanks, Sam.' She laughed. 'But you know I'm trying to give up drink. It isn't easy. I find myself craving for it at breakfast.'

'Oh, live while you can! I'm the same. We're all like that in our generation. Booze and drugs. My secretary said you were anxious about something important. What's the problem?'

Dorothy drew breath, trying to gather her thoughts for a momentous argument.

The silence made Fall anxious. After he had spoken to Roth a short time ago, had the painter phoned her? Should he assume that she knew the gist of their conversation?

'I broke off a meeting,' he added, nervously.

'Sam, I've got hold of a book from the university medical library. I should be resting for people coming round this evening, but I've been up half the night reading. I can't get through to Kaplan. Could you speak to him yourself, or get hold of Roth and talk some sense into him? He won't listen to me. He gets angry or evasive. If he doesn't listen to someone, he's going to be dead before we know where we are. Do you understand?'

'No! I can't grasp a word of what you're trying to tell me. What's this all about, Dorothy? Try to calm down and explain to me. Please.'

'Those drugs he's on.'

'Well? He needs them.'

'No, he doesn't. Listen to me, Sam! This is what Tofranil does to you. Listen! I'm quoting. "Dry mouth, palpitations, constipation, blurred vision, precipitation of glaucoma, sweating, dizziness, weight gain . . . urinary retention, nausea, vomiting, tremors, confusion . . ." This is what Valium causes: "heart palpitations – "'

'Only in some cases, Dorothy. Don't get alarmed. Len isn't one of them.'

'How does anyone know that? He's drinking as well. God

knows what state he's getting into. What the hell does Tofranil *cure*?'

'It cures depression.'

'Len's depressed, too! Don't you think anybody with all those ailments is going to be depressed?'

Her referring to her husband as 'Len', as in the earliest days, had slipped out unguarded. Usually she called him 'Roth', like nearly everyone else did, except Fall and sometimes the gallery people when they wanted to condescend. She had made the slip out of tenderness, thinking of him in his vulnerability as a child.

'Dorothy! See reason! Side effects only affect a number of people and nobody has all of them.'

'Len has! Sam, I don't want him to die – '

'Come on, Dorothy! Pull yourself to– Dorothy, are you crying?'

'Oh, Sam, I can't stop! I'm sorry . . . Can't you see what they're doing to him, Sam?'

'What is it you're reading from? Some quack herbalist's journal? Some long-haired veggy book?'

'I'm reading a standard work on prescription drugs. Don't insult me. I've seen the results, too, with my own eyes. Sam, I've stumbled into someone living round the corner who's been on drugs for some time.'

'Oh?'

'A Mr Parker. I meet his wife in the shops sometimes and yesterday we started talking at the supermarket checkout. Apparently his mother was one of the goyim who used to do Sabbath jobs around Harehills. She used to go to the Roths because old Saul Roth wouldn't let anyone belonging to his own household even light a fire on the Sabbath . . . Sam, Mr Parker's like Roth. He's become totally unsociable, hides away in a bedroom, can't bear to speak to his family; is over the moon with happiness one day and near suicide the next. He's been on Tofranil and Valium. His wife's sure it's because of the drugs.'

'How does she know that?'

'A wife does know these things.'

'Dorothy! Dorothy! Superstitions!'

'Well, I went to see Mr Parker. It was all too similar to Roth's condition. A carbon copy of his behaviour and psychology. My suspicions sent me to the library. It was all there. Sam, the worst is, Mr Parker lives all the time with drawn curtains. He has an allergy to the light. Imagine: Roth, of all people, not able to bear the light. How could he paint?'

'I'll do what I can to speak to Kaplan, Dorothy. I do understand. Calm down and leave it all to Uncle Sam. Maybe Len can be eased off. You just have a nice party. Set your mind at rest. I wish I could be there.'

'Oh, thanks, Sam, thanks! I'll leave it to you, then, thanks!'

'Have a nice day.'

'And you.'

——It is that occasion when I 'interfered' fifteen years ago that is so haunting. 1966. It isn't that I have a bad conscience about breaking up Roth's affair. If it embarrassed him, so what? I was fighting for the preservation of our love! Struggling for what I *knew* was good for him. I did it when the ghastly knowledge soaked in that I enjoyed the world only with him, and that life ahead without him was endless.

I was possessed by terrible jealousy that Roth was giving some part of himself that he hadn't shown to me to another woman. Because we ourselves fantasized, I imagined the most terrible things. I saw those two developing more and more subtle, inevitable and demanding love scenarios.

My interference wouldn't have had any effect upon that little tart, Rebecca Marks. She was an impervious little cow; a badly brought-up child who couldn't help but turn out as she did. Joan Kilburn, 'Mrs Kilburn' as Roth continued quaintly to call her, was a different kettle of fish. Her husband had given her a baby and she stayed married. Still is. She was taking on Roth as a lover, oh, very Byronic, but she seemed to be deceiving him (maybe they were deceiving each other) that they were in love.

I sent her copies of Roth's letters to me, from when *we* were in love. In retrospect, I know how naughty it was of me. But you have to understand how it was at the time. Mrs Kilburn and I (we never actually met, though once I caught a glimpse of her) were obsessed with plotting and counterplotting.

While we two contested, using every ruthless device, what did Roth do? Grew his hair long, because Mrs Kilburn found it romantic. Oh, what fools men can be! He'd no idea what was going on between Joan Kilburn and me. What bit he did see through, he found flattering and funny. Mrs Kilburn and I were about as funny as a Stalin seven-year plan.

I know the lies that men can tell when they're under the influence of a woman determined to get her own way. I was going to puncture them.

As well as sending the letters, I wrote and told her the truth, the *truth*: Roth thought that maybe with someone else he'd be able to sire a baby, I told her, but he'd already tried and failed with that whore Rebecca Marks, and I didn't know how many other women.——

27

Sam Fall poured himself another tumbler of whisky.

Thank goodness Dorothy hadn't realized that he had been speaking to Len earlier this morning. If husband and wife really did get together, there'd be problems for him and for everyone.

As it was, Fall had enough trouble with a black eye, and cuts were healing on his face. To shame him before an unavoidable lunch date at the Groucho Club, two toughs hired by a client, a famous actor, had followed his car. Trailing him along Euston Road and Pentonville Road, they trapped him under a railway bridge near Priory Green Estate.

Some more beatings could be on their way from Roth; these days Fall had to be careful where he drove or walked. (Though he didn't do much walking.) The thought of Roth's unstable centre of gravity brought out gooseflesh on Fall's arms.

The whisky, at least, he did not worry about. In 1950, his head had first been turned by boozing in the company of legendary drinkers whose lives, no matter what the reality, were charmed by glamour. Fall, as a young man, 'hating drab accountancy', had collided with Dylan Thomas in Soho and his course was set to be star-struck by the glitter in a bar, in a glass, in a club.

Sam cultivated an appearance that was a mixture of all Soho's drinking artists. A Sixties figure right into the Eighties, Fall let his lank grey hair reach to the nape of his neck. Over his pink or yellow shirts, he rarely wore a tie. After a trip to California, he was one of the first in England to move around his office in jeans and sneakers, but he still did not look youthful. Fall's figure, alas, was pear-shaped, baby-helpless.

And his emotional affairs were in a shambles. His wife, saving their two children from a 'monster', had run away from his sexual proclivities. She had then found herself to be hooked on them, finally making off with a sadistic policeman. The development amused Sam; except that she also took custody of their country cottage.

Fall had recovered quite well. He sat on arts committees and judging panels, and he was invited to exclusive prize-givings. His London home overlooked a Bloomsbury square, so nobody, even the postman, could say that he had done badly.

Although his front office there, except for its untidiness, was like any other, with mail baskets, computers, desks, filing cabinets and papers all over the floor, his home beyond was like nowhere else. From bathroom to attic it was an ad hoc store of contemporary art, much of the best and a great deal more of the worst. Over walls and floors, the art seemed to be in motion. In a tidal wave, it said everything about Fall's character: indiscriminate, wealthy, acquisitive and restless. Author-signed, prize-winning novels, poets' first editions, autographed photos of actors and actresses, paintings in every style that had been in and out of fashion for the past twenty years, sculptures, art glassware and pottery had been arranged, disarranged and stacked around the rooms; much of it resting for only a short time before being consigned to cellar or attic as new work came in. There was a large Roth landscape of North Africa over the drinks cabinet.

Fall's handling of the Inland Revenue had made his name a byword as champion of the oppressed artist. He would 'open a file' for a promising artist in exchange for examples of work, and they were so grateful to pay out of the only surfeit they possessed, that of their talent, that they never ceased the habit of giving him paintings, books or *objets d'art*.

When a desperate potential star first turned up at Fall's, Sam offered an awesomely overbearing tumbler of Glenfiddich. After a noisy, dusty bedsit in Archway, Islington, Whitechapel, Hammersmith or wherever the shifting artistic fraternity had lodged at the time, it was flattering, with a whisky in one's hand, a seductive armchair swallowing one's backside, to be staring at the tops of unvandalized trees through tall Georgian windows.

Fall would listen carefully. (Occupying himself with his spectacles: taking them off, blowing on them, wiping them.) Brushing the hair from his eyes, he would smile and say: 'Bring me all your receipts and leave the rest to me. Never mind the fee. Let me come round later and choose a picture. That saves *me* from paying taxes, too.'

The first accounts were generally simple. By mid-career, when Fall had gained supremacy, holding the secrets in his head and the documents in his filing cabinet, the artist was likely to find that Sam chose a painting worth considerably more than an appropriate accounting fee.

Fall could be persuasive, even bullying when necessary. From the outset he cultivated his victim's gratitude. Fall's ragged, artistic appearance was disarming. Until the moment when he was moving in for the kill, he chattered about poetry, theatre and art. His rumpled earnestness made him look like anything but a schemer. 'Though he probably isn't very efficient, you can trust a man like that,' clients remarked – until they learned better, when they would say: 'There's no point in having an accountant who *isn't* crooked. The important thing is that he's on my side.'

The client soon learned that an arts accountant is all things to all men. He is their confessor and their adviser over affairs of the heart. Fall offered services as an unpaid (Fall stressed that) agent for their careers. At the moment he told everyone who had some glitzy prominence – as actor, politician, journalist or whorehouse owner who charmed on the chat-show circuit (he had two of those) – to write novels; publishers were crying out for books that already had a handle to them.

Sam worked his way in as family friend and adviser of the most important, so that they could not do without him. This served also as a bait for the less well accepted, who grew envious.

Clients found Fall at the bottom of the manure heaps of their divorces. He arranged the hospitals and rest-homes where they went to dry out or die. They were unable to discover what happened to the deeds of their properties that he persuaded them to place in his care until, eventually, they travelled the slow road, as slow as Fall could make it, towards disillusionment. It was when they were planning to leave him that the real bills poured in, for back tax, legal fees to divorce lawyers, and hospital care. The bills generally made them stall over leaving. Artists' wives often did not realize until they were widowed how dependent they had become. They usually discovered this on the day of the funeral, when Fall could be as soft-footed as an undertaker, and very understanding about their ignorance and confusion. Removing and replacing his spectacles, he had a remarkable bedside manner, as one might call it, with widows.

Other artists caught on to the fact that their affairs were in a parlous state when Fall was not available to answer phone calls and the secretaries gave standard excuses. He was 'in a meeting', 'away on business', 'out at lunch'. The clients might eventually burst into the office, in person or by proxy, with varying degrees of aggression and persistence. This was the stage at which Fall depended upon that apparently disorganized, loquacious public-relations lady in the outer office; the one seemingly always making mistakes, or asking disarming questions about one's kids at inappropriate moments, but who always got her own way. Sooner or later, clients were bound to suspect the truth: Fall had used the deeds of their possessions as collateral to obtain money for short-term investments. Some of these crashed.

Roth flattered himself that he knew his accountant, but what he did not know was that Samuel Fall was also his gallery's accountant; nor was he aware that Fall received a salary from the Station as an 'adviser'.

After Roth left for Yorkshire, Victoria telephoned Sam Fall.

'This is the Station Gallery. May I speak to Mr Fall, please?'

'Mr Fall's not in his office today.'

'Don't monkey with me, kid. This is Victoria Voyce speaking and I've a busy schedule. Tell Mr Fall that this is important.'

'Just a moment. I'll try to put you through. Hullo? You're through, Miss Voyce.'

'Sam!'

'Victoria! What can I do for you?'

'Sam, how much whisky have you had?'

'Why do you ask?'

As a matter of fact, the effects of Sam's restaurant lunch with a client lay heavily on his stomach, and even more so on his brain.

'Because you're going to need some more, Sam. We've just had a call from our mole in Ashby. Young Adam says that Roth is going round the bend. Quite doolally. It's going to take more than a dose of salts from your Kaplan to set the old boy right. Sam, our quarry has set off for Yorkshire on his bike. If we're not careful, Adam tells us, Roth's going to give us the slip. In the state he's in, he's going to kill himself before we're prepared for it.

'Adam's other news is that the studio is chock-full of paintings. New stuff and old, he thinks. Quite beautiful, except that the work is growing darker. Apparently, Roth can't tell that it is. Thinks that it's bright.

'Adam says that a lot of the newer canvases are mad self-portraits. Whether they're good or not, who knows? They might enhance or they might damage Roth's final status, but either way, their existence should attract attention and bring crowds flocking to a posthumous show, the critics arguing whether they're the final flights of genius or whether he's gone cuckoo. You can't ask for better publicity.

'If the madman tops himself, we've got to be in there before anyone else, Sam. Some of the stuff has to disappear. We must take the initiative.'

She meant that the Station had to be ready to move in before Dorothy, Hannah or any other member or representative of the family got there.

'I have a key to the studio,' Fall answered. 'It wouldn't be breaking and entering.'

'The least we can do to protect our interests is to take a look at the place. Sam, Mr Rosblum would like a word with you.'

'Okay, put him on.'

Fall topped up his whisky.

'Sam, how are you!'

'Fine, fine, Pericles.'

'You bin drinking this lunchtime?'

'How can you tell?'

'I can smell it.'

'Down the phone?'

'I gorra good nose. Your voice is slurred, o' course. It don't do you no good. You should be like me and never touch the poison. I had an apple, an orange and a glass of water, all by myself in the office. I need you with a level head for my accounts.'

Sam was weary of being lectured about his bad habits.

'How was your trip to Salonika?'

'You know what them Greeks are like, Sam! Every time them guys see one o' their own come back from abroad, they expect him to bring them the goodies. We Greeks discover how big our own families are, once we get back home. Nobody's had a bigger family than mine since Noah, and I didn' even know three quarters of them existed. I thought they'd all died in the camps. Them Greeks are simple people, Sam, that's why they only respond to iron hand. They think I'm rich because I'm from abroad.'

'You're not doing badly.'

'But I have such problems, Sam! Sam, we gotta do something about this Roth business. You've just been given the update. The man's a fruitcake. There's no knowing what he'll do next. We gotta get our hands on the stuff we gotta right to, Sam. We need 'em to balance our books. I just sold a batch o' Roths, big stuff, really, and it was'n a lo' o' dough. We spent good money promoting this guy.'

'Who did you sell to?'

'To Fondation Moderne.'

'Oh, I see.'

Fondation Moderne was a Rosblum 'company' which existed only as a file in the drawer of a Liechtenstein lawyer who was the 'director' of a hundred similar dummy companies, set up to launder money and pictures.

Pericles Rosblum made a point of not writing any of this down, and he rarely signed anything. When a signature was necessary, he got someone else to do it, so that if anything went wrong he could fire him or her, and claim that it was a mistake.

He carried his business in his head. 'I survived Auschwitz by having a busy head. You couldn' write things down there,' he would say.

A busy head about which you could tell nothing from the exterior. Rosblum had been expensively advised by specialist consultants to disguise anomalies of his personality; to hide signs of predilections or emotions that might be played upon in business deals. The right clothes and hairdressing and the correct, almost scentless aftershave could not hide his cocky stance nor the dangerous sharpness in his eyes. Unkind rivals still described him as a 'spiv', but he retained his notion of himself as a smooth operator.

He was the opposite of Fall, who displayed his casual raggedness as a means of getting people to trust him.

'The price wasn't high?' Sam suggested.

'They were par' of a group sale of twen'y pictures. There was a Nicholson, an early Bacon and a dozen new artists.'

'What price do you put on the Roths?'

The point of selling pictures in a group was that they could be individually valued at a figure, high or low, to suit the dealer.

'When I averaged it out, I put the Roths at three thousand to five thousand each.'

'Dollars?'

'Pounds, Sam, pounds sterling. Le's be generous.'

Sam laughed and drew a spider on his writing pad.

'I don't think even Roth will swallow it, Pericles, but we'll see. I'm sure Dorothy won't. She's the mystery factor.'

'There's no need to tell her yet. We mighta bin able to promote him berrer from the beginning without that dame around.'

'She'll find out very soon. She phoned me this morning. She's been trying to phone Kaplan, but couldn't get through.'

'Sensible guy to go into hiding! Worrra geezer!'

'She's worrying about the drugs that Roth is taking. She thinks they're going to kill him.'

'We got the obituaries written and ready to roll. We bought the film that company in Lancashire – I forgerrits name now, it went bust – made of him ten years ago. *South Bank Show*'ll snap it up.'

'And when he goes, she'll find out the worth of the pictures fast enough.'

She would also discover that many had been spirited away to nonexistent collectors. Actually, they were in Rosblum's warehouse, waiting to emerge mysteriously upon the market when the dust had settled.

'Sam, we gorra get into that studio and check it out before it's too late. Something's going to happen to him today. I got an intewition. In the state he's in, at his age, he's no hope of getting to Yorkshire and back safely on a bike. When something happens to him, five minutes later there'll be police and reporters to watch everything we do. We've gorra be in there fust. We know now that Roth's working, even though he says he ain't. He's the sort to keep on painting till he croaks.'

'Why don't you send a taxi round for the key and get up there?'

'That's whar I was ringing for, Sam, to make sure you were there. I'll call for it myself later this afternoon. Tell your receptionist to give it to my chauffeur. I've got impoitant meetings all afternoon, damn it, but I'm going up by car as soon as I'm through. I'll take some guys and the van. We'll get Adam to complain beforehand to the police that Roth's dangerous and perhaps homicidal. We can tell them we're worried about the guy, too. Then they'll pick him up in Yorkshire and we can get Kaplan to cart him off to his clinic. This morning he beat Adam up, in the studio. Dammit, I don't know his number plate. Do you?'

'No.'

'Perhaps Voyce knows it. You think of a guy with an achievement like that, Sam, cracking up like that, and you wonder what life is for, don't you? He's got so much genyus. If he had business sense as well, he'd a' probably been a success. Instead, he'll kill himself. I've seen 'em go before. Thousans dropped of their own accord in Auschwitz just from not wanting to keep on wi' the business o' living.

'When I was dealin' in them Soutines, there were others who had hold o' good pictures that 'ad slipped the Nazis' net or that the Germans had tucked away. Pictures were hidden all over Europe, in copper mines and in the cellars of country houses – just like today, when you come to think of it, eh? Only now we're waiting for the markets to rise, instead of for the dust of war to settle. Those guys could'a made money out o' pictures, the same as me. They blew their chances. And ended by blowing themselves away. But not me. What's life for, Sam?'

Contemplatively Pericles Rosblum sliced an apple into segments.
——What *is* life for? All my goddam colleagues are rollin' to perdition on barrels of whisky and overeatin', as I keep tellin' Freda. Tha's what they think life's for. Even Voyce. She's a smart cookie but sometimes she's pie-eyed after lunch. Fall takes whisky for breakfast. Thinks he shows no sign o' damage, but at the next stage, he'll be five sheets to the wind with the first drop, and after that, it's curtains. Dorothy Roth's sousing herself in champagne, instead o' taking care o' things like a dame should.

There's another thing: these couples tearing themselves to pieces – so as to hold something together! Ain't that a paradox? They ain't none of 'em got families to save 'em. That's their real trouble.

Roth's wastin' his genyus. He's got genyus, that guy. I've always said that. You can tell it by his style. It's solitary drinkin' with him these days, tha's the most dangerous sort, instead of horsin' aroun' wi' the fellars like he used to. In them 1960s parties, he used to get drunk and pass right through it; sleep it off and wake up to start again next mornin'.

Good Jews don't drink. These stoopid colleagues o' mine all star-red this stoopid habit from tryin' to shock their mothers.

We gorra settle this Roth business and then I quit! Darn nuisance about that number plate. Voyce doesn't have it either. Got Voyce to chase Adam up and he doesn't know more'n one letter of it. I suppose that until Roth does something, the police are not going to arrest him. They have enough to do.

I tell Freda time and again it's time to gerrou'a this business. You know wha' the new guys are doing in art? I ask her.

Bein' a stoopid woman, she's no idea. So I tell her. They're not makin' pictures any more. They're layin' pebbles all over the gallery floor. They wanna display marked ordnance survey maps showin' where they bin walkin'. They frame the notes they made in the rain on some moor somewhere. It's all right for the subsidized Hayward Gallery, but who the hell is going to buy it? How do you make a living?

There ain't gonna be no more real artists, Ben Nicholsons, Stanley Spencers, David Bombergs, Ivon Hitchens, Leonard Roths, Peter Lanyons, I tell her. I'm in my sixties now. Let's gerrout o' here. But Freda says she likes Lon'on. The shops, the operas.——

28

When Sam Fall thought about what life was for, he remembered the 1960s, when it had been at its most vivid, reckless and happy so that he had hardly thought about what life was for.

Pericles Rosblum and Leonard Roth indulged the same nostalgia for when London, with New York, was an art capital of the world. Also it had to do with being young(ish) then, and so Dorothy shared it, too.

The period when Fall, Rosblum and the Roths had got to know each other had been one to which the Roths had been lynchpin, celebrating with parties. Dorothy made it her ambition to become famous for her cooking.

She was out to please Roth, a working-class artist. They're all the same: because it was his ability to paint well that got him out of a working-class ghetto, he had to be given more quality than a duke in everything else – cooking, women. As time went by, fewer and fewer people mentioned Dorothy's painting, except condescendingly, out of kindness.

Their Wiltshire rectory had an acre of garden with thick shrubberies. Roth, although he loved 'nature', hated gardening, so they kept a couple of sheep to clip the lawns. They were called Holman and Alma, after Holman Hunt and Alma-Tadema, two grandiose Victorian painters whom Roth despised. The parties, flowing in and out of the house, past food, flowers and wine, went on for days and nights. Visitors came and went; were sick among the holly bushes, before returning to the fray. The vicar and his 'clients', as Roth called them, spied upon the famous, the disreputable and the eccentric, though mostly trying to pretend that they weren't eaten by curiosity. The guests danced in one room, fell about the floor in drunken debate in another room, listened to music in a third, played the piano in the fourth, fought in the back yard, took brief naps or curled up with a partner, anywhere that they could find. The vicar's 'clients' might be excluded, but plasterers from the local pub drank with London actors and picture-collecting stockbrokers. Roth told Fall that once he came downstairs in the morning and found the books cleared off a shelf for a distinguished sculptor to sleep on it.

Fall first remembered meeting Dorothy at one of these parties, staring at him 'like a witch', he said. He knew that she put real people into her small, surreal, narrative paintings and she questioned him about his life, his affairs, his mind. She painted as a diarist writes, making her subjects uneasy, and after he had unguardedly made various confessions when drunk, the thought crossed his mind that she could blackmail him. Fall had pretended to admire her talents, to enjoy her fantasy paintings and to lament that she was giving up her work, but really he was glad because it saved him from embarrassment.

For instance, once after a weekend party Dorothy painted a hyper-real version of it from a high viewpoint, as if from the top of the church tower. Instead of the guests conversing inertly, holding glasses of wine while they presented rehearsed personae to one another, they were acting out their fantasies. There was Sam Fall, spectacles glistening as he surveyed a nearby group of girls. Around the garden, the houses and cottages of the village were depicted on fire, yet no one was taking notice – except for the figure of Dorothy who was trying to warn everyone.

The wife was hardly of any account today, but in the earliest years she had been on an even footing with Roth. The Station had exhibited her work as much as his. Fall watched her being dropped stage by stage.

The first stage was when, at her own parties, Rosblum did not mind her overhearing his scepticism about her work. The second stage arrived when, it seemed, he intended her to overhear him. He could be a brute, and he liked to test his strength.

'Wha'yar think'o that dame?'

'She's cool. But she's tough underneath. She's an artist in her own right, of course,' Fall hedged.

'That's because you like-a the cooky stuff. I don't gerrit. I just don't gerrit. The future's in abstract. That's the advice I go on. Anyway, a woman can't paint.'

——Yes, I smilingly stood there, Wife of Roth, offering round a tray of drinks as if I were a maid, tense as hell while I listened to that stuff. This was in 1966 when we were holding the party in honour of Georgia O'Keeffe, who was in Britain at the time.

All women get used to men's typical reaction to one of us who succeeds in 'their' (the men's) professions. It deflates their egos, for they can see it only as a challenge and not as companionship. Moreover, it is rivalry from a supposed inferior. It embarrasses them and makes their hackles rise. Georgia made jumped-up little Rosblum twitch and hop like a frog on a hot stove.

He and O'Keeffe could never have got on. She clearly despised him. Dressed in black, as she had been since girlhood, her hair pulled back severely, her face leathery, lined and severe, she put on her grandest matriarchal manner for the toad.

That day he was wearing a green silk suit with massive lapels, and a broad, purple kipper tie. It was fastened with a gold pin that thrust it up on his cocky chest and made him even more like a comic robin. (On other occasions, he actually wore a tie with a bathing belle printed on it – this was before the 1970s, when at last he learned to hide, rather than display, his lack of breeding.) He still had a habit, picked up from holding his own on postwar building sites, of rubbing his lumpy biceps when he felt insecure. He was a fifty-year-old, wealthy, supposedly cultured art dealer, not a callow youth. The contemptuous hauteur with which Georgia surveyed him was enough in itself to upset his vanity. She drove him to anti-feminist excesses, unusual even for him.

'Sam, a woman's meant for creatin' babies,' Rosblum said. 'A dame that don't have a baby, don't have proper feelings. And a dame with a baby don't have the time to paint. Not without neglecting her baby, and that wouldn't be natural. So they can't put no natural feelin' into their art. That's why she can't paint pictures. It's a contradiction. Not masterpieces. Get me?'

'A little tough, Pericles.'

'The truth _is_ tough. We both know that, even if some o' these pansy artists don't. You ever heard of a dame can paint real good? This O'Keeffe ain't nothing. She's just a seven-day wonder because the women support her. But all that them pictures tell you, them shapes she paints, is that the woman wants a baby. Get me?'

'Excuse me, Mr Rosblum.'

'Wassat, honey? Oh, thank you.'

He took a glass from me, and thinking that was all I was offering, he turned away. I knew that the man was a smooth worm, yet my heart was pounding. I was very angry. All that about babies!

'Excuse me, I think you're wrong.'

Rosblum smiled condescendingly. He thought that I couldn't get under his skin: a man who had outfaced all ranks, from German guards to lordly diplomats.

'It's my opinion that the reason women have not been "great" is because what "great art" is, is decided by men,' I said.

'A woman who's married should stop playing, whether it's with art or anythin' else, and gerron with it. You've Roth to look after. Now _there's_ a guy, and he's your responsibility. Anything wrong with looking after him? You chose your mission and should be proud.'

'You know Athens, Mr Rosblum? You've been in the Benaki Museum?'

'The folk art?'

'Yes.'

'And the National Museum of Greek Art, too? Not the Archaeological Museum, where the ancient sculptures are. I mean the museum on Vassileos Konstandinou where they exhibit the Greek painters.'

'Nobody goes in there, kid, but I bin in there.'

'Nobody goes in there: exactly! Hardly anyone. I've been in there, too, Mr Rosblum. Your national collection where, as you say, only men have produced the "art". In the whole tradition, a hundred and fifty years since the Turks left Greece, not a single woman is represented. What have the men produced? Pompous imitations of what was fashionable abroad. Pretentious imitations of Ingres' and Delacroix' scenes of battle and rape. Impressionism and post-impressionism. Self-portraits in whatever styles were fashionable.

'Unless they are being raped or adored, women are in the background of these pictures, making coffee, serving wine, denied any part of the action.

'The Greek national collection shows you how men define what is art. If you want to find what women did, go to the Benaki Museum. Weaving, bridal dresses, fabrics, carpets. Matisse would give his right hand to have produced any one of them. But it wasn't called art. It was only what women did. Despised and anonymous.'

'Except that Matisse could do more than reproduce traditional patterns. He was able to make variations,' Sam Fall interrupted.

What did that matter, I thought, if the quality was there?

I said no more. Like one of the women in the background of the men's 'domestic scenes', I slid away with my tray.

When we discussed it afterwards, Roth, you could not understand why I did not make an ally of Georgia.

The reason was that, although Alfred Stieglitz had died in 1946 and I never met him, I questioned whether her relationship with him had been as perfectly supportive of her as the legend supposed.

To tell the truth, I thought it bitterly ironic that, as I saw it, he had used her to paint his male fantasies for him. These then became excusable because they had been executed by a woman; excuses, disguises, denials being necessary in the 1920s and '30s, when most of them had been painted.

I know that O'Keeffe denied that her work depicted female sexual organs, even though it seemed so obvious to me. Why did she deny it?

I know there are many who think that if a woman paints anything at all other than babies or gardens she is 'oversexed';

and what the hell does that mean, anyway? They'd never say it of a man, no matter what he painted. It would be admired as 'erotic'. Nevertheless, I could never see O'Keeffe's work, even landscapes, as anything but variations upon juicy vaginas and breasts. Had these been painted by a man, they would have been attacked by women as fantasy pornography, I believe.

I have, too, come across the bizarre phenomenon of those, stumbling across an exhibition of women's art, seeing (shall we use as examples) scenes of sexual horror, or of nude male vainglory, who comment that they thought 'it was done by perverted men'. My own humanist pictures have been denounced as obscene.

This misunderstanding comes about because maybe women artists are turning pornography on its head, in order to comment, to satirize it.

What, after all, is pornography? Porn fantasy consists of falsifying the nature of sex, typically of the opposite sex, in order to raise false hopes in it. It is the raising of the false hopes that does the damage, because it harms one's relationship with one's actual or possible partner. Therefore slush fiction is as dangerous a form of pornography as any other. Taken seriously, it corrupts; and no matter how fantastic, true pornography has to be believed in order for it to work.

But one can caricature sex, can imitate the pornographic mode, in order to comment on it.

Now. It seemed to me that Georgia painted fantasies on behalf of her lover – just as she dressed to satisfy his fetish for women in black. It seemed to me that they had lived out an intricate sado-masochistic relationship, in which Georgia was submissive.

This would have been fine by me. What disturbed me was this terrible irony: O'Keeffe's puppetry at Stieglitz's beck and call was presented by women themselves as an exemplary relationship.

We used to see a lot of the Rosblums through the 1960s, and we moved out to Wiltshire at their recommendation, when they bought a manor house nearby.

'Better than Alois Brunner's, eh?' Rosblum announced when he first entertained us there.

He was still haunted with unseemly envy for the mansion of the head of the Gestapo in Salonika, which must have been the grandest house that Pericles had seen by the age of twenty-four.

That first party at Rosblum's was held on a Saturday afternoon and some of the guests were ferried in by helicopter from Paris. Within a security fence, in grounds that you could not walk in safely without referring to guards and dog-handlers, were sited statues from the first to the third centuries AD, smuggled out of Greece and Italy. There were sculptures pillaged from medieval churches. There were Islamic paintings and Buddhist figures – the flotsam of the underground trading in art, if one chose to look at it that way. As Rosblum had put the thought of Brunner into my mind, I wondered if the Gestapo chief's home had been like this, at least in Pericles' imagination; for he had only penetrated the mansion (he claimed) as far as the prison and torture chamber in the basement.

'In Salonika, there was a butcher named Aristotle. There was a policeman named Plato. My father must'a seen I'd become king of a golden age,' Pericles Rosblum joked.

A marquee was spread with champagne, lobsters, cold game, pies and salads. Half a dozen servants, who seemed to know what artists are like, watched us like hawks as we poured – questioning, hushed sometimes, chattering sometimes – excitedly over the garden, through the orangery and through the house, which seemed the more spectacular because it was not yet properly furnished. In huge, almost empty rooms, the antique furniture, sculpture, pictures, icons out of Greek and Russian churches, looted ivory and tribal carvings from Africa were still crated, covered in dust sheets or lying casually against the walls. Rosblum's pride in all this was so great, he was happy for us to stray even through his bedroom, where I found myself in a group bedazzled by one of Freda Rosblum's many wardrobes. It was twenty feet long, spilling furs, shoes and handbags. Like the art, it bore the labels of having been culled from many places: Paris, New York, Milan, London, of course, but also Sydney, Brasília and Madrid. Even Moscow was represented, by a fur hat.

The wife of an international dealer can live like Imelda Marcos. Freda Rosblum had developed that polished look of the overfed, international spoiled, when the unrealistic opinions held in the head put a glaze upon the outside. Freda was the more callous and savage from having, like her husband, been in a concentration camp, having spent her childhood there. Terrible experiences don't necessarily make one humanitarian. They may make one more ruthless.

I also remember our first visit vividly because it was then that I got the hang of Pericles Rosblum's character. He said he put all this together 'for Freda and the kids' and it is true that he indulged himself very little. Under the flamboyance there was a driven, self-punishing ascetic.

Rosblum was clearly a family man, proud of his son's school blazer, his daughter at public school too, and there's no need to say how envious I was of his family. But what did his love and pride mean?

His family was an extension of his vanity. It was another possession. He was proud to claim that, as well as filling a house and grounds with art, he who came out of the cauldron of the Balkans could found an enviable dynasty, too.

His overwhelming need was to be admired. He had no scruples about what he did so long as those around him admired him for it, and so long as there were a lot of people to do so. He was a little man who had to seem big. Anyone who showed a crack in their admiration was finished. Imagine how difficult it was for Freda, who had to keep it up all the time. I don't know how they are together now, but the day she ceases to be in awe at everything he does, she'd better look out.

She isn't one who needs lessons in how to survive, though. Her price for her admiration is that he should spoil her; she who can never be satisfied. That's how she keeps her hold on him. I'm sure they've worked that one out.

Roth could do or say what he wanted because he was an artist; he was Rosblum's raw material.

But me – !

Even so, I think Rosblum realized, too, that I had grasped yet another key to his character; one that was even deeper than his need to be admired, though linked with it.

He was without inner resources other than the blind, icy ambition for sheer power. His success had depended upon his buying the right people to tell him what he should do. It had begun with mere luck, the Soutines found in a hen shed, and this had provided his first capital with which to buy people. Rosblum realized I knew that his show of power amounted to a gift for spotting whom he could make use of, and the luck to profit by his pathetic dependency.

I was one of those who had known him before the major transformation of his personality from flashy spiv to administrative zombie, and I didn't pretend that I hadn't seen two Rosblums, as others pretended. I didn't pretend I didn't know that he re-groomed his appearance as he chose his pictures – because his advisers told him what was best for him.

Once I'd turned uppity, Rosblum increasingly grew suspicious and wary. Hiding his fear of me, as men often do try to hide their fear of women, or bluster their way through it, he showed me his hard, negative side; one to which Roth was impervious because he was never shown it.

Rosblum's strategy was to build up my husband at my expense, but it took me years of frustration to catch on to what was happening. Because of the man to whom I was married, Rosblum could not ignore me completely. Instead, he condescended. Rosblum is practised at treating artists as if they are children. When he started referring to me as 'the little woman' I ought to have seen that, so far as he was concerned, my days as a serious painter were over. I ought to have realized what was the cause of the strain I experienced in dealing with the gallery staff; of the repetitious 'mistakes' they made over my affairs; of the new mixture of iciness one moment, politeness the next; and of the delays over arranging an exhibition for me.

I should have been given a show every year. Two, three years went by. When at last I was granted a showing, it was at an inauspicious time, in January after everyone had done their

Christmas spending. The catalogue was flimsy and late and there was little attempt at publicity.

I would have valued some disillusioning honesty, instead of wasting so much of my time. Eventually I saw that the increasingly nervous state I was being reduced to was preparing me for when they would be elbowing me aside, not only as a painter but as a wife.

They were heading for when they would control my husband's medical affairs and his estate.

29

Roth used to say ('Roth used to say . . .', 'Roth said . . .'; those phrases always in my mind!) that all the elements of an affair, the reasons for its success and the causes of its downfall, are present in the first minutes or hours.

I was attracted by the mission of saving him from his destructive self. I can still see him, arguing, shouting, hunting through the pubs of Fulham, Kensington and Hampstead for a critic he intends to beat up; fighting with another one in the street outside a gallery at a private view; ostentatiously pissing in the fireplace when drunk at a party; at another 'do', as he calls them, throwing glasses one after another at a wall, until everyone departs except us two, crying with remorse upon the floor. I used to believe that his self-destructiveness was a kind of war wound in his soul.

When we met, Roth wasn't yet making money. I was, and I also had a legacy. I could paint without worry because I was one of the last members of the middle class in Britain to employ a live-in maid. I could get on with my painting because of her – as a male artist can work because he has a wife or a mother. On my own behalf I hardly thought about cleaning, cooking and shopping.

After visiting Roth's studio, the first thing I did was discreely to pay off his most pressing bills. I turned myself into his housekeeper. He was living in Hampstead, which was then not an expensive or rarified 'village', just a happy one, and he carelessly owed money in every direction, for milk, for food at the grocer's, for coal, for clean shirts which he was unable to claim from the laundry; for everything but paints and canvases – he always found the cash to spend on those. It took me half a day to visit and pacify the tradesmen. I did it secretly, as if ashamed. I reclaimed his shirts, took them home by taxi to Highgate and had them ironed. My Spanish maid gave me quizzical looks, but said nothing. I ordered a load of coal to arrive without his knowing.

I'd say that I was a woman of independence, for 1951. I had walked out of an unsuitable marriage with such aplomb that I had skirted most of the potential disasters, so I believe. I knew how to move through the domestic oceans with quiet and stealth, without raising storms. With the minimum of strain, I think, I had acclimatized my then husband to my leaving. I had manipulated my fulfilment, which was the privacy of a Highgate studio, with the skill of a successful business manager. Now I was abdicating.

I was in love. I discovered that I wanted to love and to be loved, more than I wanted to paint. Thus I set up the pattern of sacrificing myself. It was mostly without Roth having asked for it; accompanied by his taking it for granted, and my resenting it, secretly, burningly. I blamed him for not seeing what I was not prepared to show him. I thought he should have seen it for himself.

Two weeks after we met he was already painting with more energy and conviction. I did not worry that I myself hadn't stood before my easel in that time.

As well as being obsessed with him, I had already lost confidence. I felt crushed even by the differences in our studios. His manly command of his space, his large chairs, easels and tables, made me think that my studio, with its delicate furniture, littered with bits of collage material, cloth, paper, scissors, and with curtains at the window, was trivial – *feminine*. Why was I so stupid?

While Roth produced large pictures, broadly painted with large brushes and a mixture of oil and turpentine medium, I painted small but intense canvases, closely worked over with sable brushes, and almost entirely using oil as a medium, like certain pre-Raphaelites. With the hyper-realism with which I depicted an edge of lace, say, it was said that I invested a portrait with an air of the surreal even when the pose, the subject and the composition were banal. I had recently broken through to intentionally surreal compositions in which my quirky, personal observations and flights of fancy were distinctive. I was introducing collage into my oils on canvas. Using *trompe l'oeil* techniques, I painted such subjects as heavily lipsticked tarts floating with angel's wings over landscapes and townscapes, where no one looked up to see; or scenes of London EC1 with bankers and businessmen going to their offices unembarrassedly naked, except for briefcase, umbrella and maybe bowler hat or rolled newspaper. When the critics wrote their few column inches about me in the art journals, they pointed out that I tended to paint extraordinary subjects with an emphasis on the fact that no one took any notice. I am still moved by that, still taking it as my subject that people tend not to take any notice.

Now that Roth has gone, maybe I will fill my time painting scenes of our blind and absorbed love while the malign spirits that destroyed us hover in the dark air.

After meeting him, my imagination fell into impasse. My mind full of this man, I spent my time thinking of what to do for him, what presents to buy, what clothes to wear to delight him.

Two weeks after we met, I surprised him by turning up at his studio with my basket full of twigs that I had collected while walking across the heath. The first nip of winter was in the air. As I crouched over the fireplace, lighting my sticks and my coals, I felt my back burning even more than my face, because of his eyes upon me. Of course he saw me stiffen, as he saw everything, though I tried to continue quite naturally.

He told me in later months that my presence in a room, or when we went somewhere together, made the world sing. I felt the same way about him. Only necessities like the danger of falling under a bus could pull his eyes away from me, he told me.

'It's so kind of you to do these things,' he said with un-Rothlike politeness when I brought the sticks. (I believed I was already having a civilizing effect on him.) 'My mother used to say that a visitor should always bring something, no matter how small. Do you know what an extraordinarily *giving* person you are? I've noticed you with lots of others, not just myself.'

Talking about his mother brought us closer and we found ourselves making love for the first time. I can't remember how it came about, but he used condoms that he dashed out to purchase from the barber's shop at the corner of the block.

In those days, the purchase of condoms was a seedy business. A man didn't walk openly to a girl behind the counter in Boots. They sold them in that odd bastion of male privacy and intimacy, the barber's shop. Yet I remember thinking he didn't behave as if he was doing anything unusual. I had an uneasy thought that he went regularly to the barber's for that purpose. I sensed that the bed he led me to was already haunted.

And, of course, I didn't yet know that there wasn't any need for us to use condoms at all.

Roth started taking me to art galleries, while my maid must have wondered why I was out all day. The visits were more intense than any I had paid before, because previously I had gone alone, or with parties from the Ruskin School in Oxford where I had studied, or with friends or family who were only semi-interested and wanted an entertainment before tackling the more important business of shopping. Roth, unlike anyone I had met before, would tolerate no dilution of his concentration.

At the Tate Gallery's 1955 show 'Modern Art in the USA', I felt attacked by something brutal, masculine and alien. Especially by the Jackson Pollocks, which were so aggressively virile. White lines like spurts of semen had been thrown over many of them, on the messy floors where Pollock laid ('laid'!) his canvases.

After a walk through, my admiration mixed with a shudder, I wanted to get out; if not to go home, then to soothe myself among Dalís, Max Ernsts or the pre-Raphaelites, who were my own pictorial antecedents. Roth, however, was overcome in a way I had not met in anyone before. The Pollocks and the Rothkos inspired in him a mad intensity of looking that was frightening.

My wanting to leave the gallery, but not daring to, was my first experience of being hypnotized by love, like a rabbit before a stoat. All the normal discomforts, the airlessness, the heat, the tiredness of my feet, troubled me the more because I was afraid to leave.

It was in the Tate, the National Gallery and the Courtauld Collection that I found I was afraid of arguing with him. It was because I was more concerned to be loved than to be part of an equal and therefore possibly disagreeing relationship.

He would drag me into the city and make me spend the whole day looking at only one or two pictures, which *he* chose. After a couple of hours he took me out to see the light on the river or for him to enjoy a beer. Then back again to stare at Rembrandt's self-portrait (the one in Kenwood House) or Van Gogh's sunflowers in the National Gallery – two of his favourite paintings.

My happiness had seemed previously unimaginable to me. Oh yes, I reminded myself many times, mentally pinching myself to make sure that I wasn't dreaming, the joy was real and true. I was consumed by the beauty of his body. I could look at nothing and nowhere else, and people in the streets returned looks of alarm at our happiness.

Years later, Roth admitted that when I went out his time was half wasted in waiting for my return. While I, too, felt attached to him by an invisible string. As if he were pulling me in.

In 1956 we gave up the tenancies of both our flats, got married at Highgate Registry Office, and travelled Europe. He had not visited the great cathedral cities since the war and I had not seen them at all. The paintings were beginning to surface from hiding. Everywhere, from cities to small towns, was still untroubled by tourism and the great sites gained both mystery and dignity from the marks of neglect or war-battering. I can't believe how easily we went through my inheritance, and how glad, too, I was to spend it all in a couple of years.

Returning to London in 1958, we set up home. No maid, no luxuries any more. But big, Victorian houses were not expensive. Before moving out to Wiltshire we lived in Rosslyn Hill, in a double-fronted villa with a decaying attic, leaking skylights, powdery beams and, outside, a garden overgrown with roses. I painted a three feet by two feet canvas of that garden, a picture now in a public collection in Zurich, and it was executed in one of the two studios that we adapted out of the bay-windowed rooms at either side of the front door.

This was perhaps the best period of our lives together. Being without money was a new world to me with fresh, small pleasures. Making cheap jewellery look expensive, for instance; or twice a year carefully choosing one new dress to buy, instead of taking half a dozen every month without thinking about it, as I had done before.

We had no one else to consider and we acted spontaneously. If work was not going well, perhaps we would walk, even in the rain, over the heath. One is not supposed to know about happiness while it occurs, but I was aware of it, although occasionally a strand of cloud threaded across my mind when I feared that it might not last.

Once *Harper's* magazine photographed us leaning over a bar (how else?) and described us as 'the Fitzgeralds of Fitzrovia'. 'The sparks flew tonight when the Roths took to champagne,' reported the *Hampstead and Highgate Gazette*.

I had discovered, you see, that when I was drunk, I was no longer afraid of him. On the contrary, I could say what had been suppressed; say it even more fervently because of the suppression. But it came out wildly and dangerously. Instead of an explanation, drink turned what I had to say into ferocious attacks.

Attacks, because Roth wasn't capable of allowing happiness to last. He often said that he was 'only able to judge people by pushing them to the edge'. Contentment! He didn't know the meaning of the word.

It was his theory that both love and art were vulnerabilities – and that this was part of their beauty and vitality, not of their sadness. Maybe he had to prove to himself that they *were* vulnerable.

It was at the very height of our happiness that I found out.

'No! *No!* I don't want to make love. I just don't. I *won't*. Oh, Leonard!'

This was before we first set out for Europe, in 1954. We had been together for three years.

'Why? Why not, my darling?'

I have never been able to bear his lying to me. All dignity goes with it; and I cannot bear to lose my admiration for him.

After he'd repeatedly questioned me, I told him: 'I can smell another woman on your body.'

It wasn't merely perfume, as a man might pick up from a brief kiss. It was the juices of another female, rubbed off over his whole body, as can only happen when sweating excitedly together, making love. I dared not fully imagine it. My mind would not let me.

'Some whore!'

Of course, I know; the 'other woman' is always a 'whore'. That's what he said to me at the time.

My cries turned into howls. It was his first infidelity. How could he be so insensitively reasonable about it?

I discovered that the only way to recover from the horrifying iciness that overcame me, and which I *must* overcome to escape my loneliness, was to remember and foster the love I had previously felt. I forced myself to repeat my familiar acts of love, washing his brushes, making sure his coffee hadn't grown cold, until eventually love came back.

We recovered and were more passionate than ever.

We married in order to seal that act of faith. But after we returned from our travels, fresh infidelities occurred, and more often through the irresponsible years of sexual 'liberation'; that euphoria peaking between the pill in 1965 and the discovery of AIDS. Merely for the sake of the 'experience', couples went to bed as readily and meaninglessly as they would deliver a good-night kiss. Men and women woke up in the mornings not remembering the partner at their side.

Until I made him take sperm tests, Roth and I were baffled by our inability to conceive a child, and in the late Fifties and early Sixties I taunted him with looking for someone who would be seduced into motherhood. For at first, since I had no child from my first marriage either, I had assumed that the 'fault' was mine. Women do.

Today, I believe that he wasn't unfaithful out of desperation to prove his potency. That was only my own paranoia. His infidelities occurred because he was unable to resist a new world of experience. It usually happened when he was drunk, and when he got into the company of groupies. Roth's acolytes were mostly naive middle-class girls freshly arrived in London and overexcited by their realization that the pill gave them control over their fertility.

The period deluded so many as a happy one, but the abandonment of marriages led to a generation of children growing up warped and uncontrollable. Tell me I'm old-fashioned; I've a right to be, at sixty-six. Even at the time, it did not appear to me a happy state. I am what in those days was called, with a tinge of contempt, 'the faithful type'. At each of Roth's infidelities I thought: How long can we continue to be lucky? Each time, it could be suicide for us. Thus Roth began to live with what he seemed to want and need, which was the risk of destroying our love.

I learned that my husband actually needed a little pain, trouble and rejection, and I picked this up from the implications of other things that he told me. For example, he said that the war had taught him that pain was a door into an initiation and that lying beyond was an experience that was magical and transcendental. It was a new idea to me. I had no suspicion that he was leading me on to our inflicting pain upon one another.

Sometimes men longed to repeat the fear they had endured in battle, he told me. Men and women who had been tortured obsessively recalled their punishment cells, unable to discover feelings in later life to match the intensity. Some of the Nazis' victims, he claimed, lived in shame at their secret longing to recapture the fine thrill of their fear of a knock on the door.

Roth had come out the best in most fights, he had escaped the war lightly, his life had been little troubled by sickness and, out of perversity (he admitted), he needed to taste the alternative.

'I see,' I answered. For it seemed to me that suddenly I had learned a great deal.

At the time, he was explaining why he plunged into reckless dangers: balancing on the edge of a cliff in Cornwall; baiting Moroccans in a bar in Perpignan; wrecking a canvas that he had been working on for months; walking out of happiness.

War had offered Roth nothing so intense as the danger which he himself engendered of losing my love, he told me. No feeling in his life had been as strong as his jealousy when the dread took root that I might be looking for another man.

I realized that he was trying to provoke me with his infidelities. He told me that no pain was comparable to his feelings when he looked at men at whom he had just caught me staring.

I never stared at other men. Yet the phenomenon of his self-induced jealousy confronted me, out of nowhere, violating my feelings.

As his other affairs followed, I tried to understand and be positive. I reasoned that out of choice I had abandoned my own art in order to succour his, and his infidelities were part of the artistic confidence that I was feeding. He needed to be periodically unfaithful because, through a new relationship, his imagination was excited into making a leap forward. The world that had been growing stale was freshly made and of a new colour. His work moved on.

30

If Roth was not to be rejuvenated by a fresh woman from time to time, it had to be done with a new landscape.

Our first travels, in the Fifties, were modest. Our furthest limit was Spain.

In the Seventies, the need to escape ourselves being even greater, and Roth's muse growing ever more voracious, we toiled for days over the remote mountain regions of the world, often in appalling weather, looking for sites for paintings. We risked our lives for weeks on end in the desert. I daren't think any more about our trips through Africa. We've camped in hot marshes where the mosquitoes were the size of bulldogs. Always lugging canvases, boxes of oil paints, easels, brushes, sketchbooks; travelling on the backs of donkeys, in rickety jeeps, on camels, in leaking boats, or clinging to our possessions in the guard's vans of unreliable trains.

Always we moved southwards, seeking an antidote to the north.

I feel as though our being travellers is what defines us. I see our journeys, including voyages in my own head – our fantasies – as the essential metaphor of my life, continually being carried by some means I do not understand, hopefully into somewhere better, somewhere strange.

Simple train journeys came first in my life. As a girl, then as a young woman, I took them to set up a different rhythm in my body and to flash different places before my eyes. Boys and men were encouraged to adventure, were allowed to go for 'rambles', as they were called in the Twenties and Thirties. Not, in those days, a girl, or even a woman. So I invented excuses: shopping, visiting an aunt.

My first marriage, like a train journey, had been in hope of travel and change. Through it I indeed exchanged one place, one beautiful place, for another: Devon for Sussex. When I found that it didn't make any difference because my inner life wasn't altered by it, for some years I grew antagonistic to all lovely scenery. 'Beautiful places are no substitute for people,' I used to say. What effect places had depended upon how one lived in them, I learned.

Upon what was going on in one's head. If bored or unsatisfied, the surrounding beauty reflected only one's boredom. Everywhere I went until I met Roth – Devon where I was born, Oxford where I attended the Ruskin School of Fine Art, Sussex where I first married, and places visited on holidays – I stared and stared. 'What are you staring at? What do you see there?' asked my father, and then my first husband.

I could not answer. I was trying to penetrate the obvious beauty of my surroundings, but was finding only the reflection of my own loneliness. At least people *spoke*, but the silence of these places was anguish.

And then what did I do, but fall in love with a landscape painter?

With Roth, life has been an adventure; yet it has come about through responses to places.

The places were exciting because we shared an inner adventure, too. Our life was a conspiracy, taking us to regions where no rules from the outer world could reach and where no morality could help.

Words, too, were journeys. From the minute I first spoke to Roth, back in 1951, it was his words that took me and made me know I was attached to him.

We met in the Station Gallery where we were both exhibiting in a mixed show. Feeling the pluck of different directions in our first exchange, it was so intense, progressing so rapidly, rushing without control of our tongues until reaching the heart of each other's feeling, that when we spoke to a third person later, an acquaintance of Roth's to whom I was a stranger, that person had thought we had been lovers for years.

Later, instead of joining others at a restaurant, we walked through a rainy night along Marylebone High Street and into Regent's Park; he in a tweed jacket that indoors smelled of cigarettes, I in a mackintosh with a tartan-lined hood. It was as if we had known each other for years, having been merely apart, missing one another, and having so much to tell one another. I can still put my hands out and touch the wet leaves of the plane trees. Still. Oh, I wish . . .

Whenever we made love, our words poured before his semen did. Oh, his voice, his voice! Whispering, feeling under the bedsheets, he led like a priest conducting me through the labyrinths of a dark temple. As often, I led him. When orgasm came, I felt it run through my womb and right through my body, reaching up to chest and throat, then clouding my head. All day afterwards I could feel him inside me and I carried his smell over my body. Like an animal, this was how he claimed me.

In early days together we talked a lot about 'fate'. Roth said the war had taught him that if you did not trust your fate, fear would make you a nervous wreck.

It was also the war that taught us to distrust such words as 'fate' and 'destiny', because of the use Hitler made of them. We learned to see them as part of the machinery of evil and to dislike even philosophers using such terms. After the war, there was thus nothing esoteric left in politics – esotericism had been disgraced, as doubtless our Wiltshire vicar's fascist family had disgraced it on our lawn in the 1930s, and there was only consumer-realpolitik left.

Personally, I was so lost in the certainty that I was grasped by fate that I could not conceive of my whirlwind not being beneficial to everyone else. (*Is* there any other form of love? From my experience, I doubt it.) I felt I had been chipped out of a concrete wall. Once in the light, I was so dazzled by golden fortune that morality was a cold and feeble candle to hold up to it. I could not believe that everything would not come magically right for the whole world.

It didn't. Travels threw me out of reach of familiar settings and places, so part of the trouble in those mosquito-bitten, dust-blown, dried-up villages of mean lives and noble myths where we lived for much of our time was that we had to compensate with a colossal love for each other. In our isolation, each of us was painfully sensitive to any failure to give the other sufficient, compensatory attention.

After 1968, when we tried so hard again to cure our problems through travel, we found ourselves wrecked upon our aloneness, as two, welded into one, against the world. That one was stronger than a dozen separate souls, and it needed the strength in order to survive.

It was in 1968, after Mrs Kilburn, that we started to make journeys in real earnest. You couldn't possibly call us holidaymakers any more.

We dwelled in houses here, flats or hotels there, but the lives we burned out were the same.

In the end we could hardly distinguish one place from another. Couldn't remember which countries we were in, without checking the shop signs. Big, bare rooms that Roth hunted down for studios. Suites in decrepit spa hotels. Farmhouses and barns deserted by farmers. Backwater railway stations in mountainous country. An obsolete morgue, a slaughterhouse, an abandoned school, in which country? These all filled with pictures, while our bedrooms became stuffy with the ghosts of fantasies.

I must think about fantasies, which have been so prominent in my pictures, such as they are, and in our lives. Did they begin for me with lies? Lying to my mother so that I could keep assignations with boys; or so that I could take some secret train to – anywhere?

I think I realized as a child that my 'lies' were the essential truth about me. I was inventing fictions that explained my inner self. The 'truthfulness' that was urged upon me at school, church and home was no more than a façade hiding a building structured differently underneath, within which an unsuspected life beat.

Our fantasies triggered surges of closeness. That was an unbelievable, drowning sensation. Our skins ceased to be barriers. Skin became no more than an atmosphere through which we floated into one another, a mist in which our two selves mingled. With it came longing, as if pouring from a fountain. To come anywhere near one another, to kiss ever so lightly, brought orgasmic joy.

Roth confessed that he was roused to an erection at night by thinking about what I had been wearing during the day. Was it that he was aroused purely through his eyes, as I was through my ears? Or, he told me, he was stirred by imagining me at particular moments when I had caught his fancy. Was the word 'erotic' sufficient to describe it? The embrace that went beyond the physical, absorbing the flooding of the psyche, erupting in such quantities of images, experiences, thoughts and feelings.

A shared fantasy made us feel we had given everything of ourselves to each other, with the outer layer peeled off and the core revealed.

Asking questions, making suggestions and registering their effect, I had found out all about him. I discovered what Roth hardly knew about himself. I got under his skin.

Whispering as he stroked the petals of my entrance, he, also, uncovered my secret thoughts.

At first in my life I had kept my imaginings for painting. It was Roth who lifted them off the canvas.

Sam Fall, a glint of surprise and pleasure in his eye as he surveyed my pictures for the first time, had instructed me in female fantasies such as I would never have guessed at. These were certainly not mine – not some of them. Fall was quite an encyclopedia. I don't know how he found out, for he wasn't 'experienced' with women in the usual sense. Dogs and monsters figured. He told me that women imagined themselves as being the earth ploughed by some massive farmer; as trees stirred by a whirlwind; as being mounted by a beast. A remarkable number were variations on one archetype, which was that of sky god, or Wagnerian tempest, pouring over fertile, submissive earth.

Those were their private dreams (confided to fatherly, ambiguous and ambidextrous Sam Fall, probably after an expensive dinner), while public ones, in the evening, over a snack, watching TV, were Clark Gable, a Daimler radiator grill, a country estate and a woman with her hair blowing in the wind.

At first I worried about what had been running through my mind. When I found myself only waiting for the night to conduct me back into that other world I feared that I was growing sick, hooked on some immoral drug. My imaginings seemed destructive because they turned topsy-turvy all that I believed in. All my morality. It meant murmuring the words for latent feelings that seemed monstrous in the daylight of a world built upon kindness, tolerance and fairness.

Sexual fantasies fortified our extraordinary sense that we had lived together in some previous time. Maybe it was merely that we were indulging in what all humans share, the collective memory. But even on the evening that we met, when we walked in Regent's Park, we felt we had lived together before.

This was probably what was most seductive about our fantasies: they put us in touch with past archetypes. What were the *Odyssey*, the *Oresteia*, the *Bacchae*, the processions of Lapiths, centaurs and abductions carved in stone, but dramatizations of those same scenes that haunted us in lovemaking? Surely Euripides, Aeschylus and Phidias would have understood us.

Roth never worried that our games might result in permanent harm to our love by making us unable to distinguish between reality and unreality. I could not understand how he, an artist, could be so blind. Probably it was his greater painter's egoism that saved him from falling into a pit.

I painted my fantasies, and they were the prime material of my art, but I knew the difference between fantasy and life. But he lived even more compulsively and uncritically inside his own head than I did, for he got in the grip of his inner world and couldn't get out. He couldn't distinguish where fantasy ended and real life began. His inner life was self-sufficient, and though at one extreme he could be wildly gregarious and convivial, he was also able to be solitary for long periods, lost in his own mind. He seemed just as happy without any person near at all.

Except, mind you, myself. Oddly enough, I, who could not bear social isolation, was happy to occupy my own bed and room. Roth, who could continue for months without social life,

began to grow quite mad when I was not with him to hold him
back. My satisfying his patriarchal demand for constant love was
what saved him from being destroyed by his inner demons.

Doubtless he has been spending his last months pretending
to be a noisy and extrovert survivor in that Hertfordshire village,
shaking the local pub to its foundations, frightening the locals,
but I know that, many times, he might kill himself in the night.

That is what made me desperately telephone Kaplan and
Fall.

Yet Roth's dependence on me, coupled with isolation, was
what I had been unable to bear, finally, in Greece.

I felt immured in the nunnery of his mind.

In Greece, Roth's ultimate fantasy was (don't laugh) Tolstoy's,
Gandhi's, Fra Angelico's, St Augustine's, Savonarola's.

Chastity.

Give up the struggle and restlessness! It was 'like being un-
chained from a lunatic', he quoted Socrates. He became excited
by a vision of peace in mind and body, of self-containment, and
of energy preserved for work. Meanwhile he seemed to think he
would be able to feel for me the sensations that he most treas-
ured; desiring me, yet never suffering the tiredness and dullness
of being satiated. Admiring and worshipping an icon figure.

The artist's sensations for his muse-queen. It was the state of
medieval sculptors, architects and stained-glass-makers when
they created their images of Mary. He pointed it out himself; he
knew what he was doing. The fact that they could never possess
Mary was the source of their images' power.

It appealed as a way to deal with his fading erections, about
which he'd been worrying for years. Such nonsense! I laughed at
him. He worried as all men worry; but he, who was more active
than most men, was more anxious than most.

Is the extinction of the light worse for artists, poets and
philosophers? Do they both fear it and in consequence embrace
it more recklessly, their need to conquer fear being stronger than
the desire to live?

'Don't you think that religion has done enough telling us to
pretend to be dead while we're still alive?'

I reminded him of what he himself had said.

But Roth chose it, not for the sake of the peace as he pretended to believe, but for the thrill, the frisson of pain.

For the sake of its intensity. In other words, to generate feelings for his art.

It would not have been so bad if Greece, so bright, noisy and extrovert, had not been terrifying under the surface. Life in those hot countries, where Roth found it possible to create, all floated upon death and madness. The gaudiness that scalded the eyes was ever ready to topple into an equally extreme darkness. Death lurked so near that one was never allowed to take life for granted.

In England, I had never thought of death in such a way. If a rabbit died at the roadside, if a murder was committed, I never thought of it as an expression of the underlying spirit of the place. But when someone died in Roth's chosen homes, it seemed to be the voice of the country, the scream of its history.

I remember first seeing them slaughtering goats for Easter in Greece. In Britain it would have been done discreetly in a shuttered slaughterhouse and the trussed joints, unrecognizable as ever having been parts of animals, would be displayed in a shop far removed from the killing. In Greece they strung the live beasts up by their hooves from trees at busy roadsides. They butchered them in sight of everybody. Of all of us. Me in my Easter dress. They grilled and ate them at tables nearby, even while fresh beasts were being slaughtered. I saw them gloat over the doomed beasts' terror at the smell of freshly spilled blood. They dragged the carcasses through the dust in front of us as we sat at our table. The butcher whose flat we rented in the Peloponnese did that often. It was a torturers' country. They held their dances and fêtes inside butcher's shops, so that a joyful type of music came to be named after these places: *harsapiko*, 'of the butcher's'.

I revere life, and I hated what I saw. The macho, empty-headed callousness. But Roth drew the energy of his painting from this surrounding sense of life's brevity, cruelty and uncertainty.

In Spain, they had called the awareness of death's closeness *duende*, and they believed that art could not be powerful without it. That underlying scream, *duende*, was the true subject of Roth's painting. If some mysterious atavism of the soil did not exist, he couldn't paint.

Meanwhile, I grew more and more to long for a 'normal' life. That is, for a peaceful one. For relationships with ordinary people and to talk to them about their idols of television, politics and pop culture; those figures whose names I did not even know any more after I had been living a self-centred, or, rather, Roth-and-his-art-centred, life abroad.

As the years went by of being wrenched to different parts of the globe, not working myself, I came to feel that I did not exist except as a shadow of Leonard Roth.

I hear his voice burning out of the past. We are sitting in the open air, in the hot shade from a brilliant light, under the pines in which the cones are cracking from the heat. He spreads his big forearms on yet another of the many garden tables at which they have sprawled through drunken afternoon leisures all over the world. I could measure out my life by such times spent with him. This one is in Greece and it is retsina bottles for which his arms leave little room. They are mostly empty bottles, so it doesn't matter that his careless gestures topple them sideways. I know the geography of all the hairs on those arms. Their swirls and their eddies, gold thickening into black. I know their history; for instance, the process of their coarsening during the male menopause; and this is but a minor part of the collected observations in my vast archive of love. In the background, olive trees are noisy with cicadas as I listen to one of his many anecdotes which now scald my memory.

'Titian painted a portrait of the Pope,' Roth announces drunkenly, waving a cucumber in the air in the same vigorous way that he moves a brush over his canvas. He isn't one for watchmaker's movements, for mousy gestures. His face is shining with the cheerfulness with which alcohol warms him. 'The Pope said: "I don't look like that!" '

In one of those inexplicable changes of mood without transi-
tion typical of drunks, Roth looks at me menacingly, as if I am
Titian and he is the Pope. Maybe a pope's expression *is* crazy
with position and theology, as Roth's now is with alcohol.

' "*You will,*" Titian answered,' Roth growls. ' "*You will!*" '

Similarly, have I, Dorothy Gaddis, been transformed into
Dorothy Roth: Leonard Roth's creation? Did nature indeed
imitate art?

Roth dissected life, dissected me, so that he could put me
together again as he wanted me to be, the way he assembled the
ingredients of a painting. I became a figment of his imagination,
and so was ill at ease except when in his orbit. I found myself
looking enviously at women whose personae fitted their characters; they appeared comfortable. I, for my part, didn't know
what was myself, and what wasn't, any more.

He understood how I felt. I told him. He saw it. The strain in
my face.

But we went. That is, he travelled on painting expeditions, and
I went with him. After the first few trips I did not take my own
paints.

Three years in Spain, two years in North Africa, a year in the
Middle East, one year in Italy, a year in Greece, a couple of
years in the Pyrenees . . . I forget where else. Spurts in foreign
countries split Roth's work into periods, followed by vacuums
until he found his bearings again – through more travel.

Did our final quarrels arise because he had reached the peak
of the cycle? Because it was all downhill after that, although he
didn't realize it at the time?

It was on my mind that I was ageing and that I had no
children. No link at all, not even through art, with the future.

I worried that he was instinctively discarding me, his muse,
as Picasso had done whenever it was time for a new type
of work.

If I was going to be lonely, I wanted my pride. I wanted to be
the one to take the initiative.——

31

Roth believed that travel was a simple matter. He never considered the complications. You just got up and went. He enjoyed to childishly wander, for example, the lanes of France, without destination, stopping five miles down the road or fifty miles, for a night or for a month, every day open to choices and to the thrill of what might lie around the corner. If one lived in the right spirit, every walk down the street was an adventure.

Travel rejuvenated the sensations of childhood, when you also didn't understand the language, nor know quite where you were. Everyday objects became freshly interesting. Once more you grew excited by the blue of a train, the green of a bandsman's uniform or the different light reflected in a bottle on a table. You sensed the different air as you walked out of an airport. You surveyed shelves of unfamiliar tins on supermarket shelves and saw once again what you should never have forgotten, that the bands of bright labels were as beautiful as a sunrise.

But one pleasure did not preclude another. He was irked by those who ask if you prefer town life to country life; the north to the south; Greece to Italy. Love of the desert did not spoil his pleasure in the city.

Roth had always been attacked with reasons, either why he shouldn't indulge his travel passion, or why he shouldn't visit the places he chose. Victoria Voyce would tell him that some other type of landscape would be better for his career, 'at this point in time'. Collectors wanted him to return to the site of his last successful paintings. His sister Hannah would moan: 'How can you hope for a family, living that way?'

Political reasons were among the most cogent. It had been for political reasons that friends opposed Roth's decision to visit Greece in 1974, when he had done some striking work. Greece was still under the Right-wing dictatorship of the 'colonels' and Roth was advised not to go for the same reasons that he shouldn't eat South African oranges. The English Left, which filled the artistic and intellectual circles of that day (where were they all disappearing to?), was very strong on shouldn'ts and friends condemned Roth by telling him that he had no grasp of politics.

They were right. He had so little understanding that in the early Thirties he had enrolled as a communist, without considering that he knew nothing about the realities of the USSR. Being young, he played with ideas, welding together everything that interested him, dressing himself in any persona that caught his fancy in an intellectual review. It took the evidence of communist art to change his mind. 'We had hopes of a revolution, something brave and good, and what happened?' he burst out. 'A frightened old woman's art! A timid pecking at the past, dead and dull!' He gave up communism because of the poor quality of its art. He couldn't believe anything that communists said, after that.

Roth learned to resist well-intentioned friends, whether the hammering was with Left-wing ideology or with artistic theory. He must follow the promptings of something subtler, but at the same time grander, and less accessible to reason: himself.

This came only after the discovery of himself, which was in the manner that we all do it: tinged with regret that self-realization comes so late to build a life upon what one truly is, and not what one has decided out of vanity that one would like to be.

It arrived only after he had learned that, while in the trap of other people's expectations, one becomes a compromise. Unless one is brave, selfish or foolhardy enough to make total breaks, one remains an outer skin over an inner secret. Thank goodness he'd had enough savvy to resist their demands to get himself killed in Spain.

At last Roth learned to reply: 'An artist acts out of his inner life, a composite of feeling, instinct, introspection, dreams and reason; not out of reason alone. Where is there any art of quality that can be called, properly speaking, either communist, capitalist or any other "ist"? Art's sources are more complex. We turn to it because it questions and broadens those ideologies and rationalizations.'

This was something that Roth had thrashed out long ago in arguments with his father.

Roth had occasionally taught part-time in colleges of art. First, because he needed the money, when he lived in Hampstead and used to go to Camberwell and St Martin's. Later it was for the sake of the companionship, when he was in Wiltshire and used to travel to Bath. In these institutions, when he said he was travelling for artistic and not for political reasons, colleagues told him that he was making excuses to evade what he found morally difficult. But what were his fellow teachers doing that was so self-sacrificing? Reading the *New Statesman?*

He could never stick academe for long before going back whole-heartedly to his studio. Words had nothing to do with painting; they merely muddied everything. He had learned that as a student, when no one had ever stopped talking.

He would bear it until the suffocation of substituting words for brush marks became too great and he fled. Painting was a revolt from words. It was the activity of those whose sphere of expression is outside words. One of art's appeals was that no one could tell precisely what you were saying. You had to be interpreted.

Even from the earliest days in which Roth's friends had been eloquent with reasons why he should not do as he desired, he had thought it curious how, when you might be about to burst out of the field, people come at you with arguments for clipping your wings. Roth's only regret was that he had sometimes been persuaded.

Artists are selfish. Dorothy, bursting out in anger, said so, often. It was inevitable and necessary. For better or for worse, art could not exist unless the artist was given his head. Generally what one regrets is not what one did, but what one didn't do, and Roth realized how much more rapid his progress would have been towards what, in the end, people liked of his, and how much less damaging its execution might have been to everyone, in the end, if he had always gone straight for what he had wanted.

32

A year ago, in the spring, after they had wintered in Leeds and it had seem particularly drab and inhospitable, they had fled to Greece on the Laverda. Canvases, paints and brushes were transported ahead, while sketching materials were carried on the bike.

Again, they hoped to purge their marriage in light and heat, and to get Roth off antidepressants. At this time he was taking Elavil, but he was still sane enough to distrust drugs and to see the sun as a last chance to cauterize the problems.

As always, they had each made not one journey, but two at the same time. One was a procession of towns, sea and countryside; meals, meetings and paintings. Parallel were the journeys that they were each making in their heads, testing their relationship in a furnace of travel.

Roth had his growing obsession about ageing. He could not look at himself without thinking he had lost height. He moved his shoulders reluctantly, in dread of hearing the bones creak. He felt miserable about himself when he came close to Dorothy's body, for he had been a good lover. Not merely forceful; a good one. ('Less force but more art,' he complimented himself, quoting Rousseau's mistress upon her preference for Jean-Jacques after her episode with Boswell.)

Nowadays, the Roths made love about once a week; depending upon what you called 'lovemaking'. Often it was no more than mutual masturbation to prove that something was still there. Often he merely lay inside her, often not a great deal of the way, and did not come. Sometimes a month went by without their making love. At their age, even to these two expressionists it would have seemed ridiculous to play sex games. On all fours, to chase each other around the legs of the furniture, for example, pretending to be lizards. Their lovemaking was drying up from lack of stimuli.

Although Dorothy said that 'sex didn't matter', he felt that through impotence he was losing her. She knew only too well that what happened with Roth's glands depended upon what was going on in his head, which in turn depended upon what had entered through his ears, eyes and hands, but she wasn't going to do anything about it. They had passed that stage, she thought.

Dorothy, as well as he, was hunting distraction in the pleasure of travel, but what she required to be distracted from was her fear of a nothingness following her having given the best part of her life to Leonard Roth. And her terror of his growing tired of her.

Hence she was impatient with his egoistic fear of losing virility. For too many years she had been watching him disappear into deeper and deeper unrealities which were stimuli for feelings, for art; starting with drugs, then adding mental fantasies. To Dorothy's thinking, Roth's fear was an exaggeration in order to turn normal ageing into yet another fantasy; to turn it to account as feeling.

She wasn't having any.

'Old age isn't bad,' she said, to make light of it, quoting someone or other. 'When you think of the alternative.'

The lands of northern Europe seemed in a terminal phase before they turned into a dustbowl. As soon as Roth reached Normandy, he was given his first intimation that he might be driven to give up painting nature. The earth was sickened beyond recovery, fed with medicines and chemicals.

Perhaps this was exaggerated by northern France having served for so many twentieth-century battlegrounds. It was exhausted. Many cities and towns were still rickety, unrestored cripples. For miles, nothing changed over the new deserts of Euro-farming. The forced and unvaried green produced by herbicides and nitrates, he interpreted as the colours and tones of a spiritual sickness.

They pushed southwards as fast as possible. Thank God it was spring! During the summer, three million hedonists per day would pour down motorway and *peage* – the hell tracks of France and Italy – before seeping out into a diaspora over the south. Already, it was like being pushed through a mincing machine. There seemed little difference between one end and the other except temperature and rainfall. On the way were the rivers in different, lurid colours, purple, yellow or acid green, and the towns under different densities of pollution.

Occasionally the Roths strayed from the main routes. He made sketches at roadsides, in danger from French families who threw their cars around the corners, unable to understand why anyone should linger en route to restaurant, casino or the sea.

The Roths stayed two nights at a farmhouse *chambre d'hôte*. There the door was never locked. Monsieur Bontemps, the farmer, plied the Roths with home-made plum brandy and explained how he trustingly planned to pass his life's work, his farm, into the possession of his sons while he occupied himself with lighter work and the needs of his grandchild. His wife sat knitting by the window. Roth hadn't seen a woman knitting for years. The whole experience seemed a condemnation, reminding Roth that in a great compartment of life, family life, he had not made a success. While Dorothy was playing with a Bontemps grandchild, he hardly dared look at her.

But the Bontemps mode of living could only be found by stepping aside, by following a byroad, pretending that international capitalism and communism, the EEC, NATO, the Warsaw Pact and the pollution didn't exist. If since the 1930s Roth had seen human rights improve – for how could they not improve after the Nazis? – he had also seen the human relationship to the land deteriorate. Everyone who took the trouble to be informed knew that it was the same story from West to East, from pole to pole.

Every square inch of Europe was blood-soaked by warring nations, to what end? That the nations should all disappear. That Europe should be occupied by the new aristocracy of polluting traders who did not care about nationalities. Their boards were international and could meet in or exploit any country. There was plenty of business energy, but none of the spiritual kind.

This trip was different from the others. Crossing the plains and seeing them in this light, he already felt that something was coming to an end, for Europe, for life – for Dorothy and himself.

From Ancona, they crossed the Adriatic on an old ship of the Calais–Dover line, recommissioned by the Greeks and renamed the *Phedre*. Phaedra! She who destroyed her children, as a name for a ship! Already they were entering the bizarrely mad, *duende*-ridden world of Greece.

They arrived in the northern port of Igoumenitsa late at night. Rejecting the offers of 'room-er to rent, you wanna room?' from unsavoury characters who hung around the port gates, and not liking the town much either on their dark-time tour of it – the big, functional, empty bars that seemed all glass and metal; dingy stores where only men sat drinking; the rubbish on the broken pavements – they shot over the mountains of Ipirus and camped by a river where the nightingales sang all night in the thick, deciduous trees by the water.

The following day they settled into their booked hotel in Ioannina. A crate of stretchers, canvas, paints, brushes and paper had been sent there in advance, with breathtaking trust in the haphazard authorities of shipping company and rural coach. Everything had arrived intact. Roth immediately set to unscrewing the crates, assembling the stretchers and pinning on canvases. He arranged paintboxes and brushes on a bedroom table. He did it as if it was the most important matter in the world, not only to himself, but to everyone else.

As always, Dorothy felt a pang of jealousy. She envied his haste to work, his energy, conviction and single-mindedness.

What made him in a hurry to start was what had streamed over his eyes as they crossed the mountains from the river, and even burned his sight from the waste ground visible from the hotel window: the Greek spring. Greece was different from the remainder of Europe, for pesticides and large-scale farming had hardly reached it. There was a creaming of spring flowers. A particular bloom arrived one day everywhere, then vanished as quickly, to be replaced by another. A brilliant rippling of what the Greeks called *orgasmos physos*, 'nature's orgasm', travelled the land. And the perfume! The world was so thickly scented, it was as if he had dipped into a pot of honey.

But for a few days, and as usual in the shock of the south, he was too overwhelmed to paint. He circuited the countryside on his bike, revisiting places that teased him. These lay before his eyes before he fell asleep at night, and yet left him unable to make a decision. He returned to the hotel more exhausted than if he had worked hard.

He was back with old, familiar but exciting feelings of having to adjust to a more intense world. The heat, even in May, seemed to melt the senses he had made use of in the north. If he had brought reproductions of his previous pictures, the brilliance would have rendered them meaningless. When he tried to paint, he could not get used to the glare of the paper on his knee. His sweat dripped on to his colours. He was reduced to stupor and torpor until his only desire was to escape the discomfort, creep out of the inhospitable glare and sleep off the heat. Though anxious to paint, he did not know where to begin.

As he had boldly refused to bring an emergency supply of Elavil to this country where the drug was all but unobtainable, maybe he was suffering withdrawal symptoms? A thought that could make one panic. But he didn't think that was so. It was a matter of getting used to a place. This was a process of simplifying into order, colour, movement and tone which, magically and mysteriously, was a way of finding its underlying spirit.

His advantage was that he recognized his subject as soon as he fell upon it. Having the ability to dream complete paintings, their forms emerging through reveries beforehand, he had known almost before he set foot in Greece what he was coming for. He wanted to invent equivalents in paint for sounds, smells, atmosphere, as much as for the conventionally visible. He wanted forms and colours for the rattle of cicadas and the massive orchestra of noisy insects; for the taste and smell of dust, the feel of thorns tearing the flesh, and the scents of crushed figs and oregano.

He had only to wait. In the end he would abstract out of the confusion, from the torrent of sensations, the spirit of the place; an 'abstraction' of nowhere else but there.

At last he broke through a barrier, and embraced the dressing of flowers. Once he had started he could not stop and he went out at every dawn for a couple of weeks.

He began with watercolours. On blocks of Winsor & Newton's fine-grained, acid-free paper, twelve by nine inches, he made studies out in the open, before the sun grew hot. He nested among the blooms like a bird, a mouse or a child in Eden. To be able to flood the paper quickly, he mixed small jars of basic colours beforehand in his bedroom. On site he worked with tubes rather than blocks of colour. Sometimes he overlaid by drawing lines with watercolour pastels to give him firm, strong marks, which yet could be softened and diluted.

Roth used watercolours first because with a new motif he had to work out a fresh pictorial language. For this he needed to make small, rapid studies, looking intently, analysing colour and tone. Through study after study, not hesitating but concentrating on essentials, he simplified more and more, progressively leaving out what he found did not interest him deeply. As soon as the sketches threatened to turn into decorative abstracts, he went back to his original perceptions of the place.

He settled to haunting an acre of hillside by the ancient theatre at Dodona, forty kilometres from Ioannina. The limestone stairs and seats were swept with red or yellow poppies, flowering grasses and multitudes of other flowers.

There would never be any shortage of fresh subjects, for the wild flowers changed daily as the goddess of the spring moved northwards. As Roth followed her patterns, he felt like a medieval artist worshipping the doings of a saint, or like an atavistic ancient worshipping plants, trees or scents.

After a week he felt confident to tackle a four foot by three foot canvas. Roth, in his bad Greek, negotiated with a sheep farmer for the storage of his easel, oil paints and the canvas he intended to work on for several days; also for bamboo rods on which to stretch a canvas shelter against the sun.

A taxi transported his materials and Roth followed on the Laverda, reaching the site at five in the morning. While a flock of sheep jingled their bells and the helpful farmer sat, paced and circled, full of curiosity, round the hillside, Roth, under his shelter, squeezed his colours around the rim of his palette. He did this in his usual order of warm colours changing to cold, so that he could dip his brush without thinking and still keep his eye on the canvas. He loved the physicality of everything to do with painting. As his body stirred among his paints, excitement ran through him from his toes to his head and the tips of his fingers.

He spent the first day in covering the glaring white, new canvas as quickly as possible. He used the oil so thinned with turpentine that it looked like a watercolour. Thus, in a single span of work, he created the organization and design of the whole picture. Because of the quantity of turpentine, it was dry by the following day.

Then, more slowly, with thicker paint and less and less turpentine, he built up other elements. With half-closed eyes, he adjusted the tones. He enriched colours. Gesture, the direction and speed with which paint was applied, affected the dynamics. The shepherd marked his hesitation from time to time in the movements of his hands.

Nearby, among the thorns and flowers, all day the sheep bells rang through a mutter of scratchings and a warm smell of sheepshit and fur. The shepherd circled and sat. Occasionally he rushed out at his flock with a hissing noise, sat down and then circled once more, obviously mystified by this even more patient, motionless foreigner nearby.

Sometimes the shepherd stared downwards, as if searching for the answer or for something else that had disappeared into the earth. Maybe the old man was uselessly looking for the same thing as himself, the painter thought.

The whole spring landscape of Greece shone, sang, called, cried and mocked with its superabundant potency.

33

——Roth returned to me at noon for a light lunch (olives, tomatoes, onions, feta cheese, olive oil, bread and retsina – often too
much retsina) and a siesta. He was quite a spectacle as he came
down the road on his bike, various artist's objects hung on ropes
around his shoulders. The town paused to watch. You know how
the men have time to sit outside the cafés on the main roads
in Greece, sipping coffee and water, playing with worry beads,
watching.

As Roth dismounted, big, dusty, full of painting, full of sun, as
on so many occasions I felt eclipsed.

For years I had assumed that my own painting had been merely
a phase of my life and that now I 'lived' instead of 'painted'. I
would rather not paint at all than do only a little, ineffectually. The
smell of turpentine gave me nausea and I believed I had become
allergic to it. I convinced myself so thoroughly that there have been
moments when a whiff of Roth's studio and the accompanying
chords of Bruckner, Mahler or Brahms have made me rush to the
bathroom and heave. I have then compounded my masochism by
not telling Roth, or by blaming it on something that made it seem
my own fault. Eating what was not good for me, for example.

Whether he was worried about ageing or not, Roth had plenty of
youth and virility for art. I marvelled at it and recalled what he said
about Beethoven's late quartets: that he was grateful Beethoven
could be bothered to write them. I had thought 'bothered' a very
odd word to use. Of course Beethoven could be bothered! The
eccentric verb seemed more profound when I realized that, in
contrast to Roth, I couldn't bring myself to paint.

I believed that it had to do with my being a woman. Women,

less often than men, can be 'bothered'. This has to do with the fact that, when women do not sacrifice their ambitions for love, they are regarded as freaks. (At least, the women of my generation were.) For men it is the other way round. A man who lets go of his talent for a woman's sake is regarded as a wimp. This is rationalized – by men. 'Men strive for perfection, women for completion,' as Jung put it.

'You have only to think of the basic metaphor of the body,' Roth added, confidently. Oh, *most* self-assured. 'The circle of the womb, contrasted with the erection. There isn't any ideology that can change the physiological facts which lie at the basis of male and female activity, including art.'

Roth might draw upon some female inner self, but in the actual act of putting images on canvas, there is no doubt that he paints with his penis.

I soon felt my familiar strains. Equally familiarly, he failed to notice them. He was too wrapped up in what he was producing. He was swamped by his ego. He was mounted on his penis.

When I talked to him about his first Greek pictures – the wet canvas which, with a great deal of neurotic fuss on the part of Roth, of noisy interference from the driver, was brought back by taxi from Dodona, and the watercolours with their multicoloured streams over the paper – he said he had been 'capturing the spring'.

I thought: There are other times when he talks of art as an act of worship, of submission to a goddess. Yet how easily he uses the language of male domination, and those rapacious words traditionally used to describe the male attitude to an excited virgin! 'Capturing', 'attacking', 'commanding' a theme; 'dealing' with a subject, 'laying' or even 'executing' an idea. He talks about painting as the Turkish pasha in this very town of Ioannina (where Byron had visited his court) might have talked about women.

He paints with his penis, and yet he worries about his physical potency.

I wondered if I might be able to escape from his penumbra. If I might be able to pick up my brush again. If there might be a feminine, nonrapacious, noncolonizing form of art which I could explore.

34

Roth completed two oils. I thought they were good ones. Down the noisy, bazaarlike streets where the craftsmen dwelled – tinsmiths, carpenters, coppersmiths with wares clustered like golden grapes around their doors, iron-workers and manufac-turers of rubber buckets out of old tyres – we took his drawings for his device for a packing case.

We found a carpenter in a shop where on a carpet of woodshavings stood perfectly made tables and cupboards awaiting obliteration under French Empire-style veneers and polishing. He was instructed to make cases that held the two canvases face to face, but separate so that they could continue to dry in transit.

I don't know how the carpenter managed to take in the instructions, for our common language was minimal and he kept looking me over, as Greek men do; even a sixty-five-year-old bag like me, if she is dressed well; that is, not swamped in black as his mother doubtless is. I wore sandals and had toenails painted electric blue, at which he stared and smiled.

The packing case was put together, however. It was late, and involved a foiled attempt to cheat over the price, but was quite well made. A taxi took the crated pictures to a forwarding agency, and we too could move on.

South, south, into the Peloponnese. It was now the beginning of June. In no time, the wild flowers dried up and died. The earth was covered with a golden tinder. The dust was so fine and ubiquitous, it had a scent and gave a texture to the air. Summer was announced also by the deafening noise of cicadas and the whole countryside sizzled as if frying in oil.

The next consignment of canvas, paint and stretchers waited at Argos and we took it by taxi to a small town perched upon the mountains.

The countryside was so vibrantly alive that you could barely look at it even with protected, screwed-up eyes, yet the town was dark and soaked in death. It seemed wrong that the soil there was red; it should have been black, like everything else. It was a place that had been tormented by war since the beginning of its history. The shut-in, narrow alleyways smelled of drains, dust and rotting meat. One-armed or one-legged men sat in the cafés before plates holding boiled sheep's heads that looked as though they had been dug out of ditches or graves. Widows stared; women in black, like charred screams, their silences expressing their agony.

They, and the mutilated men, never went into the countryside for the pleasure of it, but only to labour. While we were there, a man thrashed his teenage daughter for taking a stroll through the olive groves, and her screams rang through the town during the siesta hours. He could not conceive that she might have an innocent reason for her excursion. What, then, did they all think of us, who took walks every day? They eyed us with open curiosity; we strangers who indulged ourselves with smart clothes (relative to theirs), or alternatively had the freedom to be almost nude if we wished to; the freedom to move, move away, go on holiday, work in another country or stay eccentrically here and indulge our mental agony. They sometimes heard us arguing.

We rented a flat consisting of a kitchen, a *saloni*, a shower and two bedrooms. It belonged to the butcher, who chopped up his meat beneath our floor, sometimes until one o'clock in the morning. Our arrangement would have been quickly made if we'd had to deal only with his wife, a woman grim with realism, who obviously handled business affairs. But the butcher had to make continual objections, so as to extend the opportunity to ogle my blue toenails. Our discussions took three hours and involved the opening of two bottles of Metaxas brandy. Even then, the butcher had to come round on the following morning, dressed not in his apron but in his suit.

On the wall of our apartment was a photograph of the exiled King Constantine; the bloody stains of squashed mosquitoes; and, of all things, a cheap oleograph of John Constable's *Salisbury Cathedral from the Meadows*. It was furnished with grotesque items from an unmarried daughter's dowry which, fortunately for our sensibilities, the butcher insisted be kept covered with dust sheets. It prompted the reflection, though, that our stay would be no more than very temporary.

There was no space for a studio, but then Roth painted out of doors.

Out there, in summer as in spring, I'm sure the vitality mocked Roth's sense of ageing.

Nature, in all the places that he chose to face her, didn't give him time to frame her nicely and count up her details. She was either spitting and clawing at his face, scalding him or threatening him with her armies. You need your youth for that sort of fight. Motionless as he was (in itself an image of impotence and age?), I know that the heat attacked him almost unendurably. He painted with a towel over his shoulders to catch the sweat, and continually had to wipe it from his eyes. There were rustlings in the grass. Snakes weren't too much of a danger when one marched through the countryside, because they heard one coming and they were shy, but when one remained still, they might arrive unawares. Hornets and other flies were apt to settle while one's mind concentrated elsewhere. I worried about him; I drank; and I rambled about alone, which I'm sure made the women chatter.

However, his dangers and discomforts compelled Roth to put down only important statements on his canvases, without being tempted to qualify, to weaken them. To see them was what I was waiting for all day. I was excited by the results, anticipating what they would make of them back in England. When working quickly and not on his guard, energetic, compulsive marks could emerge and surprise him, driving up from he did not know what roots.

I think that in the Peloponnese he finally freed himself of the last residues of illustration, uniting mass, form, colour and gesture to express his relationship with nature. People tell me how much they've loved seeing his pictures in galleries. I can't tell you how wonderful it was to watch them growing; the paint still wet.

That had to be my compensation for not having children. His pictures were the most important thing in his life, and it was rapidly happening that our joint delight in them was the central joy of our love.

He could rely upon this marvellous thing happening because of those earlier years, when he had studied nature so patiently. Perhaps only I know with what patience he worked, and with what anguish to be sure he was getting it right. It was the foundation that made the difference. Because he had trained himself to analyse underlying form, by continual life drawing, by creating precise landscapes in his early years, strength was lent now to his most abandoned and rapid self-expressions. I know this has become unfashionable in the art schools; but I believe in it. Roth believed in it.

In the very act of performance, I think he knew that he was creating the best work of his life. An artist always does know this; not with his mind, his hope or his vanity, but because of some inner surge. The old-fashioned word was 'inspiration' – a taking-in of breath: the numinous breath of the muses.

He was mad with the excitement of it. I think that I, too, contributed a little. But he hardly noticed me.

When Roth returned to me at the flat there was a mad look on his face. It seemed like anger. I think it was desperation, after his tussle with light and heat in the dried and swarming grass. But every time I saw him, I thought: Has he found out about the butcher? For if he'd known how often the butcher had come round, smirking – you know what some of these Greek men are like – he would have been angry enough to kill him. I spent much of my time fending off our landlord. I didn't tell Roth. He didn't ask.

A madness out of the furnace of light and heat was expressed, too, in his gait. It inspired the children to throw stones, and the haunted, bewildered men and women to cackle or stare even harder. Eventually, as he daily carried canvas and paint, the people of the countryside respected him and gave him the freedom of the road. It was because he was burdened, and this they understood.

Back indoors, all he desired was rest, and the coolness, and my cosseting. Tipsy though I often was, slugging my way through anything I could get hold of, retsina, sweet red wine, those sugary liqueurs, I always had something fresh prepared for him. Grapes. Cheese. Tomatoes. Myself.

He cleaned his brushes. He washed away the taste of salt lingering from sweat trickling into his mouth. His mind was still swamped by the colour changes of the day, gold turning to hazy violet in the heat, and back to gold under the lowering sun. It was full of the light's shifts over the hills and the movement of slabs of shadow; of the decisions he had made on canvas of where to assemble mass and tone, and at which point to arrest the movements that had wheeled before his eyes all day.

Sometimes he hardly took a glance at me.

He wanted to evade the problems of my drinking, and what it implied: my dissatisfactions. He wanted to complete his painting, and then immediately another painting before thinking about other problems, so he deceived himself that these could wait. He forgot that always in his life there had been another painting to be completed, so problems were always lying unsolved in the wings. All that he talked about was painting.

There have been seminal pictures in his career which have led him into confusion for some time. Unable to grasp the lessons and implications, he was unable to move forward, but neither could he go back. The effect of this upon others, and especially upon me because I was closest, was potentially disastrous. I knew it so well from the past. His temper was deranged, so I knew I mustn't tell him about the butcher. Indecisive in his work, Roth was indecisive in his life also.

At best, it made him impossible to live with. At the worst, I had to fear that something new in his art might mean that I would be abandoned. Even now, at his age, I had reason to be jealous of his eyes surveying the Swedish tourist woman who talked to us once in the café.

A crisis occurred, he was looking for some solution to a canvas, and this time I thought that perhaps I had suffered enough. Considering what else I was putting up with.

He suddenly stopped talking about his problems as a painter. He said that a hardness had come into my face and I wasn't listening. 'What are you thinking about?' he asked me.

'I'm not thinking,' I answered tersely, ferociously. That was our familiar code for *I'm not going to tell you*. I began the habit when we were in Wiltshire and thoughts of babies were on my mind.

I couldn't even begin to tell all that had flooded into my mind. Pouring through a drunken haze, they were the memories of thirty years of unresolved angst.

Way back in 1960 I might have held an exhibition in New York. My enthusiasm for it died as I realized that I would never be able to assemble enough work, because at the very time that I should have been working for it Roth wanted to move from Rosslyn Hill, saying that *he* couldn't paint there, and thus we went to Wiltshire. I hadn't told him how I felt. I simply dropped the exhibition hope and said I wasn't ready for it. I watched for his reaction to this news and found that he hardly felt it. All he seemed to feel was relief that I didn't object to our move.

Often he has complained that volitions in his work have been frustrated but he seemed not to notice that, for me, volition barely got under way.

Here I was, as usual simply waiting, while he painted. An ageing woman, scrubbing off nail varnish in an attempt to frustrate the slaverings of a Greek butcher.

I kept thinking of Ioannina, haunted as it is by old cruelties from the pasha's court. Disobedient women from the harem were drowned in that lake across which I had often stared, aghast. When I thought of those females, I often saw them dancing. That is what women did when enslaved to jaded older men whose appetites had died. They danced, to titillate their senses. Until called upon to dance, they waited. I also waited in limbo. Waited to dance, to amuse.

If I'd informed Roth of my discontents, he would have called it 'carpet bombing'. I have tried to tell him before, and the saturation merely creates smouldering rubble.

My husband, bless him, shares with all neurotics a physiological, paralysing fear of other people's troubles, even those of his wife. It's not that he is an unkind man, or lacking in generosity. As in Cézanne, who also couldn't bear people being close to him, it is an illness rather than a character fault. On other occasions, Roth might spontaneously cut off his arm for a comrade – isn't that odd?

So out of all my secret or at any rate subdued complaints, what could I select that he might understand, or that I hadn't articulated before without effect?

'Tell me what's wrong,' he repeated, more urgently. As if he really wanted to know.

'It doesn't matter. There isn't anything you can do about it. It's my problem.'

I thought: You care more about art than you do about real people, that's what's wrong. You create emotional crises in order to energize your painting. Having encouraged catastrophes, you don't know what to do with them, except in a painting. You don't want to do anything about them. Can't even see why you should. Confronting nothing in life, only in art, has become a habit.

He could not understand why I would not be consoled, would not talk to him, and that night would not make love to him.

He tried to soften the tension by telling me that he was sorry. But he did not even know what he should be sorry for, and I did not respond. He believed that I did not answer because I was crying and hiding it from him.

'This is awful,' he muttered.

It did not help. His egoism again, I thought; he is thinking of himself.

He tried to overcome my resistance with the familiar, first gestures of lovemaking, stroking my thigh. I gave him no encouragement, and it became almost a rape; the kind of squeak and whine in the bedsprings that made the butcher beneath us bang so hard with his cleaver. He seemed to be trying to split sheep and goats in half, that night.

Meanwhile I succeeded in pushing Roth away. Assembled in my nightdress against his side, I felt like a sack of rocks. I was biting my knuckles so that he wouldn't know I was fighting tears. Yet I was also proud and strong. I had said no to him and it had been successful. There was the frisson of a success that I hadn't believed I had the nerve for.

For the time being, I wasn't afraid of him any more. Not spiritually. Physically, maybe, but that didn't matter as much.

35

Even at the height of my anger, either of us might have turned over and the result would have been as intense a lovemaking as we had ever experienced. It would have been a thrill of light after darkness, forgiveness following hate.

But there was something that I had not expected, and of which I became aware as I lay awake. I realized from the subtle movements of his limbs that the risk to our marriage excited him.

What with a frustrated butcher masturbating a meat cleaver into the groins of sheep beneath me, and an artist finding it exciting merely to lie rejected at my side, I, Dorothy Roth, sixty-five years of age (I mustn't keep going on about my age), felt like the Empress Theodora, Catherine the Great or Leopold Masoch's *Venus in Furs*.

A fantasy had taken its grip. That extraordinary phenomenon had recurred to stop us turning in forgiveness towards one another. Now we had gone so far that only the fantasy of rejection itself, with its hanging doubts, its complicity in the perverse, produced that glow. I realized that rejection, as a way of finally defying impotence, was what he wanted.

It suddenly struck me as being a most magnificent hubris: a fantasy that would cheat, if not death, at least old age of its prize.

Now I recalled the manner in which Roth had first admitted his excruciating fear of losing virility, as well as potency. Although we were able to talk openly about almost everything else, instead of telling me boldly what I knew already, that his desire was no longer automatic, he felt the need to whisper the news in the night-time as if he were tempting me with the most delectable of all our fantasies.

On that night in Greece, I felt something pressing against my back. My words of rejection had excited the 'old man' to the erection of a stallion.

We laughed about it afterwards. Something bright had happened. There was fun in the world again.

A few nights later, when lovemaking once more threatened to decline into routine, when I wanted something to drive away thoughts of the butcher and his disgusting shop littered with horrible carcasses, I teased Roth by hinting that this might be the last occasion I would allow him to enter me.

I felt him grow inside me even as I said it.

'The last time for a week,' I added. 'Maybe for a month.'

'Perhaps it will be the last time this year,' I said a few nights later.

As it so wonderfully excited my fading husband, I began to tell him, many times, that this would be 'the last time of all'. No matter how often I repeated this idle threat, in the excitement of the moment he always seemed to believe me.

Soon, I was keeping myself from him for over a week. As it was a game, Roth did not try to make me change my mind. Yet I still loved him so intensely that I could grow moist just by looking at him when he was calmly painting, or sitting quietly opposite me.

Then came the reward of the night we had been waiting for. It was prepared for with full ceremony as if it were the coming-together of Solomon and Sheba. Perfume (Mitsouko, by Guerlain) after a shower, special clothes. Dressed in my exotica (what I had brought with me was exotic in this mountain town), I needed to exert a great deal of effort to avoid the eyes and, by now, the grabbing hands of the butcher. A special meal and wine.

We went through this process several times.

Roth's frisson, wondering whether I had really offered myself for the last time, grew more and more greedy for intensity.

It consumed more and more of our time and energy, like a cancer.

36

Our disappearances into fantasies were marked by a mixture of withdrawal and zombie-like ecstasy, as if we had taken poppers or met the Virgin Mary in dreams. Such states cannot last. Sometimes we found it exhausting to live in the caves of our imaginations. From time to time, one or other of us tried to stop the new indulgence.

'No more of that! No more games! We've had enough!' Roth would announce, smiling over a half-consumed bottle of wine. We would back off and feel relief at being 'normal' again.

Soon I would miss in him some intimacy and yielding, some flow out of his body that came with confessing and fantasizing, and I would make suggestions again. I had little else to occupy me but drink, and my lonely, shocking strolls.

We were hooked. In the excitement of release into the unreal world once more, we would tumble into our great, perverse, joy-pain. And so on, in this cycle, hardly knowing where we were or what we wanted.

As he persisted forcing me to reject him, I began to realize my real anger against him.

We were staying on in this ghoulish place because he was doing such good painting here, yet – odd paradox for a painter – it made him blind.

That was typical of our married life. To the end, he knew nothing about the butcher's advances or why I was averse to going into his appalling shop: the sheep's heads, the cans of huge eyes, the flies, the smell of meat rotting in the heat. In Roth's obtuse blindness, he failed, or refused, to see that I was angry with him for compelling me to reject the man whom I loved.

As on previous occasions, all that could overcome the true coldness I now felt was to remember my previous love.

I was confident that I could keep this business under control, because I felt I understood it. 'Trust me,' I begged.

But having made a start, I found that I had to go on making it steadily more exciting and definite. Naturally, the threats ceased to have effect.

We were continuing to sleep together, and my rule was easily broken. Maybe we were back to back, but before long I would be woken by his newly virile erection. First I would ignore it, then pretend to be angry. Then we made love.

Despite ourselves, despite what we realized and the dangers we had talked about, we found ourselves travelling down a hill without brakes. And I gave many a push to the wagon.

We *had* to go on. Now, if we stopped our teasing games of destruction and rejection, I soon saw what I wanted, what I missed; there was some fountain that could not pour otherwise. It was the fountain of himself. The intensity.

We tumbled again, drew back, then tumbled. At each return, we found it more hypnotic.

I was excited in my own way. I was rid of the age-old slavery of sexual penetration. I felt I was in control and, in a way I had not expected, I was regaining my independence.

I also found that denying sex could be more sensual than fulfilling it on a tired night. After our pact, the aura of each other in the flat, in the café or in the countryside, not touching, knowing that we would not touch in bed either, was ecstasy. This weird separateness was deeply sensual.

It appealed to me as a form of spiritual purity. I've always had a weakness for Christian virtue, you know; the village church, or overcaring for my husband. I closed my mind to the memory of the joy I'd had once and convinced myself that I was released from some tiresomeness, some toiling, some waste of energy, physical, mental and spiritual. I praised chastity as a source of peace.

I told Roth it would help him to concentrate upon his art. I threw back his own argument that he had been giving to sex the energy that he needed for his painting. Look at Van Gogh, I said; the passion and energy he could put into his work because he had to be satisfied with occasional visits to a brothel.

The inspiration did come from Roth – didn't it? Because it was I who was provoked to declare the terms, one could forget that it was he who was manipulating the cruelty to himself. But he certainly was. He was compelling me to inflict pain, in a game in which everything was the opposite of truth. In the real world, things it was necessary to deal with were being ignored, and we were buried so deeply that we hardly noticed. It was this that most filled me with real, not feigned anger, and drove me finally to turn fantasy into reality.

Why was happiness boring him so much that he had to drive us into this mad, cold desert?

He was offering himself as a victim, but to what? What had mankind done that Roth should atone for it? Was it even some twisted, guilty consequence of being a Jew; something that I, a gentile, could not understand?

But it was not that he was seeking atonement. He was hunting pain entirely for the sake of its intensity, generating feelings for his art. ——

37

Roth found himself in a dilemma. He discovered that his work and his perceptions were basically sexual. But he'd known that all along: it was part of the hubris of fantasy that he forgot.

Sexual activity, he also found, did not bleed him of energy. Sex was the way God was supposed to be: indivisible, undilutable. It bred energy. He learned the secret of why Tolstoy wrote so barrenly and so morally after he abjured sex. When his sex was murdered, the openness of his perceptions was murdered with it.

Too late. Dorothy had decided to leave.

It was the end of July; the summer was over and everywhere was burned; if I stay here drinking, it will kill me, she thought. He doesn't even notice.

While making preparations for leaving, she performed tasks as if she were staying, so that Roth did not quite, not *quite*, believe her. He half thought it was an extension of their fantasy.

Their last day held a strained morning and a tender afternoon. While she ironed his clothes with her travelling iron, he exerted self-control to keep his distance, though inside he was torn with desire to get close, keep close, curl up. There had been a moment when at the far side of the room she had stood quite still, offering her lips as in the old days. He had looked at her for a second, but when he stirred, she turned away. He did not follow up his impulse and later he felt that had been their true last moment. Her face then became imprinted upon his memory.

In the afternoon they walked, together but apart, through the countryside, discussing, discussing. Both their faces were

ravaged with tears and they did not care what the peasants
saw.

Dorothy explained that she needed to be by herself to get her
confidence back after a life focused upon his needs. Otherwise
she'd no longer be of use to anyone and dead in a couple of
years. She needed distance between them for the sake of her
sanity and health. She wasn't going to humiliate herself for
him any more, making experiments with life for the sake of
generating feelings that might pass into his paintings.

He pointed out that sometimes it had been she who had
opened the door when it would have been wiser to have kept
it shut.

'Only to please you,' she snapped.

They talked and excused and planned and forgave, as they
had done many times before, until they were so tired that they
went to bed – together – in the afternoon. They were like two
wounded animals, consoling themselves in a burrow.

'I'm sorry, I can't make love,' he said.

'If I thought you could, I wouldn't have come to bed with
you.'

Dorothy told him that she had always feared that the day
would come when she would wake up and find she did not love
him, didn't care. What she had feared most was the loneliness
of that feeling.

'I would like to go to Prospect Terrace and be by myself for a
time,' she said.

'Yes,' he answered.

'I might discover you again, there. Your spirit. But what will
you do?'

'The gallery will find me somewhere to stay.'

They fell asleep, back to back. He awoke finding that he had
turned round to her and she was crying in his arms. They rose,
lest the temptation of lovemaking beckoned. Everything they
did, putting on clothes, staring out of the window, was as
ceremonious as the Last Supper. Every movement carried the
weight of symbolic gesture.

'I cannot bear any more pain being screwed out of me for the
sake of art,' she repeated yet again as, in the village square noisy

with departing passengers, animals and taxis, they awaited the
Pullman to Athens.

She had never thought that her life would end in the
Peloponnese, but here it was, she said; and it brought a sort
of freedom, in its way. Their life together had consisted of great
ecstasy but also great pain. She could never have imagined such
ecstasy; and he was the only passion of her life.

'I'd like to send the pictures to be stored at Prospect Terrace,'
he said. 'I don't want the gallery to have them, yet.'

'I'm glad you trust me.' She paused. 'Good luck,' she whispered.

'And you,' he responded.

'When you know where you'll go, let me know what you want
me to send you from Leeds.' She laughed. 'Pictures, I expect.'

She had looked as people do at sad departures following a
failure: very vulnerable. He was contrite and ashamed at having
let her slide away and was disgusted with his own stupidity.
From the minute he watched her depart, he was anxious for her;
protective of someone whom he was no longer in a position to
protect.

It was amazing what strength Dorothy summoned when she
needed it. She had talked about the tears that she knew were
waiting for her on the journey home, but it was he who, once
he was alone, was struck down; could barely do anything; had
no confidence, only anxieties.

His first action was to go to their regular café, where she might
phone him. He started on imported beer, which the proprietor
thought proper for a foreigner. He drifted into tippling back the
cheap retsina which was drawn out of barrels and sold in flasks;
lightweight flies floating on the surface, heavy ones lying on the
bottom.

She did not telephone. Staggering against walls and olive
trees, he went back to their rooms. He passed the butcher, who
looked pleased with himself. Who seemed to have questions to
ask, but didn't know how to frame them.

Roth stared at the self-portrait he had screwed out of himself
during these last days. Already it looked as though it had been

done a long time ago, by somebody else who used to live in his room. It was the picture of a ghost. It was by a different person. The flat, too, was different. It had the glacial remoteness and silence of a museum. The persons who had once lived in it did not exist any more.

He was fully occupied for a while in arranging the crating and transport of his paintings to Leeds. But after two days he was struck down – as emotions catch up after a death. Trying not to think of her *every* minute of the day, he found that, except for the recall of incidents connected with her, his memory was shot to pieces.

He began what turned into a new life. It was one of planning diversions, in a panic, lest they did not succeed in diverting. Once the paintings were dealt with, he drank more and more heavily.

He found himself howling after her. The first time, he was standing in his room. The next, he was among the olive trees, facing the direction in which she had fled. Sometimes he tried to invoke her by shouting her name, accompanied with grasping gestures of his hands.

After stumbling from a taverna, where his stay had been memorable although he himself could not remember it, one morning Roth awoke gripping the trunk of an olive tree.

He had been there most of the night and was roused by a hot, brilliant morning, of the kind that brings everything and everyone out of doors in Greece so that there are no secrets: everyone's sins, quarrels, celebrations and disasters are on display. The woman who had found him was running back and forth over the burned field, waving her rake and yelling.

The next person fetched to the scene was the butcher's wife. Then came the butcher, grinning contemptuously from the cab of his pick-up truck in which a frozen cow was thawing and bleeding. Half the town quickly turned out to coerce Roth to the doctor. It was as much because the doctor spoke English as for any other reason. Since there was nothing else so important for the crowd to talk about, they waited outside while the mad painter reeled into the surgery.

The doctor appeared to believe that darkness in itself was prophylactic. It was like being in the dream-inducing chambers that cured the sick at Epidaurus. The curtains were drawn and the silent room was filled with dark, high cupboards. Plunging in from the August light, Roth needed time to make it out. Beyond a cluttered desk that was lit by an old-fashioned reading lamp, its light so faint that it mocked the very idea of light, was a leather armchair and a couch. The air was heavy with cigarette smoke, for at eight thirty in the morning, the doctor was already chain-smoking. Ashtrays were full. His dark and bedraggled suit was filthy with ash.

He prescribed Valium, which was Roth's first meeting with that drug.

Immediately after prescribing, the doctor scribbled out his bill, his tongue between his teeth and licking his thumb as he wrote, like a semi-literate tradesman.

38

Dorothy did not give him a chance to forget her. After a short silence, she wrote or phoned the café almost every day – which did not help him to stop drinking. He thus traced her route through Greece and Italy, but she told him where she had been only after she had left. He had a week of struggle, or was it two weeks? He couldn't remember. Then he followed her, having made an astute guess that she would linger in Florence, after she wrote him such a tender letter from there.

The midsummer city was crowded, gaudy and savage. The drifters of Europe and America gathered on the Arno Bridge, or squatted under the walls of palaces. They wore different clothes to Renaissance times, rode motorcyles instead of horses, but otherwise it was the same scene of the beggars and the poor outside the walls, while the rich were inside the palaces. Now the rich were the tourists, looking at art. Roth was even caught up in a knife fight on the Arno Bridge. The spirit of Florence, savage with the contrast of rich and poor, magnetic because of its creations, had not changed.

Roth did not need to make his way to their friend Maria's flat. He bumped into Dorothy in the Piazza della Signoria: one of those spots on the earth's crust where, if you pause for a moment, someone is certain to poke a camera in your ear, flash a light bulb in your eye, or you will be swamped by people pouring out of a coach. The crowds barely gave a glance at the architecture, sculpture and painting they had supposedly come to see. Their guides barely allowed them to, as they shepherded and hurried their flocks, who stared at their guides, with their

flags, blue, orange, white, as if that, and not the art, was what
they had come for.

In this confusion, two eyes met. Old wife, old husband.
Above them, Donatello's sculpture showed Judith raising her
knife to behead a kneeling Holofernes.

Dorothy was still not too old to blush and be confused with
delight. They stared and smiled at one another over coffee.
When Roth took his pills, Dorothy's heart almost stopped with
love. She thought – still she thought – that it was only she who
could hope to cure him.

Then Roth made the mistake of taking Dorothy to the San
Marco Monastery.

It turned out to be a mistake because something else was
there besides, at the top of the stair, the ethereal Fra Angelico
Annunciation. Down the passageways, they entered the cells.
One after another showed the cruel, crude, bloody, masochistic
pictures painted by Fra Angelico's fellow monks whom, futilely,
he had trained to paint, and who believed themselves to be
imitating the master. The disgusting, split-open heads of Peter
the Martyr, spitting blood. These cruel pictures must have
driven the sensitive Fra Angelico mad.

As the air seemed full of bad omens, they let go of one
another's hands. At the end of winding passageways, they
entered Savonarola's cell. Before his public burning in that
square where Dorothy and Roth had met, the heretical monk
had been granted two rooms, a window in each. Each window
was closed with a heavy shutter. Within it was another very
small shutter, about eight inches by four. If the monk could
not resist peeping out, hanging in one of the peepholes was
a small but perfect bronze model of a devil's head, grinning
voraciously, horns erect and tongue hanging greedily. In the
other peephole there was the head of a monk, presumably to
remind Savonarola of the most specific of all temptations in a
monastery: the flesh of one's fellows. Thus the ascetic, if daring
to take a glance out into sanity and life, into the sunlight, the
garden, was driven back to the perversity of those cells –
their paintings of crucifixions awash with blood, of the devil

rising from every conceivable temptation, even from a goblet of wine.

The monastery reminded Dorothy of their own claustrophobia. She knew too well the horror of this succulent turning-in upon oneself, this dreadful temptation to isolate and consume oneself in secrets and fantasies.

It was the one temptation that even the monks had succumbed to – had in fact cultivated – while resisting so many others. To live so totally in one's inner life, whether as monk or painter, was a form of exile. The whole monastery demonstrated not transcendence and spirituality, but how one could choke upon internalized life.

Dorothy ran out of the building. Oh, to be in the bright, clean light, with the sun on the clean, green leaves of the lemon trees!

But perhaps it was impossible to escape the darkness, once one had stepped into it. The inner world had savage claws.

Roth chased after her, in panic that she was ill. Whenever she was ill or clearly unhappy, every other concern fell away and all he felt was a need to be near her, to comfort her.

She could no longer stand their life together, Dorothy told him. He was two people and she never knew which one she was with, her lover or her destroyer. Their life together had grown like that horrible cell, with its two small windows covered by padlocked shutters. She prophesied schizophrenia for him. She was afraid of him and wanted a divorce.

39

In mid-afternoon, the drab light of Leeds seeping into the room, Dorothy drained another bottle of Moët et Chandon. Earlier, she had sipped steadily, but there always came the point when the alcohol took her over and it was like plunging into a fire.

She felt herself hovering on the brink.

Before it happened, she telephoned Victoria Voyce. She asked for Victoria and no one else. A woman-to-woman chat was on her mind.

'Mrs Roth! What can I do for you?'

The tone struck Dorothy as over-brisk. She wondered why, and it made her switch to addressing the gallery manager as 'Miss Voyce', which was not a good start to an intimate conversation. Incoherently garrulous, Dorothy tried to list her complaints, starting with the price they'd let the last batch of pictures go for. Roth never noticed this kind of thing, but despite their separation she had managed to keep in touch to some extent and she'd seen the accounts. A few thousand pounds each for pictures to Fondation Moderne – whatever that was – didn't seem a lot of money.

'Have you sampled Sam Fall's champagne?' Victoria Voyce interrupted, gaily.

'How did you know about that?' Dorothy felt stung. 'Can you smell my breath? Are your spies in the street?'

'Now, now! Sam Fall said he might send you a crate of Moët et Chandon to celebrate the last sale. We did put a couple of pictures through recently. Perhaps you haven't heard. The champagne was just a kind thought. Nothing sinister.'

'How much did the canvases go for?'

'Offhand, I really can't tell you, Mrs Roth. In fact I'm not sure that I should.'

'A crate of champagne is a very nice present, Miss Voyce, but not when it's to celebrate a canvas going for less than it's worth. That's what's been happening.'

'It's difficult to sell your husband's work at the moment, because he doesn't send in anything new and his career is suffering a longueur. In our opinion we're doing rather well for him, under the circumstances. I think we might already have a buyer for one of the Greek landscapes you let us have. We have talked about all this before, you know.'

'If Roth isn't working, it's probably because of the drugs that he's being pumped with. It seems, with your support or advice.'

'He needs them.'

Dorothy dropped her defensive tone and broke down, pleading.

'Miss Voyce, I have to tell you, because I believe you'll understand – I'm at the end of my tether with worry about him. I'm – yes, I'm drinking, I'm drinking myself silly. Listen, Miss Voyce! You must understand how I feel . . .'

Dorothy hesitated.

'Has Roth been to see you? Is he with you now?'

'No! Should he be?'

'I only wondered – thought perhaps he might.'

'Miss Voyce . . .'

'I'm listening.'

'There's a man around the corner from here who's been on Tofranil and other drugs for some time. Mr Parker. He stays in bed all day because his senses are deranged and he can't relate to his family. His social relationships have broken down. He keeps the curtains drawn because he can't bear the light. He's a cabbage! At one moment he's high and a bit of the old Mr Parker comes back, who was a great storyteller, I'm told. A famous bon viveur in the public houses. The next minute he's in depression. He's an awful sight, sweating all the time. His eyes are glazed. You should see him. Then you'd be able to understand what's on my mind. For pity's sake, try to help!'

'Calm down, Mrs Roth. There must be something else wrong with your friend.'

'There isn't! It's just side effects from overdoses. His wife's an intelligent woman. She's watched it happen, steadily.'

'How long has he been on medication?'

'Oh, years. Ten years.'

'Roth's only taken the drug during this last year, Mrs Roth. Please keep it in proportion, for your own sake.'

'And he's not as bad as that – *yet*! But he's on his way.'

'Please don't worry, Mrs Roth. We are all concerned about your husband's welfare. Perhaps he needs another short rest in the clinic. He couldn't have anywhere better than Kings Langley, you know.'

'Miss Voyce, if Roth is put away again, he'll kill himself! Please listen! I *know* he will. He'll stash away a supply of pills, get someone to bring in a bottle of whisky, and he'll end it all.'

'Mrs Roth, take a hold of yourself. Your imagination's running away with you.'

'I *know* him.'

'Well, no one cares more than we do at the gallery. We do have a stake in his future, after all.'

Or in his death? Dorothy didn't have the nerve to come out with it. She wasn't even conveying to Miss Voyce that she was suspicious.

40

Near Sheffield, Roth first hit a truly northern landscape. On both sides of the motorway was the flattened land, littered with bricks and bits of wire, where British Steel had once operated. His mind inventing rosy pictures, he had forgotten how much dereliction there was.

Looking beyond, Roth could see a line of hills. They were ten miles away but he knew what was there. A scribbling of walled, grey lanes, a sprawl and tangle of stone villages. Breaking the moorlines were outcrops of millstone-grit rock. Soon, he would reach it. His head spinning, his heart pounding, dryness in his mouth, he accelerated through fast traffic, straight down the outer lane, ninety-seven miles an hour. He made it to over a ton, his face caressing the petrol tank.

The faster Roth went, the more he seemed in command of a huge, invisible drawing over the earth's surface. He knew that the greater the speed, the more dependent he was on meagre threads; the thin wire of a brake cable, nuts and bolts of suspension, thin rubber tyres. He with his faculties impaired. Okay, okay! At least he was on a high, for once. That not better than a depression? He was flying. He was a tightrope walker, balanced on the string of his hallucinations. If he was giddy, why blame the Tofranil? Wasn't it the excitement of flight?

He loved the Laverda for being dangerous. Like all motorcycle masochists, T. E. Lawrences of the motorways, though he was skid-fodder at one hundred miles an hour, yet he was blissful.

He pushed the machine on. Daring to take his eye off the road, he saw that he was doing a hundred and ten. But he still had good eyesight and concentration. Even impaired, it was better than that of any cop on the road. No one could catch him. He had outwitted police cars before, and loved the chase.

As he shot off the motorway, a police car appeared behind him, but it was not until he had slowed down for the junction, and although the cops took a good look, he was not followed.

In the crowded, old industrial valleys of West Yorkshire, they were tearing down a dead world. He had forgotten all this demolition.

He saw frantic activity, angry, frustrated, unhappy and a little bit mad, with an energy that sprang from the destruction. There was so much wreckage on either hand that no one else, apparently, took notice of even half of it. Factories everywhere were demolished or half-demolished. Almost every house and alleyway corner had its own bit of private wrecking going on. Someone would take down a wall and leave the stones by the roadside. Old doors and window frames had evidently been left, sometimes for months or years. Destructiveness was a release from the ancient, tribal sense of injustice in the factories.

Roth glimpsed a chap absorbedly drawing his brush loaded with green paint around a hole in a rotten door. So used to seeing broken things, he mustn't have realized there was anything foolish in preserving a rotten door. Nobody seemed any longer to understand what to destroy, what to preserve and what to build.

Roth smiled to himself. He had once heard of someone in West Yorkshire who stole an abandoned railway station, taking it away, stone by stone, lorryload by lorryload, without British Rail knowing about it for months. It was eventually found in a garden, resurrected for peacocks or ornamental ducks or fancy sheep, or some such genteel-rural fad.

His eye caught a sign, badly painted on the wall of an old factory: *Hire a reck. £4 a week*.

On other walls was written a single, anarchic, unequivocal message: FUCK OFF.

How strange the mind could be, building up a perversely blind love of a place because it was familiar. He had preserved the memory of a region that was warm, kind, excitingly chaotic.

One that could be hospitable to all, because of the diversity of its history and its types. Now he found the correlative of what was angry and bitter inside himself.

The truth was that Roth's home no longer existed and his real home was in his mind. It was in the old myth of an original paradise, which had never existed except as a metaphor for the womb. Maybe Roth's home was only to be found in that intangible, still unrealized, tantalizing painting which flickered at the back of his mind; the one that had glowed since his youth and of which his separate pictures were fragments.

The landscape was rejecting him. A deep anger poured out of every wound. People burned anger here as they used to burn coal, getting life and energy from it. This was what Rebecca Marx apparently understood. Soon there would be riots, of a kind unintelligible in Ashby.

'It's gone! It's over!' the grey summer sky cried. 'Go away! Get free!

'FUCK OFF!'

Roth did not fuck off. Filling in time, he drove around West Yorkshire with the anger of a bluebottle trapped in a jar.

He parked his bike in a crowded coach park by a river. Once he stopped moving, he felt dizzy again and had to cling to a wall. Only his trajectory could keep him balanced and alive. His eyes in any case could not focus. His mind could no longer hold more than a single obsession – that of the confrontation that had brought him here. Some thought like that would be vivid for a time, then it would vanish; it was like painting on snow.

By now, he was way beyond blaming Tofranil. In fact, he believed he needed another dose. How much had he taken today? He couldn't remember. O Lord Jehovah, his mouth was dry; his heart was beating; he must have more pills soon.

Keeping his eyes lowered to guard his footsteps and to shield him from the hurt of light, he joined other crumblies who were pouring out of the coaches, and legged it towards a Tea Shoppe. Ah, yes, this was Holmfirth – he realized where he found himself. A television comedy series had made the town like a medieval shrine to saints. Postcards and mementos of the actors, and guides to the sites, were displayed in shops which originally had provided the functional ironmongery and dowdy clothing of a mill town.

Although the café was busy, the rattle of teacups and the rustle of plastic macs was almost the only sound. Roth sat at a gingham-covered table in a forest of goods for sale; corn-dollies, antimacassars, stripped pine and tourist books. Jocular verses warned that anything broken had to be paid for. They must have had many breakages because it was difficult for anyone not a midget to move at all. Visitors, compelled to creep around like mice, were frigid with silent gentility. Hannah would love it. He could bet that she watched the comedy every week.

(He ought to visit her, but he couldn't face the lecture, the advice and the quizzing.)

A girl in a frilled, pink pinny brought Roth his tea.

The old folks munched and stared silently, balefully, like grazing cows, as he arranged his pills upon the tablecloth.

'One . . . two . . . three . . . No, not like that!' he scolded himself, loudly. 'Try this way!'

Even the rustle of macs and teacups had ceased. He was in a silence like the end of the world. He didn't even notice.

'One . . . two . . .'

He looked up and realized that hurriedly averted eyes had been staring at him.

'Good afternoon!' he announced into the general air.

Sets of eyes returned him furtive looks of alarm, then buried their glances back in the teacups, afraid of causing trouble.

'I said, "Good afternoon!"' Roth insisted a little more loudly, refusing to act humble because of his dreadful appearance. He settled his ferocious glance upon a gent wearing a tam o'shanter, clutching a folder that announced: *Nora Batty's Wrinkled Stocking*.

'Good afternoon,' the gent whispered.

'Don't cause trouble,' his lady hissed.

Roth popped the Tofranil, one, two, three.

The frightened flock at one table was rising and fleeing.

Roth stared hard at the backs that were ignoring him. 'Do they execute you if you speak in here?' he asked.

Others were leaving. A stampede was commencing. The woman behind the cake stand looked terrified.

The tam o' shanter gave Roth an embarrassed smile and fidgeted with his envelope. It was meant to be decently inaudible, but you could pick up any sound in here; the fall of a cube of sugar into a cup, the quiver of a leaflet.

Roth rocked back on to two legs of his chair, and as he watched people leaving the café, he plucked a large book of sentimental photographs of Yorkshire from a stand. He flipped through the lush colour plates – sheep and meadows, moors and woods; pretty stone villages with not a modern building or motor vehicle to be seen.

Views appeared to be graced merely because the author declared that once he had stood and looked at them.

The little waitress was at his elbow. She had that dull, bland appearance of a Jehovah's Witness.

'What do *you* think of this?' he asked her, as with his oily thumb he obliterated a lichened church tower.

'I'm sorry, sir,' she whimpered.

'Tell me what you *think* of this stuff you sell. It's not your fault.'

'Excuse me, sir, I must ask you to leave,' the woman behind the tea urn interjected.

'Ah, fuck!'

Roth rose, noisily, clumsily.

'This is my fucking home!' he shouted.

He upset a rickety little table draped with bedspreads, antimacassars and aprons.

'Okay, okay! I'll pay for it.'

'Sir!'

'Okay, then! Fuck it!'

The café was now only half-full. The torpid movements of those who were accustomed to dying slowly and politely over tea and cakes, whom no event would shift and who would probably sit through a fire, became completely frozen.

Roth still had the offending book in his hand.

'Fucking visual chewing gum!' he shouted and, fulfilling the impulse he'd nursed for some time, he flung it at the window, which shattered in a spray of light, like a water-fall.

At last, the shop sprang into pandemonium. Even the most decent crumblies were knocking things over while they shouted – yes, at last, shouted – for the police.

Roth was out of the shop, running down the hill, sorry because he had not left the poor girl a tip.

Time, at last, for Roth's first drink. And more pills – or had he? – no, so far as he could remember, he hadn't swallowed them, after all, in the teashop.

Country pubs had not yet opened their doors. To find one that he remembered – the Fleece, was it called? – he was compelled to lock up his bike and walk through town streets that had become a pedestrian precinct; first they had been cobbled, then tarmacked, and with changing fashion they had been recobbled. He shared this lonely place with two lovers and a bearded man lying horizontally with a bottle in his mouth. Still stumbling against walls, chuckling over his memory of the faces in the teashop, he found his pub among the altered streets. Seeing at the bar a glass box displaying sandwiches – bright-red tomato and bits of slippery ham – Roth, though still without appetite, remembered how little he had eaten that day, and he took something out of duty. He did not speak to anyone, except to make his request. Roth might have been the better for some casual talk, but he felt as much a stranger in his home district as he had in any foreign country. He sat alone in a corner with his pint of beer and his sandwich. He swallowed six pills, after due consideration of the pattern they made on the tabletop.

Looking slyly out of the corner of his eye, he saw them. *They* were watching him. *They*. He could see them lurking in corners of the pub, pretending to be nonchalant tramps, lovers, or strays out of offices who were waiting for buses home. You think you can kid me? To hell with them. Probably half the police force in West Yorkshire were out looking for him. Did he care?

He hadn't earlier, but he did now. He neurotically sensed persecution in the air. His hands were shaking. His stomach was churning with junk food. What was his mind stuffed with?

In a mirror, he saw that his face was white. He existed in a different world from anyone else. The space between him and others was an invisible frontier. When the barmaid, too, eyed him suspiciously – has she called the police? – he guiltily left.

It began to rain. Everywhere seemed full of stone, because it was wet. Along the valleys, winding miles were shining like broken glass. No police were trailing him yet; a panda car came towards him, surveyed him as the police do survey the rider of a powerful bike, but did nothing.

Roth, with a mixture of drugs and alcohol making his brain as murky as the bottom of an old canal, at last made his way to Leeds. Approaching headlights splashed on his windshield like hot wax, running and melting. What leaves had managed to emerge were already being torn from the trees. Some had turned yellow without the interlude of summer and they splattered on the fairing. All was grey, or grey-blue, with the odd touch of unseasonable, sickly yellow. The only flowers were the television sets in dark windows, entertaining the older folk who had driven bored youth out to scream through the towns looking for the apocalypse.

He went through Leeds centre, along the Headrow, and at the far end turned left, through what had been the Leylands and was now a desolated area of road junctions and high-rise offices. Not a home to be found.

In Harehills he reached the first belt of surviving houses, where there were now as many Pakistanis and West Indians as there had once been Jewish tailors. Doors, windows and brick walls were painted yellow and purple. Gardens, gutters and roofs were as neglected as those of huts in a place where one might expect earthquakes, famine, droughts and floods to remind the inhabitants that life is temporary and fragile. Death-wish Pakistanis and West Indians were crashing gloriously around the streets in their beat-up old cars, and it gave the area an atmosphere of Calcutta or Port-au-Prince. Indian children in silks were playing on the pavements. The little girls, in emerald and silver, had their skirts lifted by the breezes. It was very different from those districts where you hardly see people but only hear their stereos and choke in their car fumes.

In this notorious area, peaceful in the daytime, was embedded Prospect Terrace.

In appearance, the terrace had survived as an island of Edwardian sedateness. Except for its incongruous inhabitants, the street was the same as it had been in Roth's childhood. The rows of bow windows on either side were still intact, even preserving their original gloom. In Roth's boyhood, all the streets of middle-class Leeds had been faced with doom-laden front rooms, only used as places in which to lay out the dead or entertain the half-dead, once in a while: visiting aunts, rabbis and priests.

Roth parked at the end of the street on a 'landscaped' parking space where houses had been demolished. He padlocked his helmet to the handlebars.

On his feet, once again he had to lean upon something. He paused for a moment, panting, until he felt the blood return to his face. He heard music and other noises down the street.

Strangers were drifting towards the party. Okay, okay! This is it! Feeling for his house key in his pocket, Roth walked down the road, slapping his palm with his gauntlets.

Roth arrived at the façade of his home. Gagging with emotion, he surveyed it for a moment, his glance starting at the roof and the gutters, running downwards.

The door was open and he walked into the crowded hallway.

41

Imagine! At my own party I saw Roth's tall, black, rabbinical figure. In that instant, that is how I thought of him. I know I was drunk. But I saw a rabbi striding over the tundra, over the central European steppes. A fierce ghost out of history. It was as if Jehovah himself had walked in.

Roth, though he had supposedly spurned his Jewish background, grew steadily more Jewish in his nature as he grew older, becoming like his father: dogmatic and mad. He looked so menacing. I did not yet know that he'd been tearing around his homeland like a black avenging angel.

In a second I was flooded with the old claustrophobia, hatred and fear. The fear was natural enough. The hatred was because of my fear. In truth, I was hating myself for being afraid, and was turning it upon him. And it was love, too, love, which was turning into hatred because it had been blocked.

A very female mixture, as I told myself at the time.

I moved towards him. What else could I do? He had already got into the front room. I suppose I could have shrieked. Or waited for him to do something. He himself, I noticed, did not stir.

I was aware of no longer being dressed in old trousers and jersey. And glad, too. Isn't that odd? While living alone I had drifted into the company of that doleful, extended family of women who have suffered bad experiences of men. These were the people I had invited to the party, and I had intended to wear the type of clothing that they wore. Track suits and trainers. Then I changed my mind and put on a summer dress that I had not worn for a year.

For, believe it or not, I had half expected Roth to turn up. Mind you: I had thought this before today – for instance, it struck me a week ago, in the way Roth and I have often known what the other was doing or thinking, even when we were miles apart.

I was wearing a loose dress, elaborately patterned with flowers. It was one of his favourites and he used to claim that he could smell the flowers. I was 'like a herbaceous border', he said.

There seemed to be no one else in the room but he – you know the cliché. I know we were both drunk; the state in which clichés are so haunting. But there *was* an aura around him. His appearance had raised the temperature of the sex war already simmering in the room. My guests, like a herd of nervous gazelles, continued to graze upon each other's conversations, yet their tension registered the presence of a nearby beast of prey. There was a certain jerkiness of movement. Sentences were abandoned partway through, as glances were snatched at him.

I was smiling, or trying to, but Roth continued to glare. Why was he glaring?

'Why did you let those bastards take my pictures?' he said.

Oh, that. The question I had been dreading having to face, sooner or later. Believe it or not, it had slipped my memory, temporarily.

I came close to that familiar bulk, smelling of bike oil, turpentine, linseed oil, leather, sweat. I was already hypnotized by love. As of old, once more I was preparing to act out of character, to adapt myself to him. I disliked myself for it, even as I clung to my smile. It was as if my smile were on another person's face, or carved upon a mask. The mendacious words were already forming in my mouth.

(Of course, all this is how – I think – I remember that I felt.)

This was not the time to answer his question about his pictures. But he repeated it. The disarming pleasantries that I had ready-formed, and of which I am ashamed, melted in my mouth.

'They only took one or two,' I said. 'I had to let them have something, to get them out of the house. The best ones are still in the attic.'

I put my hands over my face. What a start! What shall I do? I looked up again.

'Roth, I don't want you to leave, not now that you're here. But please behave yourself! Don't spoil this for me. Let's not talk about the pictures now. Let's have *some* minutes of peace between us. Eh?'

As shorthand for all that I could see was wrong with him, I added: 'You look so tired.'

Roth smiled, God bless him.

'I don't care about pictures,' he said. 'I care more about you.'

It wasn't true, but I appreciated the intention. 'What have you been doing?' I asked.

He laughed. I knew he wanted to touch me.

'Drove around a bit. Threw a book through the window of a teashop in Holmfirth.'

'You *what*?'

I burst into a loud laugh, too, which was partly hysterical, and I leaned my body in his direction, like a tree in a wind.

When I looked up at him, he seemed rather pleased with himself, like a child.

'My God! Oh, Roth, Roth, my darling!' I leaned fully on him, now. That chest.

'You don't change, do you?'

His arms were about me.

'What about the police?' I asked.

He merely wrinkled his nose.

I touched it. 'You're crazy,' I said.

'Mitsouko!' he exclaimed.

'I'm glad you're here,' I said. 'Why don't you take off those stinking leathers,' I added, standing back. 'They're filthy. They're old-fashioned. Why don't you get some new ones? You look like George Formby in *The TT Races*.'

There was a memory! I hadn't intended to touch something as deep as that. We went together to see Formby in *The TT Races* three or four times in – 1952?

'Stop nagging me,' he said. 'Let's have a glass of wine. I'm not on a bender.'

'Roth, I've been so worried about you. You can't imagine . . .'

'*I've* been worried about *you*.'

He sounded a bit cross, as if it were a complaint.

'You look hot.' I spoke quickly. I wanted, somehow, to keep him off drink. 'Why don't you take those leathers off and put them upstairs? Hang them behind our bedroom door,' I added, quietly.

I suppose I had been talking to him for ten minutes by now, concentrating exclusively on him. I think we must have been interrupted from time to time, but do you know, I cannot remember that. I remember no more of my party than one might recall of the crowd in a street that is the background to an accident. While he was away, I flung myself into my neglected duties and thought: already I'm sacrificing my own life, and what I should be doing, for him.

When he came downstairs again, I recognized the same clothes he'd been wearing for years: those old, black, paint-scabbed corduroys and a woollen check shirt.

He was making, not towards me, but towards the bar.

'Roth, come and meet . . .'

I struggled to divert him, but he was pushing through my guests with the blind, drugged purposefulness that I know so well; that I so much dread.

'Roth, oh, please!' I was tugging at him. 'I'm so worried about you!'

'Worried?'

As if it were the most surprising suggestion in the world; as if he had forgotten what I had said, and what he had said, too.

He filled his glass to the brim. He used never to do that with wine. I loaded a plate with food for him. I didn't need to ask him what he wanted – he used always to let me feed him, as a mother feeds a child. I heaped up Lancashire cheese, celery and brown bread.

He was slopping wine on the cloth.

'That's your mother's cloth,' I scolded.

'Why worry about me? I'm all right. Who the hell are all these fucking numb people you've filled my house with? You've not let them into the studio, have you? Is it locked? Are *you* painting?'

'How many milligrammes have you taken today?'

'Oh, I don't know. Fifteen, maybe.'

'Fifteen?'

'Maybe twenty. To be honest, I forget.'

'You *forget?*'

'I forget, fuck it.'

I tried to take the glass from his hand, but I stumbled against his chest as, smiling, he held the glass high above my head.

'You're drinking it as if it was beer. Where's your bike?'

'At the end of the street.'

'Are you going to stay with me tonight?' I pleaded.

Isn't it pathetic. But I couldn't let him stagger away on that bike. He had fought his way to see me. That was very moving.

He did not even deign to answer me, but surveyed me with an archetypal look of male victory. Having captured me, he was holding me in suspense until he decided whether he wanted me or not. Isn't that dreadful? And it was my own fault. I didn't know whether I was resentful or pleased. My friends would be horrified. Agamemnon must have looked at Clytemnestra in that way – before he knew what was coming to him.

Perhaps that was the reason she threw the net over and stabbed him in his bath.

And I kept hiccuping, from the Moët et Chandon. I haven't mentioned it, but I'd burped several times already.

'Yes, I'd like to stay,' he whispered at last, though it was hardly audible. And by then I had become angry.

'Come and meet some people,' I said.

I led him off.

He hated being led.

'My husband!' I announced, proudly. 'I'd like you to meet Roth.'

42

Even though it was summer I had built up a huge fire, for the sake of being welcoming, and the pair of us settled on a rug on the floor. Between us stood a bottle of white wine, a freshly opened bottle of Moët et Chandon, and two glasses, the correct ones for the drinks. We forgot about drunkenness. Gave up on it. I felt it was only by being drunk that I could care a bit less about all that had been on my mind for so long. To hell with it. I decided to enjoy the relief of flowing with the tide. Who cares?

Level with our faces, legs were dancing. Lights were pulsing and music was lilting or throbbing. I couldn't tell you who was putting on fresh records for me. I can't tell you anything about what was said to me; only what Roth said. I never imagined I'd abandon my party to run its own course like this; but then, the best parties are always run by the guests. I expect the word had gone round that we had much to straighten out. These women were used to straightening-out sessions. They spent their lives on them, and never got anywhere. They understood us.

At any rate, we were hardly disturbed. I felt lying between us a tenderness that was both massive and terrible. Yes, terrible. It was frightening in its rawness. I knew that over its horizon lay greater hurt.

I couldn't possibly let him leave in the state he was in, and yet I knew it wasn't going to work with Roth, finally. The impression his entrance had made on me was an image nailed in my brain. The tall, rabbinical figure, mad as his own father had been, smothering me.

I remembered too clearly how in Greece he had refused himself to me for the sake of a frisson; his own frisson, yet making it look as though I were doing it to him. Cat and mouse.

Our lives had been a horror movie and could appropriately be filmed in blood Technicolor.

I couldn't go through that again. Sooner or later, I would have to tell him that there was no going back to the old ways; too much blood under the bridge. I knew that we had reached our finale. Yet I had asked him to hang his leathers behind my bedroom door, I had asked him to stay, and this made me dread the more having to tell him, eventually, that our life together, if not our love, was over. For our few remaining years, some solution had to be found to save us from gobbling each other. I had no idea what. Although I couldn't look after him, I was certain that a further stay in hospital would kill him. But more than ever before did I know that for the sake of my sanity, I must remain firm.

We sat there for, oh, I don't know how long. Sometimes Roth was cross-legged and I was lounging; sometimes it was the other way round. Though I was drunk I can remember every moment, every movement, every word, every expression. What I find difficult to recall is how long it lasted; it seemed eternal. Today, I can unroll it before my eyes like a film, any time I want to.

Sometimes a spark fell out of the fire and Roth picked it up. I was amazed that it didn't burn him. He did it so quickly with his nimble, tough hands. Sometimes we were nudged by the legs of the dancers. Occasionally we put out our hands to touch or stroke one another, to fill or lift a glass, while we talked, talked, talked.

We had the whole past year of intense life to catch up on. Through a drunken haze, we bludgeoned those great subjects that matter to a pair at the end of a long life. I think we believed that some truth would be hammered out, at long last, like a fine oil out of hard seedcases.

I went for two more bottles of wine. As I returned, I swirled my dress. It was a girlish gesture that I could not help making. I was soon embarrassed by it, thinking it showed how drunk I was. But Roth looked pleased. He told me that he had missed me: catching up on my party duties, I surely hadn't been away for long. It was so bitterly ironic that our missing one another felt like the old days in Hampstead when we met.

We sat together and touched again.

'There must be a reason for all this pain. A purpose to it . . .' I began.

I was trying to get round to what I really had to say to him. I wanted him to stay – in every fibre of my being I longed to care for him – while rational fear told me to book him into a hotel, call a taxi and hope that he would go quietly.

'You can't say it hasn't been a life that we have shared,' I continued, laughing. Hypocrite. But, God forgive me, I wanted to make *him* laugh.

It worked. With a laugh, too – not of humour, but of warmth – he asked: 'Do you think about death?'

He told me that he believed we had never discussed this subject because we had shared the common assumption that it was a gloomy one, best left to sanctimonious funeral parlours and to vicars who wanted to bully the living. However, in the time he had spent alone he had found that looking towards the exit had not oppressed him. On the contrary, it had filled the world with a glow. He could not pretend that he had solved any mysteries by facing that direction from which others diverted their attention, he said; it was as great a secret as ever. Perhaps there was only extinction, and life had no purpose, being a time-filling game. But that was the worst of all the conclusions that one could come to – and that one seemed all right to him. No one had the answers; and the more realistically one stuck to the evidence, the more one was driven to admit the unexplained. The very fact that there was a mystery, that there were possibilities, was what illuminated the corners and made them dance.

That is the gist of what he told me. I was getting lost. Either he couldn't explain properly or I couldn't follow, or both, because we were drunk. And I still wasn't saying what I had to say.

I spoke about Mr Parker, gibbering and unable to communicate with his family, suffering his highs and lows after being hooked on overdoses, and squatting in the dark. He was on my mind, at some level or other, either haunting me beneath the surface or right at the front, giving me the shivers, all the time. Whenever Mr Parker was nearest to being rational and calm, I knew that there was one subject that he, too, was thinking about above all others; the one that neither he nor anyone would speak of, even through euphemisms, and would never mention by name: death.

Angrily I had told myself that I must confront this and speak my thoughts to Mr Parker, for nothing else could possibly matter very much to him. I could never do it. I could not help my very first words sounding pretentious, and my courage would fail. It seemed an impertinence to be instructing Mr Parker about death. When death was real and not theoretical, it was too awesome to speak of that about which one knew nothing.

And I thought that, maybe, at the back of Roth's mind he was angling to discuss how we would be taking care of each other in our final frailties. In other words, how I would care for him. How could I tell him that I couldn't do it anymore, that I was worn out? What I wanted, desperately, was to get Roth to see the need to take care of himself. I do blame myself for stupidly thinking there might be an answer other than the fatal clinic. But that was why I talked to him of Mr Parker.

'We should be planning how to spend a creative and healthy old age together, not fighting like this,' Roth told me in such a slow, sad way.

It was absolutely true but it was ironic, because that was not at all the direction in which his life was driving.

The conversation was growing positively leaden from alcohol and we were both falling asleep.

I thought that it was time. I put out my hand and stroked his arm.

'It's no good, Roth.'

That was the way it came out, at last.

'Pardon?'

'It's no good.'

'What isn't?'

'Us.'

I tried to smile. I think I succeeded. Probably it was like

something modelled in wax. My head was like a block of wood with a single, solid pain.

'It's no good our going on, you know. Let's just give it up in some – friendly way. Please stay tonight, tomorrow maybe, *but* – '

I saw Roth grip his glass and stare fixedly at it. I thought he was going to crush it, or throw it. How like him!

It made me angry. For some reason I was not, for once, afraid. He slackened his grip, and with the other hand he wiped his brow from which sweat was dripping.

'I'm going to phone for a taxi,' I blurted out. I did not really mean it. I was really trying to frighten him into calming down. From fear, confusion and drinking all day, I could hardly stand or think. '*Please* don't make a scene, my dear – '

'That fire!' he shouted angrily. 'In the grate! It's too fucking big! You'll burn my fucking house down!'

'Roth, please – *please* let's stay friends!'

He was on his feet as I pleaded, so that I had to stare up into his face.

I sometimes suffer the terrible thought that it was I who drove him to his destruction but, also, it was he who drove me to that point.

At times this has struck me as an echo of his own belief that he was responsible for his father's death, that Saul Roth's suicide was inspired by the revolt which he himself had inspired in his son.——

43

Roth burst out of the room. Pushing through the guests who tried to ignore him, he climbed the stairs. Climbed too fast, with a heart such as his. He could hardly see.

He passed the bathroom. A smell of fresh oil paint – a scent which his nose was always eager to catch – came from the back room, where the door was half open.

He took a quick peep at what was on Dorothy's easel: the figure with a wolf's head approaching the girl on the bed. The picture seemed mysteriously aimed at himself, and guilt made his heart stop.

On his mind, too, was his first impression of Dorothy today and the wreck that marriage had made of her. Something about the way her hair was cut shorter than ever before, but without attempt at style or art, had reminded him of an asylum inmate. The strain had showed as a strange intensity. She had developed the kind of face that one shunned.

He reached what had once been Dorothy's and his bedroom. It still held the bed in which Roth had been conceived. Angrily he went in to snatch his leathers. He remembered the delight he had felt when he had hung them there; how he had noticed the double bed made up for a single person, and the preciously feminine air of the room. As he had rambled through his house and taken in the small dilapidations consequent upon Dorothy living alone, he believed himself necessary, he thought he was missed. He believed he had patched his marriage. It even led him to plan what he should do tomorrow: put this house together again; make it shipshape. Now those reflections seemed to have taken place years ago. He did not have the heart even to climb the attic stairs and take a look at his studio. He thrust himself into the foul, familiar leathers, and zipped himself up.

He fancied he heard shouts from below. He reeled against the landing wall. He thought he could smell smoke. Dorothy's guests were rushing up and down, like flies at a windowpane.

'Fire! Fire!' Roth muttered and tried to point. Tried to tell them . . . explain.

Guests looked at him, some worried, others amused. Then they seemed to get the message. So he thought. As he leaned against the wall, shivers down his back and sweat over his face, they were pouring down the attic stairs from his studio. What were they doing up there? It was as if they were unpeopling a canvas, some great battle or crowd scene; a Delacroix.

At first, they were peering in expectation of some exciting surprise. They'd see! Some were giggling. Others were determined not to be taken for fools. Then they, too, seemed to panic, as Roth yelled, down the stair and up: 'House is on fire! Get outside! World is on fire! Leave everything! Get outside! Get outside!'

He might have rescued Dorothy's canvas but he was caught in a press down the stairs. He found himself rushing, pushing, stumbling, hearing curses. Hearing, actually, a laugh. Why laughter? The house seemed more crowded than it had been and the strength of frightened, angry people was colossal.

He was weakened, weak at the knees, looking for Dorothy. Where was she?

The fire had been started in the parlour grate, of course. The burning planks had tumbled on to the carpet.

'Roth!' Surely he heard her shouting, as he stumbled through the door? Had he brushed by her, a moment ago?

He was out in the street and it seemed that no one was there. Hardly anyone. A few, who were looking at him. Some stood with arms folded on the step. He staggered. No Dorothy. Where is she? Where was she?

He looked up to see if people were clambering out of the windows. He expected to see flames pouring out. No. Yes, there were. Were not the tiles swarming with half-clad figures who had climbed out of the studio's dormer window and were struggling on to neighbouring roofs? Others were dropping from the lower window sills.

Roth staggered away up the street. Helmeted himself. The weight of the helmet almost toppled him. Mounted his bike. He could laugh! Ha! Ha! Yes, yes! All was dreamlike.

Focusing his attention, Roth drove fast, heaven knew how he did it, down an empty motorway. There were only a few convoys of trucks shuffling through the night.

He did not stop until, on his left, he saw the dawn and he was home. He roared into the village, went over the kerb through the ready-open gates into the churchyard. He could still see Dorothy. Saw her on the path, under the olive trees, down to the sea. He gritted his teeth and leaned over the fuel tank, willing his grief into the fairing. He followed the church path from the porch, round the tower to the boiler cellar. He bucked over the grass and wove among the gravestones.

Bedroom curtains were twitching. He circuited the graveyard once more. Revved the engine. Challenged them to come out of their holes, the bastards!

More lights were switched on. Again he circuited the graves. Again. Again. A slightly different route this time, dipping under the sycamore trees. Round again.

He saw a police light flashing on the road. An ambulance behind it. Then another car. Who's whistled up this cavalcade? Why, Sandbach, the bloody JP!

He'd do another circuit before they caught up with him.

The cars and the ambulance pulled up at the gate. Two policemen and a man in a white coat. And Dr Kaplan?

Round the graveyard again. Round. Another one.

His dreams of the previous morning. What else was the world but a circuit, a spinning wheel, a coil of anxiety, a tarantella, a merry-go-round?

GLYN HUGHES

THE ANTIQUE COLLECTOR

As the real male world rushes to the trenches of the First World War, an ageing music-hall drag-artist writes his memoirs. Fugitive from the drudgery of a Yorkshire work-house, his often bewildered, wryly humorous account of 'other' women and the two elderly men whose fantasies he fulfilled provides a unique slant on the differences between the sexes, and a memorable portrait of the times in which he lived.

'Excellent . . . the evocations of time and place, from a period as brutal as it was sentimental, are deeply felt and as indelibly signed as Blackpool rock'
Norman Shrapnel in The Guardian

'A fine portrait of ambiguous sexuality and a wonderfully eccentric perspective on nineteenth-century mores'
Zoë Heller in The Independent on Sunday

'Truly an original hero/heroine . . . Hughes has drawn one of the most sensitive portrayals of a "woman" character by a male author that I have encountered'
Catholic Herald

'A *tour de force* examination of the human condition in all its horror, complexity and beauty'
In Dublin

'Glyn Hughes has excelled . . . He has transmuted the perverse into the sympathetic and the endearing . . . a moving and revealing book'
Andrew Sinclair in The Times